"How did you kill it?" Gwen said, growing impatient with my tale. Since I only had a minor wound, she didn't need to hear every painstaking detail. Gwen wasn't one who needed all the finer points of a story, just the gist. "How did you kill the dog?"

I held up my middle finger like an angry trucker. "With this."

Gwen made an audible gasp. "What?"

Keeping the finger raised, I said. "I got away from the parked car and was backing up, keeping the dog squarely in front of me. After kicking at it for the fifth or sixth time to keep it away, I tripped over the curb and fell backward. So, the dog made an attack for my throat. My one forearm blocked its body just enough that its teeth couldn't get my throat."

I wiggled the middle finger as I held it up in the air. "So, I took this finger and shoved it into its eye. I just pushed and pushed until this finger was so deep inside its skull that I couldn't see the finger anymore. Then I twisted and dug and moved this finger around in his skull till the goddamn dog stopped moving."

Gwen vomited on the kitchen floor.

A thought occurred to me: If we had a dog of our own, I bet it would've tried to lick up the vomit.

Dogs eat puke. Nasty animals.

I0545433

Acknowledgements

Thank you Mary and Bill. Cheers!

MAULED

BY CHRISTOPHER GROSSO

PART ONE

EATING PUKE AND THE DISTANCE PISSING RECORD

CHAPTER ONE

"Oh shit!" is usually the phrase a person utters when an angry dog jumping at a fence finally exceeds the height of that fence.

A fence, when it is all that separates your leg from the clench of a dog's jaw, is an unreliable fortification. I've learned over these past few days that fences—especially those green-wired, waist-high, faux-metal fences that adorn American backyards—are nothing more than mere decoration. White picket fences suck too.

Who or what are those waist-high fences expected to keep in or keep out of a yard? A grown man or woman can easily hop over one. A child can easily climb one. Deer barely break stride leaping over. Squirrels are acrobats on them. Skunks and raccoons dig under them. And dogs …

If a dog is motivated enough, backyard fences are impotent. At least they are impotent to dogs that are big enough to maul a person. If you want to keep your ankle-nipping Lhasa Apso or Chihuahua from escaping, then backyard fences are fine. Just fine. For any dog over two feet tall, backyard fences are worthless. That is the first thing I learned on the first day of my problem.

In addition, dogs are everywhere. You never realize how many dogs there are around you at all times until each and every dog wants to maul your throat open and eat your esophagus like bacon. In my section of America, the Northeast section in the City of Philadelphia, dogs are as plentiful as birds. One of the animal-saving nonprofits says on its website that 39 percent of households in America own at least one dog.

Considering there are 1.5 million people in Philadelphia, that is a lot of goddamn dogs.

That same non-profit website says of the 39 percent of households that own a dog, 60 percent own more than one dog. Shit, a retirement-age woman on Grant Avenue has four dogs, of mixed breed and size. Well, she *had* four. They nearly had me behind the supermarket, but I was carrying a gun by then and had a team, so I won, though at a high cost.
I'm getting ahead of myself.
In the beginning, I learned fences do little and Americans own way too many dogs.

At least it feels like too many dogs when every dog decides in some massive, tongue-wagging, furry, militaristic fucking cult, that if they see you they must kill you. Plus, it was *just me* they wanted to kill. Well me, and a few other people close to me. To the general public, they were the same ole pleasant, joyful, fun, snuggly, man's-best-friend doggies who loved being petted and walked and fed. Beginning October 17, 20—, whenever a dog saw me, it became a ravenous monster of snarling teeth, intent on my final goodbye.
Until October 17, 20—, I liked dogs. Then my problem started, and started rather suddenly. At first, no one believed me. I can't blame them. Of course they wouldn't believe me. Not even my wife believed me at first.
When I came home on October 17th, my wife was surprised to see me coming through the door three hours early. I usually worked till five and then had a forty-minute commute home. That day was an odd day (as I will detail) so I decided to quit early.
The front door of our apartment opens into the kitchen of our first-floor bungalow. When I walked in, Gwen sat at the kitchen table working on her laptop. She looked only mildly surprised to see me. "Look what the cat drug in," she said.
"Are you fucking kidding me?" I replied, a little more forcefully than I intended.
Now she looked truly surprised, for I was a mild-tempered

man who was, generally, pleasant and cheerful. I usually greeted my wife kindly, with a kiss. Not that day.

"What's wro—" she began, but stopped when she saw the material of my right pant leg was all torn and bloodstained. Normally I was well groomed, preppy even, wearing khakis, an ironed and starched button down with a subdued necktie to accentuate my short brown hair and clean shaven, (dare I say?) handsome face. "Shit, what happened to you?" Gwen asked.

"Poodle," was all I said and limped over to the fridge to get a beer.

"Wait, what?" Gwen managed, closing her laptop. "Lucas, what happened to you?" She usually called me Lucas, though some people used Luke. She only used Luke when she was about to orgasm during sex. I think she liked to imagine Luke Skywalker was fucking her with his light-saber.

"I was attacked by a poodle. A full-sized poodle, not one of those little yipping ones."

Gwen stood up, which was no easy task considering she was eight months pregnant with our first child. Her belly reminded me of a beer keg, which, lately, had been an enticement to drink more beer than I normally drank. Or maybe I was just scared shitless of being a father. Nevertheless, I wanted a beer just then, but opted instead for something stronger. I reached into the cabinet for my bottle of Hound's Tooth bourbon. The irony of the bourbon's name was not lost on me that day, so I chuckled.

"You got bitten by a dog? That's not funny. Sit down, let me take a look."

I did as commanded, but there was nothing she could do because it was all done already. After the bite, I drove myself to the ER where some first year D.O. resident gave me five stitches and a rabies shot. I think the rabies shot hurt worse than the bite … at least that first bite.

My pregnant wife, who did freelance public relations work for local non-profits, took a look at my stitched leg. She gave her very untrained approval of the physician's medical work and then proceeded with the grilling. *Where did this happen? What happened? Why did the dog bite you? Did you call the cops? Did you get the owner's name? Was the dog dangerous or just startled? etc. ...*

I kept my story succinct and decided to begin at the end. "I don't know what happened, but I killed it. The dog. It's dead. I had to kill it."

Gwen sat back in her chair and a hand went toward her mouth in surprise. She repressed the reaction and the hand made it only halfway toward her mouth. "Why did you do that? It's just a dog. I'm sure it didn't mean to bite you. It was probably just scared."

"Nope," I said. "It wasn't scared and it *did* mean to bite me."

"Well, it might have appeared—"

I stopped her there. "It appeared mad. It wasn't my own fear causing me to misinterpret the situation. I was walking down Kirby Drive over by Knight's Road going to a client's house. The dog was in a backyard, completely fenced. It started barking its ass off when it saw me. To be honest, I didn't notice for more than a passing second. Dogs bark at people. That is what dogs do. No big deal. So I was looking at the numbers on the houses trying to find where I was supposed to be. I was scanning the house numbers and I faintly noticed that the barking coming from this three-foot-tall fluffy white poodle was different. It was insanely loud and it sounded ..." I searched for the right word but couldn't find it so I settled on, "... angry. Yeah, it sounded pissed off. Madly pissed. Enraged even. Like pure hatred unleashed in a bark. So when I took a passing look at it and I saw the damnedest thing. The fucking poodle was trying to get over the fence."

Gwen nodded, agreeing. "Sure, I've seen dogs do that. They look like they really want to get over the fence. But they never actually get over the ..." She stopped herself, realizing this dog did get over the fence.

I knew what she meant. "I know, you're right, they never do. It is mostly just bravado on the dog's part. It's like a guy at a bar being macho who actually has no real intention of fighting. Just chest-thumping-bullshit. Dogs usually jump up and down at the fence and bark but you know they don't want to get over that fence. They are actually scared of us."

"Right," Gwen said.

"This dog *was* trying to get over. It wanted over. I saw it with my own eyes. I watched this dog backpedal ten feet and run toward the fence, leaping with all its might to clear the fence. It hit the top bar and fell back into the yard. Meanwhile, it's still barking with insane rage and keeping its eyes pinned on me. Eyes pinned on me like I was a Milk-Bone." Gwen let a smile creep onto her face. "Then—I know you'll think I'm nuts, Gwen—but the dog backed up fifteen feet the next time. It gave itself an extra five feet of starting-distance and then ran to the fence and dove. This second time, half its body cleared the fence and the other half didn't. The dog's mid-section hit the center bar. For the briefest of seconds its body rested on the top bar, balanced but teetering. The dog didn't want to teeter back into the yard. It wanted out, and it fought, trying to teeter-tot its weight so it would go face-forward over the fence. That's when I saw the first speck of blood on its white fur."

"What? Oh God, what do you mean?"

"Think about it." I reminded Gwen how a typical backyard fence is constructed. Most are three and a half feet high, metal-laced fences with a vertical post every few feet and a horizontal top bar that runs across the entire length. Rising an inch above the top bar at intervals of every four inches or so is a twist of metal from where the fencing is tied off. "Gwen, remember those little metal twists at the top of backyard fences? Like a single barb of wire? So as this fucking dog is teetering, those little mental barbs are tearing into the skin on the underside of this dog—the part stuck on the bar. The dog is kicking and twisting. Those little barbs are just digging into his flesh and shredding his skin. Blood is splattering his white fur and pieces of torn flesh are—"

"Okay, got it. Jeez-us." Her face was a portrait of disgust. "So it was hurt, I got it. Less detail next time. So did it make it over? Did it teeter over?"

I took a pull of the bourbon. "Not that time."

"Wait, it tried again? After ripping its belly apart it tried to get over again? It wouldn't do that."

"I didn't bite my own leg," I said, voice dripping with condescension. "The damn dog finally fell backward back into the yard. The thing didn't even hesitate. Its white fucking fur soaking up all that blood, with little pieces of doggy flesh—" I cut myself short, seeing Gwen was readying to reprimand me again for the descriptive gore. "Anyway, it ran in a big circle like it wanted to gain some forceful momentum and wham!"

"It cleared the fence."

"For a fact it cleared the fence, because the fucker bit me on the leg in the street moments later." I took another pull of bourbon and emptied the glass. "On that second attempt, it cleared the fence by a few inches too. Like a goddamn Olympic hurdle jumper."

"It was hurt," Gwen tried to rationalize. "If it didn't get over when it was teetering, it wouldn't try again unless it was rabid. Oh shit, was it rabid? It must've been. With the pain from the injury surely it wouldn't have tried again unless it was rabid."

I was in no mood for speculation. "We don't know that for an absolute certainty." Gwen merely looked away. "Let's just acknowledge it got over the fence. The cops took the corpse of the dog to a shelter to run a rabies test. We'll hear the results tomorrow."

Gwen nodded in agreement. I went on, only after pouring and downing another three fingers of the Hound's Tooth bourbon. "So when I saw that the damn dog cleared the fence and was free, I walked briskly away from the house. I didn't run because somewhere in my head I remembered hearing that you don't run from an animal. It will want to chase you if you do. It'll think it's a game."

"I think I heard that too, but it was about bears. You know, in the forest."

"Whatever," I said, again more angrily than I intended. "Regardless, I'm walking as quick as a man can without actually running and looking behind me the entire time. The dog is running, charging, clearing the 500 feet between us in no time, his white fluffy fur all bloodied on his undercoat and legs, barking his goddamn head off."

What I didn't mention to Gwen was how absurd it felt for

a second. There I stood, a grown-man, thirty-four years old, looking at a white, three-and-a-half-foot tall fluffy poodle and feeling more terror, fear and dread than I have ever felt in my life. A poodle? An old woman's dog? How could it scare me? I am six feet, 195 pounds, I work out at the gym and I have hands. I have hands! With opposable thumbs! The damn dog should be scared of me, not the other way around. I had size advantage and a five-fingered weapon at the end of each arm called a fist. The poodle should be afraid, but it wasn't. I was. I was afraid. I was terrified. So I froze. I was frozen in terror.

I didn't describe my fear when telling Gwen the story. "I made a quick decision and decided the best course of action was to stand still. I couldn't outrun it and chances were, when it got close it would stop a few feet from me and just bark. All bravado. Then when it saw I wasn't scared of it, or going to attack, it would take off and find a piss-scent to sniff or a lawn to shit on or something."

"Didn't the blood on the coat scare you? Make you think it might have rabies?"

It did, of course. That was the scariest part. Some part of my brain processed that very thought. *This dog is enraged enough that it wounded itself—severely wounded itself—just to get at me. I'm sure it didn't intend to wound itself, but its vigor was so overwhelming that it did hurt itself, nonetheless. Just to chase me?*

"Well, the fucking thing didn't stop or sniff or shit. It lunged right at my leg and did what you see here," I said, lifting my leg slightly off the ground.

"Did it lock on when it bit you? I hear that some dogs will lock their jaws onto whatever they bite and you can't get them to release."

"I've heard that too but no, this dog bit and let go. I stumbled back into a parked car. The thing lunged again and missed by sheer luck. I didn't do anything on that second attack. The damn dog just had bad aim and missed the mark. How could I do anything? I was still too surprised that this white fucking poodle bit me to recognize the severity of the situation. Then it lunged a third time, aiming for my injured leg and I had just enough time to get a bit of my senses back. I kicked at the thing with my other leg. My foot caught it on the nose, grazed it really, but it backed off a few feet and gave me time to figure out what the hell was happening."

"How did you kill it?" Gwen said, growing impatient with my tale. Since I had only a minor wound, she didn't want every painstaking detail. Gwen wasn't one that needed all the finer points of a story, just the gist. "How did you kill the dog?"

I held up my middle finger like an angry trucker. "With this."

Gwen made an audible gasp. "What?"

Keeping the finger raised, I said, "I got away from the parked car and backed up, keeping the dog squarely in front of me. After kicking at it for the fifth or sixth time to keep it away, I tripped over the curb and fell backward. So the dog made an attack for my throat. My one forearm blocked its body just enough that its teeth couldn't get my throat." I wiggled the middle finger I held up in the air. "So I took *this* finger and shoved it into its eye. I just pushed and pushed until *this* finger was so deep inside its skull I couldn't see the finger anymore. Then I twisted and dug and moved *this* finger around in his skull till the goddamn dog stopped moving."

Gwen vomited on the kitchen floor.

A thought occurred to me. *If we had a dog of our own, I bet it would've tried to lick up the vomit.*

Dogs eat puke. Nasty animals.

CHAPTER TWO

Feminism is dead at two in the morning. It dies when the woman beside you in bed hears a noise in the darkness outside. Darkness, feminism, and noise are insoluble elements.

My wife nudged me in the ribs, gingerly. I was zonked, having overindulged the Percocet the emergency room doc sent home with me for the residual pain from the bite. The doctor prescribed one Percocet every four hours, which I accelerated into two Percocet every two hours. Not that I really had much pain, but the mental numbness was exquisite.

"Lucas, wake up," she said, nudging more forcefully. "Didn't you hear that?"

Of course I didn't. Nor did I want to rouse from my deep sleep. Gwen, knowing the male mind all too well, gently stroked my cock. This, not surprisingly, did arouse me, from both my sleep and my genital flaccidity. As soon as she had my attention (in all aspects), her hand was gone from my swelling crotch. "Lucas, outside. The front door. There is a noise."

I didn't even try to talk my way out of checking it. I tried once about a year ago when she woke me saying glass was breaking outside and people were talking loudly. I told her it was just punks walking home from the bars tossing their empty bottles. I said not to worry about it and go back to sleep. Then she said she didn't know how my mother could have produced two sons who were so complete opposites. One earned two purple hearts in Afghanistan and the other wouldn't even check to make sure drunken kids weren't vandalizing his apartment. Comparisons to my brother's bravery in combat always stung me harshly.

So, like a stubborn child, I refused to check the noise. The next day I proved I was correct and it was only kids throwing a few beer bottles on the street. I also reminded her that while my brother was a decorated vet, I was now a Ph.D. psychologist. I further reminded her he was just a drunken asshole living on VA checks, with nothing but a couple of war stories to rattle off. Plus, he was a douche-bag who thought the world owed him something for shooting a machine gun in the desert at untrained Afghan farmers holding thirty-year-old AK47s. I didn't really believe what I said was true, but my pride was wounded. Until the problem occurred, I could never compete with my brother's bravery and it pissed me off.

Over the course of my problem, I came to rely on my brother and his knack for war. In fact, I came to love him again like I had as a kid.

On the night in question—when my wife had stroked my physical manhood with her hand to wake me instead of insulting my manhood altogether—I knew she wouldn't relent till I checked out the source of the noise. I rolled over and in only my boxer-briefs and a Hanes tee, I moved through the apartment to the front door, my mind still a hazy mix of sleepy narcotic.

Quickly, I was awake. Acutely wide awake. The noise. The fucking noise.

It was scratching. Something was scratching at the front door. We had no screen door, just a thick wooden front door. It was an unmistakable sound of nails moving up and down, up and down, up and down, with machine gun speed, pausing every few seconds, only to start again.

Scratch-scratch-scratch. Scratch-scratch-scratch. Pause. *Scratch-scratch-scratch. Scratch-scratch-scratch.* Pause.

The bottom half of our wooden front door was being scratched by claws. The instant I heard the scratching I knew the culprit was a dog.

"Lucas, what is that?" Gwen asked, standing a good ten paces behind me now, more in the hallway to the bedroom than the living room.

"Scratching," I muttered, barely audible.

"What?"

"A dog is scratching at our door."

Gwen walked up behind me now, her feminism hiding behind me in case something dangerous was within our apartment walls. "You saw a dog?" she asked.

"Listen," I said, holding a finger over my lips for silence. "That is a dog scratching."

Gwen listened and said, "It's probably just a squirrel or a raccoon. Go bang on the door and scare it away."

"Gwen." My voice caked with exasperation. "It's a dog. A damn dog."

"You are just thinking that because of—"

I cut her off by walking toward the door. The incessant scratching continued.

It was solid wood, with no window, only a peep hole. Hesitantly, as if I was afraid the door would break apart and a bloody Cujo would burst through, I put my eye to the peephole. As soon as my eye hit the hole, the scratching stopped dead. I took a step backward, alarmed by the sudden silence. I looked at my wife, who just shrugged.

Again, tepidly, I closed my left eye and put my open right eye to the hole. I saw only the narrow strip of street illuminated by our porch light. Nothing unusual. *All Quiet on the Western Front,* my mind mumbled.

I pulled my eye away from the hole and looked at my wife. She stood still, arms crossed to protect against the late-night October chill in Philadelphia that seeped into our apartment.

I turned back toward the door and looked again. Nothing but the street illuminated by the overhead porch light.

Then it happened. A shadow flashed through the light. Then another. A swinging, arching shadow moved at lightning quick speed across my field of vision. Just a quick black line of shadow sweeping through the light.

Then I saw it, for the briefest of instances I saw what made the shadow sweep through the light. It was a tail. A wagging tail.

I stepped back again from the door, a good three feet. "It's still out there."

"What," my wife said, alarm creeping into her voice, undoubtedly caused by my own tenseness.

"A tail. I saw a tail wagging."

Gwen started to walk toward the door, presumably to take a look for herself. She stopped still in her tracks at the instant, startling return of the *scratch-scratch-scratch, scratch-scratch-scratch.* "What the fuck," she muttered.

Aware that I was a man and needed to show some bravery, some leadership, some balls, I looked around the room. I don't know if I was looking for a weapon or just time for my mind to develop a plan. I found nothing.

Almost mechanically, I walked back toward the door. Again, when I was within inches of the door, the scratching stopped. When it stopped, I stopped.

My ears became alerted to a low, deep tone. Leaning my head toward the door, I listened more intently, forcing my mind to block out my other senses. What my ears heard made my heart jump. A low growl. A throaty, grave, cavernous growl from the very core of an angry animal. The core of a dog, I knew.

Fear atom-bombed my body, mushrooming into every recess. I stood still because some still sane, twitching little part of my brain that carries a man's ego said, *Be brave.* When I looked at my wife, that little part of my brain said it even louder. *Be brave, little boy. Be a big man.*

Without conscious thought, I slapped the door hard with an open palm and yelled, "Go on, get. Go. Get outta here."

I slapped the door three more times. "Get."

The low growl turned into a much louder, more vocal growl from the throat instead of the core of the dog. *That* growl my wife heard. "Shit," escaped her lips.

My open palm closed into a fist and I pounded the door three more times. "Get the fuck off my porch. Go."

The growl grew even louder.

Now I was pissed. My faculties returned and my fear turned itself into fury. I looked at my wife but did not really see her. I thought, *I can't open the door. I can't reach it through the door. How the hell do I scare it off?*

Under the door, my mind reminded me. *Slide something under the door to scare it away.*

I told myself how ingenious I was as I darted around the apartment, looking for something—anything—to slide under the door. My wife asked what the hell I was doing. When I told her, she seemed at first skeptical, but then started to help me look.

She found a wire coat hanger. "Stretch this out straight, and stick it under the door. Sweep it side to side. That'll scare it."

The growling continued and I agreed with my wife, adding that two hangers would work better than one. I straightened out two wire hangers until they were long, straight-ish pieces of metal. For added measure, I let the hook-shape on the end of each hanger remain. I believed it might, if it came to that, scratch the dog. I sincerely hoped it didn't come to that. Despite being bitten by the poodle earlier that day, I still liked dogs.

I was nervous, but tried to hide it from my wife. Steeling myself, I got down onto my belly, and felt immediately vulnerable. Something about being flat down makes a man feel weak, defenseless. I steeled myself again. I had one straightened hanger in each hand, hook facing forward. I was about to shimmy the first hanger under the door when Gwen said, "Think I should call the police?" She didn't give me time to answer before she had her iPhone in hand, dialing.

I thought that it was odd that my leg didn't hurt, but dismissed it as one of nature's gifts of survival, compliments of heightened endorphins.

The first hanger slid underneath without any trouble. I left it sitting out about an inch past the door while I jimmied the other one through. This second hanger did not make it through as easily as the first. The door was not hung perfectly straight and even. It dipped a fraction of an inch to the right. Nonetheless, both hangers were through. Amidst the loud growls of an enraged dog and the soft background noise of my wife telling an unbelievable tale to the 911 operator, like a mad puppeteer in some hillbilly freak show, I plunged the hangers into the open air beneath the door and violently moved them from side to side.

It did not go as expected.

I swept the hangers side to side. The hanger on the left hand hit something that stopped it suddenly. I presumed I'd smacked the pooch's leg. Leaving the right hanger where it was, I swung the left back and forward again, putting a little elbow grease into the swing. I hoped if I added a little sting to the slap, the dog might realize it was not welcome.

With a twist of the wrist, the hanger sped beneath the door causing a little, faint, "whoosh." Then it stopped dead, having made contact with—what?—the dog's leg? It had to be the dog's leg? I'm not sure to this day but logic said it was the dog's leg. Logic did not figure into what happened next.

Spontaneously, the hanger from my right hand was pulled forward from the other side of the door and was pulled with enough force and velocity that it sucked the hanger from my grasp, pulling it outside the door.

In a matter of seconds I had lost one of my two weapons.

In another instant, I felt a sudden tug on the remaining hanger. My hand reflexively gripped tighter. This time, my weapon *just* stayed in my hand. I can only surmise that the dog grabbed the hanger in its mouth and pulled. I didn't think at the time that a hanger—all thin and wiry—was something not particularly suited for a dog's mouth. In fact, unlike a cord of rope or a leash, it would be uncomfortable and alien for a dog to bite and pull. I knew it was pulling so I pulled back with a modicum of strength.

The dog replied with an uncanny pull itself. I almost lost the hanger outside the door. Just then, the dog sent a message, loud and clear—a pissed off, wake-up-the-neighbors growl.

Fear, not thought, caused me to yank with all the force my thirty-four-year-old muscles could muster and the hanger gave way, pulling backward until it caught. "Caught" is the correct word. I knew it then in my gut and in my heart as I know it now as fact. The hanger must've slid through the dog's teeth, wire sliding across incisors, until the hooked-end of the hanger caught the dog in the jaw. It pierced through the soft palate of the bottom half of the mouth and came out the other side, catching the dog's jaw like a hook in a fish's mouth.

The hanger bucked violently and bent upward as the dog jumped up. For a second, the hanger came loose from my hand. The bend of the wire hanger was now V-shaped. With the dog pulling in any direction but out, the handle-end of the hanger stayed inside my door. I grabbed it again, trying to pin it down flat and center as the dog reared in different directions, trying, presumably, to free itself from the fishhook.

The dog finally decided (I presumed getting a bit of its wits back), that escape was its best option. It pulled backward violently. I gripped the hanger so hard I bent it almost in a circle that wrapped around my fist. At meeting my counterforce, the dog stopped pulling backward for a second. Just like reeling in a fish, it jumped again and pulled away. This time I was ready and like a fisherman with a marlin on-hook, I pulled in the opposite direction.

I won.

The hanger gave way and jutted back toward me. I heard a loud thud hit the door. My racing mind knew it was the dog's head being reeled into the door like a fish hitting the side of the boat.

Then we both froze. The dog didn't fight or kick or buck. I didn't move my hand an inch. What seemed like an hour was, my wife later told me, a full-blown, unbelievable one minute. Or as she told the police later, "They were at a standoff for a full sixty seconds."

Fido or Benji or Old Yeller or whatever was on the other side of that door made the first move. It growled.

That growl broke me from my trance-like rigidity and I looked at my wife, who was as frozen as I had just been. Looking back at the door, I put my ear flush against it. Sure enough, I heard the low grumble of a growl from the other side.

I realized all this reeling-in had put me on my elbows. So I lowered myself back down flat onto my belly, trying my best not to move the hanger. My eyes came level with the small space beneath the door and I felt a gust of hot air that smelled like leftover meatloaf gone bad. I saw a snout, the sides lifting up and down as the dog breathed, sucking in my scent and exhaling putrid, hot filth of breath. Below that snout was a small, three-inches wide, puddle of blood.

I looked at that snout and those two beady nostrils and I wanted to punch it. I wanted to tell my wife to get the long butcher's knife. I could shove it into the dog's nose and through its nasal cavity and into its eye socket, stopping only when I had made mince of the dog's brain meat. Because I knew—maybe from the rotted stench of the dog's rancid breath or just because of the events of the past day—but I knew this dog on the other side of my front door wanted to kill me.

As I dreamed of plunging a knife into my opponent, the dog pulled backward with such a determined strength and with such purposefulness that the hanger wrapped around my fist bit into the skin, pulling my hand to the door. I felt the amazing power and strength as my hand held onto the weapon. My muscle tensed in defense, tightening my hold on the hanger until … it was gone. The hanger went slack and I heard the scratchy-scratch of a dog's nails on the concrete entrance. The dog was free of the hanger but it hadn't decided to leave yet. Its feet stopped at the edge of the porch, moving side to side, nails scraping the concrete. I knew it was looking at the door. I knew it still felt a primal urge to finish what it started.

Then it turned and I heard it run off. A second later, I heard what the dog's amazingly acute canine ears had heard much earlier than my own: it was sirens. Police sirens.

I rolled away from the door and lay on my back looking at the ceiling. I moved my hand to put it onto my forehead, forgetting that it was still gripping the hanger. When my hand moved it pulled the entire hanger into the apartment and my wife screamed.

I jolted upright and met my wife's eyes, which were pinned on the hanger. I looked down at the weapon beside me. Dangling from the hook were bloody, wet pieces of the dog's lips, gums, and other cartilage.

The dog had pulled itself free from the hook. It tore its own jaw apart to get free. Even after that monstrously painful act of self-mutilation, the damn dog stayed on the porch for a few more seconds, deciding if it wanted to attack again.

What unholy hell was being unleashed?

CHAPTER THREE

Officer McNally (I wondered if his first name was Rand, like the roadmaps they sold before blessed GPS arrived) stood looking at the front door. He shook his head slowly, almost imperceptibly, from left to right as he studied the oddity that had become the entranceway to my abode.

The bottom half of the wooden front door looked like someone had run a cheese-grater up and down it. The paint was chipped and splintered, torn away in different lengths of vertical streaks. These exposed that muted-yellow color of bare wood that lay beneath the paint. An array of splinters, chips, and particles of wood lay on the concrete. The dog's nails had done only cosmetic damage to the door, but it would certainly need some synthetic wood-fill where pieces had been torn away, plus a new coat of paint.

McNally's partner was a slender black man whose name, Officer John Johnson, was as redundant as the amount of time he made me repeat what occurred that evening.

"All right," John Johnson asked for what felt like the fifth time, "you never saw the breed or size of the dog?"

"Nope. As I've said, I saw its tail sweep through the light when I looked out the peephole. Then I saw its nose when I was face down on the ground with the coat hanger."

"It really is something," McNally offered. "What could this dog have been thinking?" McNally, true to his name, had been trying to map out the dog's thought pattern since arriving. Not wanting to remind him that dogs are incapable of developing plans, strategies or even the most simple of future planning, I remained silent. McNally had the badge and uniform and the power, so I let him ramble, annoyed as it made me. "So this dog decides," he said, and I winced at hearing the verb "decides" being used to describe a canine's thought process, "he decides he wants into your house, despite how impossible that seems to be. He decides on this house from all the other houses on this block. Why would he do that?"

I saw my wife, now the feminist once again, cringe slightly every time the cop said "he." I knew she was about to remind the officer that we did not know if the dog was a male or female. Therefore, using the pronoun "he" for an aggressive animal whose gender was unclear was tantamount to implying that aggression was a more common male trait and hence, sexist. I would add to that argument that if you met my wife, as lovely as she is, you'd know that women—females—can be as forcefully aggressive as a rabid boar.

Instead of letting my wife debate feminism with two very male Philly cops, I jumped in. "Officer, I don't … " I searched for the right words "… believe, in my experience that is, limited as it may be, that dogs are capable of deciding anything. They act on impulse and respond to their environment. They don't form ideas like us. They just process stimuli and react based upon genetically predetermined markers. They have instinctive impulses excited by stimuli garnered from the senses. Some stimuli excites certain parts of the brain. Synaptic fireworks spark at lightning speed and the dog reacts almost without any thought."

"Are you a veterinarian, sir?" redundant John Johnson asked. "Because if you are a veterinarian or biologist or some shit, that information could have been offered previously, as it may be pertinent. Some pissed-off pet-owner or something."

"No," I said, looking away, knowing my little scientific explanation was probably an insulting stimuli in the brains of these two cops. "I'm not a veterinarian. I'm a psychologist. A family-systems psychologist."

"Well then, Mister—"

"It's Doctor." I couldn't help myself. "Doctor Lucas Miller."

"Oh. Well shit. My apologies," John Johnson continued not even attempting to mask his sarcasm. "Well Doctor, I don't care what you—how did you say it—'believe, in your experience, as limited as it may be.' We are police officers and we know two things and know them well. One, we know bullshit from punk-ass punks. Two, we know dogs." Johnson moved closer to me than I would've liked. My personal space had now been compromised, or invaded, more accurately. "See we answer nine-one-one calls all damn night, ain't that right McNally."

"Goddamn that is exactly what we do."

"Whether it be some drunk slapping his old lady in some ghetto apartment or some junky sticking a gun into the flat-face of some Chinese-food delivery boy, undoubtedly when we get on scene, there is a fucking dog."

"Undoubtedly," McNally added like an alleluia to a preacher's message.

"Every low-life cocksucker who lives deep in the cesspool of low-life-living owns a dog. Don't ask me why 'cause I'd probably just say something offensive and upset your delicate sensibilities."

"That's right," McNally continued in his chorus.

"So I know dogs. I know them too damn well. It could be me and my partner here trying to calm a situation and the situation ain't no fucking good. You got some fat bitch screaming while her gang-banger boyfriend is huffing and puffing. Thirty damn cousins and neighbors are mingling about and talking shit and you're trying to control that situation."

McNally gave a "yup" in agreement.

"Then you got the dog." John Johnson leaned in closer to me. "There is always a dog. Now, despite what your psychological training and higher learning might make you believe, let me tell you one simple truth that I've learned from fifteen years on this godforsaken job. A dog can make a decision. It can look at you, size up your intentions toward it. It can determine your ability to defend yourself if it so chooses to attack you. It can decide what it wants to do with you. See, I've looked dogs dead in the eye—hundreds of 'em—while I'm standing in their home, on their carpet, handcuffing their owner. I've looked in their eyes and I know one fucking thing. I know they are deciding."

"Deciding what?" Gwen asked from the couch.

John Johnson took his eyes from mine and looked toward Gwen. "The dog is deciding if it will let you live or not."

"Okay," I said, relieved that John Johnson wasn't looking at me anymore. "I understand."

Johnson turned his attention to me again. "I don't think you do. See, I've seen a dog decide it was going to snuff the life out of someone. Saw it with my own eyes. My training-partner, when I was a rookie. We were at a domestic call and this dog was eyeing up my partner. He was on a leash but he was eyeing 'im up. I saw it—a flash across those dark doggie eyes. A flash that told me a decision had been made. A resolution had been affirmed. A plan had been devised and decided. That damn dog—part Collie and part Labrador—jumped so hard it broke its collar and left the leash and collar dangling in the hand of the woman holding him. He descended upon my training-partner like hell gone crazy. Fucked him up too. Took his nose and left eye before I shot the fucker."

"Jeez-us," Gwen said.

Johnson looked back at Gwen. "So it may sound like folklore of the street or something, but it ain't. It isn't my imagination or my hallucination. It just be. It just is. Gospel-like."

"Thank you, Officer," I said, trying to sound genuine. "I appreciate your insight."

"Oh," Johnson said, his gaze turned back to me. "Just to dismiss any preconceived notions you might have about two dumb cops not knowing nothing about nothing, I'm a second-year law student at Temple. I go part-time. McNally here has got his Master's degree. So we *get* higher learning."

"Okay, you're right. I get it." I walked away from John Johnson now, intimidated by his demeanor. "Where does that leave us? My wife and I? What do we do?"

"Damn if I know," John Johnson said bluntly, his demeanor changing instantly from lecturer of all things streetwise to a casual, almost-bored patrol officer. "Stay away from dogs and buy a steel plate for that door in case this shit happens again."

"Again?" Gwen said in shock.

"Wait. That's it? That's all?" I was still shocked from Officer

Johnson's abrupt turn to casualness. Considering what I went through both during that day and then, that night, I preferred him serious and profound. "In the same twenty-four-hour period, a dog bites me on the leg miles from where I now stand. Then, within the same twenty-four hours, a dog tries to claw its way into my house, and you aren't going to do anything?"

McNally answered. "Well, if it makes you feel any better, we'll file a report on the damage to the door just in case similar incidents occur in the neighborhood. We like to see if a pattern develops."

"Pattern? Have you been getting other reports about dogs acting weird? Attacking people and stuff?" I asked.

"Of course not. What? You think it's a doggie apocalypse?" John Johnson said, laughing a bit. "No. No weird dog calls. Just the usual cesspool shit I've been getting for fifteen years."

"Officer Johnson." Gwen stood. "Let me ask you. With all of your street-based experience with dogs and with your obvious education, why do think we've had these two—uh—experiences with dogs? If nobody else is having problems with dogs, then why us?"

John Johnson looked around the apartment again. *Redundant.* He looked at the door again. *Redundant.* Then John Johnson looked at me. "It might not be an 'us' problem," he said pointing two fingers, one at Gwen and one at me. "It might be a 'his' problem." He closed one finger and left the other squarely pointed on me. "I mean, you are the one who got bitten today. You piss off any dogs lately?"

I let a small chuckle escape. "You mean other than the poodle I killed after it bit me. Then no, I haven't."

"Before the poodle. You piss off a dog before the poodle?" John Johnson asked.

I was emphatic. "No. Absolutely not. I have nothing to do with dogs. Any dog."

"Well," Johnson said, heading toward the front door. "Then maybe dogs everywhere just decided that they don't like you for some reason that is imperceptible to us both."

Johnson and McNally were almost through the door when

McNally turned back around and said, "Or maybe you have the faint whiff of meat on you? Have you been cooking a lot of meat? Eating a lot of meat?"

I smiled, shook my head no, not even bothering to dignify the question.

"Well," McNally continued. "I wouldn't cook meat for a few days. Dogs love the smell of meat cooking. It gets on your clothes and stuff so you carry it with you."

I shook hands with the two officers and thanked them for answering the call. Gwen did likewise. "Officer McNally, just out of curiosity," Gwen asked as the two officers were just outside the front door, "what is your Master's degree in?"

"Ceramics and pottery," McNally said, beaming. "From U.A. That's the University of the Arts. I got a show next month at a gallery in New Hope. I'll drop a flyer in your mailbox."

"Great," I said. "That's great. Really. Great. Really."

CHAPTER FOUR

We didn't get back to bed until 4 am. I usually awoke at six for work and despite the excitement of the evening, I was determined to get the two hours of sleep that Old Man Time still afforded me.

Gwen had other ideas. "That was scary tonight, wasn't it? What about those cops? Such stereotypes. What is going on with these dogs today? Are dogs going crazy? It has to be just a coincidence, right? Do you think we need to buy a new door?"

"Gwen," I grumbled, exasperated. "That was like eight questions and it is four in the morning. Can we discuss this tomorrow?"

"You can sleep? After that?" Gwen asked, sounding surprised. This surprised me because she knew I could fall asleep on a moving roller coaster if I was so inclined. I had an uncanny ability to force myself to sleep whenever I so desired. "Fine, sleep. Go the fuck to sleep. I'll lie awake worrying about what could have happened to our unborn child."

My wife was a pleasant and gentle soul, but when rattled she could become defensive and sharp-tongued. We had been together long enough, and had loved one another strongly enough that when one of us got a bit irritated, the other did not take it personally. I knew Gwen and she knew me, period. I knew, as did she, that our love transcended the definition of 21st century married love. It more approached *agape*—the unalterable and transcendent love of God for mankind. Okay, that might be an exaggeration, but if ever two people could survive a maelstrom of struggle, it was Gwen and me.

Yet, since Gwen's belly had become the chalice of our first progeny, our near-*agape* love had become more stained. Worse even,
conventional. We were two over-educated, nicely salaried,
bohemian-stylized, liberal-Democrats living in the increas-
ing coolness of Philadelphia. We prided ourselves, smugly, on
our unconventional expression of love for one another. We felt
our unconventional expression of love made our relationship
uniquely more loving than traditional couples in suburban-
America. We would share a bottle of champagne in bed on
Sunday morning over *The Times Book Review* and make love with
the window shades wide open. After orgasms we'd read horrible Ted Hughes poems to one another in bad British accents. On
Saturday afternoons we would rent a canoe in Pennypack Park
before putting in our requisite hours at the local food co-op.
Then it was happy-hour Guinness pints at a perfectly faux-
Irish, posh hot-spot before dancing tipsy at the latest jazz joint.
Tuesday nights would be meeting with the "End Poverty Now"
group at the YMCA. Wednesdays were home with candles and
Thai food and ventures into Tantric sex. Thursdays were sunset
walks and a book club discussion for just the two of us over
modestly priced Bordeaux. Etcetera, etcetera. We led softly lav-
ish lives of intellect, laughter and conscience and, dare we say
it, love.

Since the chalice of her belly filled, the nights that had been
filled with music were quiet. Home was where the cares of
the day folded their tents like the nomad and silently slipped
away (to quote Wordsworth). Now home had become just plain
mundane and painfully mind numbing. Her back hurt, her
feet swelled. Her once self-image as a sexy woman had all but
disappeared. Forget Tantric sex, even European missionary
sex had tapered to a mere dribble of activity. Nights on the
town were exchanged for marathons of prenatal book reading.
Her carefree joviality and lightness of being were replaced by
exhaustive pre-planning for baby, financial planning for baby's
college and Gwen's radically altered identity from urban-
professional to suburbanite-mommy.

The change was killing Gwen and us.

Ironically, she resented the change but knew she couldn't stop it. Part of her wanted the old, bohemian, carefree self. An ever-growing part of her (growing physically and emotionally) could not resist morphing into the conventional, super pre-mom. Whereas I once foresaw a future of graying into intellectually stimulating and artistically relevant urban ascendency, I now foresaw a minivan, soccer practice, a cul-de-sac, and a potbelly in my increasingly benign future. Change was calling and change was not pleasant.

"It has been a crazy night, Gwen, I agree. I am worried. I am. Please, I have to work tomorrow. Understand? I gotta *go* to work." That is what I said, and *"fuck-me I am a stupid asshole,"* is what I thought as soon as I said it. The moment the words escaped my mouth, I knew I would be getting no more sleep tonight.

"*Go* to work? Excuse me? Did you just imply ... wait. You have to *go* to work? As if I don't!" Gwen said, her voice more than raised, more than irritated, hovering somewhere near homicidal. "How dare you! Just because I work from home doesn't make my job any less trying or tiring—"
"I didn't mean—"
"Just because you leave the house to work doesn't make your job any more goddamn important or difficult or ..." Her voice trailed off in a huff.
"Gwen, all I meant was—"
She cut me off again. "I know what you meant. You meant that—"
"Stop cutting me off," I yelled, the boom of my voice surprising even me. "Christ Almighty! I didn't mean shit. I just want to get some sleep. If I don't get sleep now, I'm going to be fucking exhausted."
"Me too," she said, shimmying her massive girth-of-impending-birth over on the bed, as far away from me as possible.
Why I said what I said next, I'll never know. Maybe it was fatigue or just plain bewilderment over the two odd dog incidents. Whatever the reason, I did it, and there was no taking

it back. "I don't work from home, Gwen. I can't take a snooze on the couch mid-afternoon."

Gwen looked at me like John Wilkes Booth probably looked at the back of Lincoln's head one second before the gunshot. "You cocksucker. You goddamn piece of shit. Like your job is so hard. It's a government job, for Christ-sake. You talk to a family, fill out your little form, get an hour lunch, off on every fucking bullshit holiday." Her eyes squinted and she looked even more like an emotional predator. "You don't even have to remove the kids from the home. If you deem, in all your pathetic wisdom, that they are in danger, you get the cops. You file your little form and order the police to take the kids away. You file your little form and order the men—the tough guys—to do the dangerous work. You don't even have the balls to face down the family and remove them yourself. I'm surprised you didn't piss your pants tonight."

I jumped from the bed to my feet, adrenaline compelling me to move. I began to speak but only sputtered out a few guttural sounds that might have been the beginning of words. I felt the kettle of emotion steaming in my body, a mixture of rage and shame. *How dare she call me a coward*, the rage said. *Fuck her*, it boomed monstrously, *I am no fucking coward*. Shame corrected me. *I am a coward*, it answered. *I was scared both today and tonight*, the shame reminded me. *I was scared when those dogs ... those damn dogs scared me.*

I looked at my wife. My eyes burned with the same mixture of rage and shame, anger and knowingness. My eyes were at once furious at her gall and pleading for her to retract the wounding words.

Gwen looked away, awash in guilt that she questioned my courage and manliness. I knew her well enough to know she felt bad at knocking me down a peg or twelve. I didn't give a shit about her emotions at that moment. She had said it and she knew its painful implications.

She also knew, as I did, that it would not be easily taken back or apologized into forgiveness. What's worse, she didn't even try.

Blood boiling but ego deflated, I started to leave the room and stopped. I looked at Gwen and her apologetic face and said, "I wish I let that dog into the house and let it rip your throat wide open."

CHAPTER FIVE

After my parting words with Gwen, I quickly shaved, shat and showered (what I called my "3S Routine") and was dressed and ready to get the hell out of Dodge. The sun was just rising on what would be, although I didn't know it, a monumental day in my life and the lives of so many unfortunate others.

Gwen never stirred that morning, feigning sleep while I got dressed in the bedroom. I knew Gwen well enough to know the difference between real-sleep and pretend-sleep. She merely kept her eyes closed to avoid more heated talk. She probably thought that by lunchtime I'd be settled down and ready to talk, calmly. I'd have rationalized her sharp cuts at my manly prowess as nothing more than reactionary utterances of anger, aimed to wound, but without the teeth of truth. Yes, Gwen assumed that by lunch, I'd have accepted that what she said was untrue (I *was* brave). Gwen knew I was brave (she was just mad). She was sorry she said what she said (she was feeling insecure about working from home and wanted me to feel insecure about something too ... level the playing field). All would be status quo again, she assumed. We would talk again later. Everything would be fine by the next time we saw one another.

As I walked toward the door that fateful morning, I thought that too. *Everything would be fine by the next time we saw one another.*

Now I can only wonder if that is true. If you are of the religious mind, then I will see her again one day when God's lottery draws my unlucky number. Well I suppose if you are religiously inclined, having God draw your number is not unlucky but quite fortunate. It would be a winning number, the grand prize.

At that time, I didn't hold any firm view of God. Till that day, the only thought I gave to religion was when I had to write a paper in graduate school about Saint Paul's almost pathological belief that human love was a window to the divine. In so writing, I found I accidentally memorized 1 Corinthians 13, the cliché of weddings, where Paul says that "love is patient, love is kind."

When I left Gwen alone, our fight still unresolved, that biblical passage was nothing more than words I'd accidentally memorized. Since that day, it has become a mantra of my life. God has to love us because I need to see Gwen again! I know God does, so I know I will.

These existential thoughts were the furthest thing from my mind when my hand froze midair while reaching for the door knob. I stood in the foyer before the front door, hand held frozen in midair, statuesque. *What if the dog was out there again? What if another, different dog was out there? Or a whole fucking pack of dogs?*

What was on my mind was fresh pain at being called a coward. When my hand stopped cold, the thought painted across my mind again. *You coward.*

I willed my hand to move and grab the doorknob, and when flesh hit the cold metal knob, it snapped me from my trance-like rigidity. I turned the knob as a cold droplet of sweat trickled down my face, despite the cool October morning. *You coward,* the droplet said.

I cracked the door an inch or so and the coward in me won out. I peeked like a scared child through the crack between the door and the frame and looked outside.

Clear. Nothing but a mundane Philadelphia morning. A bit overcast, but otherwise a typical October in the great northeast corridor of North America. No dog around. No dogs, plural. I smiled, both in relief at the ordinariness of the day and in shame at fearing otherwise.

However, trepidation still raced through my body as I

crossed the threshold and onto the sidewalk. Something still hung in the air, some venomous feeling that a dangerous unraveling of the conventional safety of life was upon me. As I hit the sidewalk at a brisk pace, the rational mind assessed the situation and made a rational decision that what I was feeling was just that, feelings. Just emotional residue from an eventful day, evening, and morning. Yes, I thought, today is just another day like any other.

Except it hadn't occurred to me till I walked toward my car, parked about two blocks away, that it was so damn early in the morning. I was in such a state of anger and embarrassment after Gwen's comments that I just wanted out of that apartment. Now I realized it was the ass-crack of dawn, and I didn't have my first appointment till nine, the typical start time for a Department of Children and Youth employee's day. I had time to kill and almost as a reflex, I reached for my smartphone.

"Lucas?" a voice answered, surprised. "Is something wrong?" The voice belonged to Lydia, and the unusual hour of my call was certainly what prompted her to ask about my wellbeing.

"Hey, no, nothing's wrong. I just couldn't sleep," I lied, knowing I could have been sound asleep at this very moment if Gwen had let me. "So I'm heading out and thought you might want to get a coffee or something. I'm bored."

Lydia chuckled on her end. "Bored? Well thanks. So I'm the person you call when you can't sleep and are bored. Just what every girl wants to hear."

I cringed a bit when Lydia said, "what every girl wants to hear." It was too flirtatious and reeked of some romantic tinge to our relationship, which, to my mind, didn't exist. I was married and just because Lydia would have wished otherwise, I did not and would never indulge in marital treason. I enjoyed Lydia for the intelligent and quick-witted friend she was but her regular need to add flirty, romantically weighted language to our conversations always bothered me. At the same time, I felt my loins begin to hum. Complexities of human interaction can be a bitch.

"I didn't mean I called you just because I was bored. I meant you are the only person I knew who would be up and showered and ready to go at this hour."

I almost heard Lydia smiling through the phone. "Oh that's much better, thanks. At least you are thinking of me showering."

She said she was up, dressed and reading the paper, which she agreed to abandon to meet me at the local coffee shop chain in her neighborhood. I was at my car by the time our conversation ended and on my way.

I reached a red light while NPR's Morning Edition updated me on the latest news of some African military regime that repressed a popular uprising. They found some dead American guy there among the human carnage. He had a tattoo covering his entire back of a sniper scope with the word "coward." I was thinking about what a stupid tattoo this is … when my heart dropped in my chest like a foul turd drops into toilet water.

An old man was on the sidewalk near the driver's side of my car, bent over with a plastic baggie on his one hand, aiming to pick up the brown pile of excrement his dog had just deposited on the ground. His other hand held the leash tethered to his dog's collar. This being a normal sight in urban America, I gave it little more than a cursory glance and looked again at the red light, wishing it to turn green. Something caught the periphery of my eye and my head snapped back to the left. The dog that had made the deposit the man was now bagging—a black Cocker Spaniel, if my breed identification is accurate—stared at me. It wasn't looking vaguely toward me, it was looking *at* me. As my eyes reached the dog's eyes, I found myself in a staring match with a dog.

I was transfixed, my eyes and the dog's eyes caught in a deadlock.

The stoplight said "go" with a green light, but I didn't move and neither did the cocker. Its top lip began to quiver, ever so slightly. I couldn't take my eyes off the dog and it leered at me, never flinching or even blinking. The quivering lip started to rise, slowly exposing the dog's teeth.

The quiver became a snarl and the rest happened so damn fast.

Almost simultaneously, the snarl became a savage bark and the dog lunged in a full-body leap toward the street. The old man was not completely upright, and when the lunge caught tight on the leash, his feeble strength could not provide a counterweight. He toppled over hard, his top half falling into the street, his legs falling on the sidewalk and his old-man's hip hitting the curb. He yelped and the leash tore free from his grasp.

My mind had two concurrent thoughts. One, landing on his hip was unfortunate because old men are always dying of hip-fractures. Two, *the fucking dog is charging at me!*

The black Cocker Spaniel slammed into my driver-side car door with unchecked speed and hit the door so hard the audible thud sounded like certain death for the furry canine. Yet it was up in an instant, jumping up onto its hind legs and scratching at my driver-side window, its mouth unleashing a machine gun of barks only inches from my face. If my window had not been closed to keep the morning chill at bay, I had no doubt the cocker would have leapt into the car and gnawed my face to shredded pork in a matter of moments. The window held and the dog scratched and clawed and barked. Its mouth and teeth hit the glass when its paws slipped to the side. Its eyes remained fixed on my own throughout, as if this dog wanted to not only tear into my flesh but devour my very soul.

I didn't pull my eyes away to check on the poor old guy who, I surmised, had orthopedic surgery in his future. Nor did I look at what was in front of me (fortunately nothing) as I stomped on the accelerator and sped through the intersection. I am not conscious of feeling a bump or anything like it, but when I looked wide-eyed in the rearview mirror a second later, I saw the cocker dragging its two back legs that were flat and obviously broken beyond use. It was laboriously pulling itself with its front legs, dragging its crippled and mangled body down the street at snail's pace, chasing after me.

The cocker's back legs must've gotten caught under my wheels as I sped off, and despite such egregious injuries, the fucking thing still wanted to tear me to kibble. What hell had I stumbled into?

CHAPTER SIX

Lydia was already seated at a table when I arrived, with one mocha for her and another waiting for me. She must've noticed I looked a bit exhausted and worn. She put it more bluntly. "Christ, you look hung-over. Fuck the coffee, maybe you need some hair of the dog?"

The reference caught me off-guard. "What did you say?" I asked, sitting down across from her.

"I said you look like you drank too much last night, you lush."

"No-no," I said, eyes scanning the sidewalk outside the coffee shop for any canine intruders, of which I saw none. "You said, 'hair of the dog.' Why did you say that? Why would you say something like that?"

She smiled at this, thinking I was playing, toying. "You don't like that expression? Maybe you'd prefer 'hair of the pussy cat'?" She emphasized the word a flirtatious vixen would emphasize. Despite all that had occurred—three dog attacks and my wife calling me a coward—part of my mind noticed how good Lydia looked. At forty-five years old, she was a bit older than my thirty-four years but she kept her body trim, tight, and her black hair girlishly long. She had sharp jaw lines and deep-set, dark eyes that dragged you into her gaze. Those eyes worked well for her. Lydia was a low-level lawyer with my employer, Philadelphia's Department of Children and Youth. We rarely saw one another at work, but we once worked a case together. We both testified in court, we won, and the child was placed in foster care. We had drinks after the trial and had been friends since. Not friends with benefits. More like friends with nuances.

Today, as on most work days, she was wearing a satin blouse and a tight-fitted business skirt that implied she was equal parts work and play. Even though I was convinced that I was under attack by insane dogs everywhere, I felt the warm wash of lust pervade my mind.

"I'm not hung-over. Just didn't get enough sleep last night. None, really."

"Oh," Lydia said, sitting back in her chair. "Out on a late-night run for pickles and peanut butter for the pregnant wife?"

Though I kept our relationship platonic, Lydia never missed an opportunity to take a cheap shot at my wife. Normally, I mildly scolded her for it but today was not a normal day. "You think I'm sane, right?"

"Huh? What?"

"Sane. In control of my mental faculties. Light bulb burning bright in the mind. You know, sane."

Lydia took a moment to consider this, again playing, toying. The look on my face must've informed her that I was not in the mood for games. "Do I think you are insane? Do I think the wheel is spinning but the gerbil is dead? No. You're sane. We are all abnormal in some part of our lives, but yeah, on the whole, you are sane. Sort of an odd question though. An abnormal question."

"I've had an abnormal day."

"Really, already? Because it's only seven. The day has just begun."

"That's what really fucking scares me."

"Whoa," Lydia said, smiling. "Dropping f-bombs this early in the morning. You gotta have a good story. Do tell. Give all the good disturbing details."

I looked outside again. A young twenty-something, artsy looking guy across the street was holding a leash. My brain seized in panic. My eyes scanned down to the end of the leash and I let out a sigh of relief. I wanted to run outside and smack the artsy douche bag in his wannabe-bohemian, nose-pierced face because artsy-boy was walking a ferret. A goddamn ferret! Only in the new urban America do you see shit like that. I sighed audibly and looked at Lydia, resolving to tell her the truth. "I'll be blunt. Every dog that sees me wants to kill me."

I waited for some response, but Lydia just took a sip of her coffee. So I waited longer, till she finally spoke. "That's it? That's your story?"

"Why don't you seem surprised? Is this something you've heard before?"

"You were bitten by a dog recently," she replied.

"Yes, how'd you know that?"

"I didn't, but you are limping a bit. Then you mention that shit about dogs wanting to kill you and I surmised it." She took another sip of her coffee. My coffee was passively cooling. "So you got bitten by a dog and now you think all dogs are after you?"

Shaking my head in boisterous disagreement, I told Lydia about what had occurred during the last eighteen hours, leaving out only the fight with Gwen. Lydia needed no ammunition for her shots at Gwen. She listened intently and purposefully, giving the occasional nod or "uh-huh" to let me know she was listening. When I finished, she took the last sip of her coffee, tipping the paper cup back almost straight into the air to get that last drop.

"Well, am I crazy?" I asked.

Her answer was flat. "You have a bite from the first incident. Gwen witnessed the second incident. If the old man broke his hip and you ran over his dog, there will be a police report for the third incident. So your story has evidentiary support. Tangible support."

"Shit, do you think I'm being sought for a hit and run? I didn't even think of that."

"No," Lydia said. "Legally, you are not required to stop if you accidentally hit an animal while driving. The law does not differentiate between a deer, squirrel, or even a dog. The old man falling had nothing to do with you. I'd say you're fine."

I exhaled. "Good. Now what about the dogs-attacking-me theory? I'm insane, right?"

Lydia looked concerned and I assumed she was concerned for my sanity. "Like I said, you did not experience these incidents in isolation. There are facts substantiating your assertions. In other words, proof. Proof, Lucas, that you've had three unusual encounters with dogs in less than twenty-four hours."

"So I'm not nuts. They are after me."

Lydia uncrossed then crossed her legs in the opposite direction. She had great goddamn legs. "All you have is proof that it did happened. You have nothing on why it happened."

"So," I said, "I lack motive."

"Correct. Why did you have three unusual dog attacks in less than twenty-four hours? What would compel dogs to attack you? Logic says nothing would compel dogs to attack you, that it is actually just coincidence."

I started to protest before Lydia jumped in.

"Yes, I know. The incidents are just too severe in nature and too close together in time to be mere coincidence. What could possibly drive these dogs so nuts when they see you?" Lydia was really getting into this, her mind searching for plausible explanations. Or maybe she was just playing along for fun. I know now, in hindsight, that it wouldn't be fun for Lydia for much longer.

"This may sound stupid," I said, "but the one cop—Officer McNally—suggested that perhaps I smell like meat. He was being cute, but maybe he is on to something. Maybe my body is naturally producing a scent that humans can't smell but that makes dogs fucking mad. Really mad."

Lydia looked skeptical. "I never heard of a scent making any animal mad. Scents make them horny or hungry or denote territories, but on all these nature shows on TV, I never saw scent make them angry or put them into attack mode."

"Yeah," I agreed. "If anything, the scent of a bigger animal scares them away."

"That's another thing that bothers me," Lydia said. "Animals are instinctual. If they see something they don't like they either fight or flight, period. They only fight over territory, mating, food, or protecting their young. Otherwise they flee. Also the dog who was at your front door last night throws a wrench into everything. That dog sought you out. That's just so strange."

I shook my head in acknowledgement and exasperation. Lydia was right. I posed no threat to any of the dogs' food, mating-pool, territory, or puppies. Yet some dog came to my front door looking for me like a Mafioso hit man. Dogs just don't do that.

Logic, it seemed, was failing.

Lydia had the same idea. "So if natural explanations do not work, than you must seek the supernatural."

I waved a dismissive hand at Lydia. "Don't go getting all voodoo on me. I'm a doctoral level psychologist and you are ..." I paused for effect. "... employed." Lydia smiled at my chiding of her professional ambition, or lack thereof. "We both should say that the supernatural is not super at all, just a natural occurrence that we don't have the understanding yet to prove as natural."

"We should say that," Lydia agreed. "I believe in life after death so why would it be such a stretch to believe something more?"

"What more?" I argued. "That dogs are somehow being driven by supernatural forces to kill me?"

"Did you Google it?"

My head shot backward in surprise. "Google what?"

"Systematic animal attacks against one singular person," she replied curtly.

"Are you mocking me?" I asked.

Lydia had her smartphone out in an instant and was plugging away. I waited patiently while she scanned through websites and wiki entries. "Holy shit," she finally uttered, not looking up from her phone.

"What?" I responded as people commonly do when someone says "holy shit."

"Afghanistan. Tribal groups in the Afghanistan-Pakistan mountainous region have been known to taint a person with an ancient hex so animals—specific animals depending on the hex used—will attack the person on sight." She was still reading the website. "It says that although these tribal people were mostly converted to Islam a century ago, they retain some ancient traditions from pre-Islam days. Maybe that's it. Maybe it is a hex. You need to see your brother."

I gave her the 'are you being serious?' look. "Really?" I

asked. "You think my brother hexed me."

"No-no. Not at all. He fought in those tribal areas of Afghanistan. He might know something about it."

I shook my head in a resounding "no." "I don't talk to my brother and even if I did, I doubt he knows shit about hexes or whatever."

"It can't hurt," Lydia said. "Besides, if dogs keep attacking you, then you are going to need a gun and your brother has got lots of those."

The obviousness of her simple, yet completely accurate, statement left me speechless. Of course I needed a gun, I realized. I needed to protect myself from whatever this thing was. Unless I wanted to wait eight days for a background check to be completed, I needed to get a loaner-gun. Knowing no hoodlums, my brother became the singular retailer for my rush-order acquisition.

"Shit," I said, standing to leave, my voice rising. "You're right. I need to see my brother. Like right now. I need a fucking gun." The woman at the next table looked up from her Stephen King novel with startled eyes.

Lydia didn't care about the woman. "Yes you do need a gun. You need to learn how to fire the fucking thing."

"Right," I said, throwing on my coat. "I'll call you and let you know when this all calms down. Thanks."

"No need to thank me. This is kind of exciting."

"Exciting?" I said, my voice thick with displeasure. "That's how you describe this mess?"

Lydia smiled her gorgeous smile. "Beats the hell out of a monotonous, boring day at work, don't it." If only she could have seen into the future, Lydia would not have been so casual in her assessment.

"I suppose that's one way to look at it," I said turning to leave. "Anyway, wish me luck."

"Good luck," she said, and paused, adding. "Be brave."

I stopped at the door and looked at her, my face heating with anger. *Be brave. Be fucking brave.* I wondered for an instant if Gwen and Lydia did talk, conversing about my lack of courage, my yellow-streak. I turned and left, and in my anger, I forgot to check the street for dogs.

No dogs. Got lucky. Luck never lasts.

CHAPTER SEVEN

It wasn't until nearly noon that I discovered what happened to Officer McNally. His incident occurred while I was having coffee with Lydia. It was much later in the day when I found out.

Officer McNally, the white cop with a graduate degree in pottery, had just finished his shift and clocked out while I was busy sipping mocha with Lydia. Having changed into his normal exercise gear, Officer McNally set off on his routine jog through the industrial park located behind the station. While McNally did not strike me as a man who exercised (his beer belly was my first indicator) he had actually just lost about twenty pounds while developing a habit of jogging five miles a day. In fact, slow-jogging had turned into brisk-running, and McNally had become an avid road runner. He even placed third in his age bracket at a recent 5k charity race. McNally, it seems, discovered a new passion besides pottery and he pursued it with gusto. His fellow police officers—typical police meatheads by all accounts—already questioned McNally's sexual orientation, assuming a man who gets a graduate degree in pottery was most certainly a homosexual. When he began losing weight and caring about his appearance, his reputation as a closeted queer became all but solidified. The meatheads assumed he was shaping up so he could go to one of those gay clubs where men take off their shirts and dance in leather pants.

One of the few colleagues of McNally's who didn't seem to question or care about the fudge-packing rumors was Officer John Johnson. As I also discovered later, John Johnson was a man who did not follow the cool crowd. He did not gossip and judge a man based solely on his actions. Also, John Johnson was a raging liberal, and besides being a badass cop with a fierce personality, he was also a man of compassion and empathy. So despite all the "homo" rumors, John Johnson offered to be McNally's partner. The two had been riding together for roughly a year.

As a side note, it turns out that McNally was not only a heterosexual, but his artistic forays in pottery and ceramics gave him access to large numbers of women whom McNally plowed through with the gusto of a sixteen-year-old. In fact, in the artsy-ceramics world of Philadelphia (who knew such a thing existed), McNally was known as a playboy and, equally, a tremendously good, well-endowed lover. Go figure.

On that morning, McNally was simply a guy going for a brisk morning run through an industrial park. It provided ample, winding pavement so that when a person ran from the police station to one end of the industrial park and back again, the entire run constituted 4.85 miles. That was close enough to five miles for McNally.

Unbeknownst to him, a fifty-five-year-old woman was outside behind the Penn Perfect Bindery and Bounding Company having a cigarette and she witnessed the whole incident. She reported what she saw to the police, which is how I came to know the story.

McNally was running on the south side of Ben Road heading north through the industrial park. On the south side where McNally was running stands a twelve-foot fence topped with barbed wire installed by a company that made copper fittings for electronic parts. Considering the street-value for copper these days, the company installed the fence three years previously. They received a discount on their operating insurance for the added protection, so the fence paid for itself in two years. They did not receive any insurance discount for the guard dog.

Samantha, or Sam for short, wasn't actually a guard dog, but rather she was the owner's pet Irish Setter. When the fence was installed, the owner realized he could bring his beloved Sam the Setter to work each day and let her run free in the fenced-off property. Sam was a nice, sweet dog, who loved to bark at people who approached the fence, but was otherwise a playful, beautiful pooch that enjoyed a good belly rub. She seemed to boost morale among the workers, who considered Sam a hard-working employee. In fact, Sam had been thrice nominated for employee of the month in the anonymous nomination basket, but had always lost out to a human employee.

As McNally ran north on the south side of Ben Street, he came to where the fence began. As always he was greeted by the full-charging, barking, and just-damn-excited Sam. McNally, running this course near a hundred times, had fully expected Sam to come charging and barking at the fence. He fully expected Sam to follow him till he reached the end of the fence. In fact, McNally liked seeing Sam and always gave the Setter a warm smile. On weekends, when Sam was home with her owner, McNally noted her absence.

That day was no different. Sam came charging from her usual resting spot about fifty yards down from where the fence began, somewhere in the center of the company's property. When McNally came into view and saw Sam come running and barking, he didn't think anything unusual.

Then Sam did something unusual.

When the setter reached the fence, McNally gave his usual smile and kept up his steady pace, but Sam, instead of just barking and running along, actually bit the fence. Not just a nibble, either, according to the witness, but a full-on, clenching bite onto the metal fence. She wrapped her teeth onto the crisscrossed metal and pulled backward with a ferocity that wrenched the fence in Sam's direction. The fence held, of course, but rocked a bit with the strain.

Both the witness and McNally jumped at the violence of the Setter's action, and McNally stumbled a bit, but recovered and maintained his pace. The witness watched, perplexed, as the dog she saw for at least six cigarettes per day behaved like a famished cougar.

The dog released her bite and caught up to McNally. She kept pace, snarling and barking with, as the witnessed described, "an unholy and god-awful bark I never heard from that dog before."

McNally too must have realized that something was amiss

and different about Sam's reaction to him this October morning. The witness reported that McNally's usual brisk pace slowed to a slow jog, with McNally keeping his eyes pinned on the animal. The dog bit at the fence again, and again locked her teeth and pulled as if, according to the witness, "she wanted to tear that fence down with every fiber of her being."

Besides the normal endorphins associated with fear, I can only surmise what was running through McNally's mind as he jogged along. *What has gotten into this dog? What on earth? This dog must be having a bad day. Thank God for fences. This reminds me of that call this morning about the dog—*
Wham!
The witness said her cigarette slipped from her fingers and dropped to the ground as she watched the dog hit a tiny space that had developed in the seam where one section of the fence met a new section. The seam was merely one section of fence peeling back and the next section of fence peeling back, leaving a few-inches gap between the two. Normally, such a tiny seam would be too small to attract Sam's attention, but that day, it provided Sam just enough space.

The Setter hit the seam like a linebacker and her head managed to poke through, stretching the peeled fencing backward. Her back legs kicked in the grass and dirt, straining for leverage, thrusting with all her might to launch her body through the widening gap in the fence. All the while, the animal barked its "unholy, god-awful bark."

McNally had now stopped running and stood for a second, perplexed, watching this dog drive itself with the determination of a grizzly to get through the fence. As the dog pushed and clawed its way through the seam, the ends of the fence's seams began to catch and get tangled with Sam's long hair. McNally watched with awe and disbelief as the Setter gained another foot of ground through the opening, not even yelping or pausing as the tangles of hair ripped from her back and hung in long, dangling, bloody twists from the fence.

That is when McNally began to run. I imagine McNally ran quicker than he'd ever run.

Turning on his heels, he took off in the opposite direction. The witness said, "he bolted at an amazingly fast speed for a man of his size," but she added, "the dog was through the seam a few seconds later and was on him in no time."

McNally never stood a chance once that dog had made it through the fence. He hadn't even cleared ten yards when Sam leaped and hit him from behind. His own momentum of running combined with the fifty-pound weight of the charging dog was enough to knock McNally flat onto his stomach. He hit the ground hard, and the witness heard an audible gasp from McNally as he hit the pavement. Sam wasted no time jumping onto McNally's back and tearing into his skin with her rather long teeth. McNally flung his hands and kicked, but he was face down, and effectively defenseless. Sam kept biting and scratching at his back until the dog finally got hold of something she could lock onto. Unfortunately for McNally, this was the side of his neck. With her jaw making a V-shape, the top half of Sam's jaw was on the back of McNally's neck, while the lower half of Sam's jaw made it partially around front, sinking her teeth into the tender, artery rich and life-dependent part of McNally's anatomy. The dog found her spot to lock and did so, followed by an insane thrashing and twisting that only further widened the monstrous tear in McNally's throat. McNally thrashed too, but in desperation to preserve his quickly ending life.

"Then like a switch was flipped, the man stopped moving," the witness said. "The man just stopped and lay still. Not a twitch or a shake. Nothing. I'll be damned but as soon as the man stopped moving, the dog let him go, looked around a bit, and lay down putting her head on her paws like she was taking a summertime nap. I wouldn't believe an animal could go from such violence to such calm in a split second, but it did."

The witness soon realized that although the dog had calmed down, almost miraculously calmed down, it had just mauled a human being. At the same time, she realized that all that separated her from this animal was a narrow street. Without even stomping out the cherry of her cigarette, she ran inside Penn Perfect Bindery and Bounding Company and called 911.

When the police arrived, they found a few unexpected

things. One was a scene of a man lying in a pool of blood and flesh and carnage that made even the most veteran officers shudder. Second, they found a calm, placid and (dare they even say it) friendly dog sitting next to the man. The dog was tranquil despite the fact that she was covered from snout to tail in blood, with chunks of flesh caught in her canine teeth. Third, they saw a small brush fire brewing across the street from the crime scene. They later discovered the witness had dropped her lit cigarette and it had rolled down the sloping asphalt into a drain clogged with littered newspaper, paper cups, and other debris.

The Penn Perfect fire extinguishers were enough to put out the small fire.

The dog went with the Philadelphia Humane Law Enforcement officers without any fuss whatsoever, and was actually quite affable during her apprehension.

Soon the cops discovered that the bloody, mangled body that lay face down belonged to a fellow officer, and despite their schoolhouse gossip about McNally being a closeted queer, cops don't like it when other cops are killed. Period.

Sam the Irish Setter died while in custody of Philadelphia's Humane Law Enforcement. Enough said.

On the television news at noon, the reporter's teaser for the story was "Not fitting for a cop to die at a copper fitting company. We will bring the story to you live."

Pun-loving pricks.

CHAPTER EIGHT

Corporal Derrick Miller, US Army, Ret., liked to be called Rick and liked to be an asshole.

I'm the first to admit it is unpopular to call a war hero an asshole, but because he is my brother, I get a pass.

Rick Miller lived just outside of Philadelphia in a wooded suburb called Pipersville. Though just a quick thirty-minute drive from Philly swank via a few major roadways, we were emotionally and socially thousands of miles apart. He lived in a free-standing, one-room efficiency dwelling on a wooded property. It belonged to a retired Marine Captain who had befriended Rick during Rick's prolonged stay at the VA hospital. The Marine captain, whose name I never knew because he was always just referred to as Captain, built the one-room efficiency as a free-standing little home. It even looked like a tiny version of a house, complete with siding and shutters on its two front windows. Inside it was just one big square, but with the comforts of electricity, indoor-plumbing, (the toilet and shower were separated as another room inside the one main room), kitchenette, and some windows. Captain, retired on a twenty-plus year military pension, had built it as a writer's office about four acres away from his actual home on his thirty-acre property. It was built just far enough away that he could walk to it each morning, yet still feel as if he was getting away from the house for undistracted work. That work was, of course, to write a great American novel.

Like most aspiring novelists, he began with gusto, walking each morning to his little efficiency, and writing for four to five hours, proud of his progress. He soon realized, as most do, that writing a book-length story is grueling work. What Captain had assumed would be an enjoyable, leisurely retirement pursuit that yielded a Pulitzer-prize-winning novel and an interview on the *Today Show* by the hot-ass Savannah Guthrie, had in fact become a painful, dreaded and exhausting enterprise abandoned as quickly as it started.

Supposedly, the Captain never mentioned his ill-fated writing career. I was once advised by Rick that if I'd ever met the Captain and I valued my teeth remaining in my mouth, I should never mention his "unfinished masterpiece." If I dared to say "failed" when mentioning the novel within earshot of the Captain then my life would be in serious jeopardy.

Since helping to move my brother into that small efficiency three years previously, I had never been back. Rick was an asshole that day and the next and soon these asshole moments had compounded into my ignoring him altogether, which seemed to suit him just fine.

That day, I pulled into the long gravel driveway of the Captain's estate and drove a good fifty yards before taking another gravel off-shoot that diverted you to my brother's small building hidden in the grounds' thickets.

I had no reason to expect he'd be home. I hadn't even bothered to call first since he never answered his phone. Even if he was home, I had no idea how Rick would receive me or what he'd be doing with himself.

I certainly did not expect what I found.

As I pulled up to my brother's bucolic bungalow, I found him standing naked as a newborn at the top of the driveway, leaning backward, pissing in a long arch, as if he was trying to set a pissing-distance record. That damn guy didn't have on a stitch of clothing, not even socks. By my own accounting, his stream of piss *was* setting a record, reaching at least four feet from cock-tip to soil.

Throwing the car into park, I was so surprised by the sight that I actually hesitated to turn the key and kill the engine. One thought did cross through my mind though. *At least in his current state of undress, I know he isn't packing a concealed gun. Chances of him shooting me are less. Although, he could piss on me.*

As if his outdoor nakedness in the broad daylight of an October morning sun wasn't enough of a surprise, what he said and did next only added to the oddity of this already odd day. While Rick finished his long-arch piss, he turned to see who pulled into his driveway. Seeing me, he looked me dead in the eyes. Shaking his considerably sized pecker (we shared this brotherly trait) to get out the last few drops, he smiled the widest smile I think I'd ever seen him smile and walked over to my car with that smile plastered on his face.

When he stopped within a foot of my car, I killed the engine and stepped out. As soon as I shut the door, my brother Rick, a war-hero asshole and (apparently) record-setting distance-pisser, grabbed me around the shoulders in a giant hug. This was not the Rick I had known previously. Despite the weirdness of being hugged by a naked man, it was the nature of the hug that really knocked me off-guard. Rick was squeezing me in a manner that was genuinely full of brotherly love. He spoke with an equally genuine sincerity. "Lucas! My little brother, Lucas. Damn good to see you. Damn good." He continued to hug me. "Lucas, I've been having terrible dreams that something bad has happened to you and I've been beside myself with worry." Continuing to hug, he added, "I know you think I'm an asshole, so I was afraid to reach out to you. Afraid of what you'd say to me, how you'd receive me." The hug continued, but had gone from weird to uncomfortable. "Now here you are and damn it, I am just so happy." He paused for a moment and added some small, but noticeable squeezes, to his embracing hug, which now was no longer just uncomfortable but downright disconcerting. "I love you, Lucas."

I had enough and wiggled just enough for him to know I wanted a release from the closeness. He held on a bit longer, giving me one final good squeeze, before letting me go.

"Wow," I started, "Rick, uh, good to see you." I pointed at his nakedness. "Good to see so much of you," my awkwardness shining forth in the bad joke.

Rick didn't seem to notice. "So you need my help, huh. Bad shit happening to you. I've been having dreams about bad shit happening to you. How's that wife of yours? What's her name? It doesn't matter. Come inside, tell me what's wrong." He started leading me toward the house then stopped, as if a thought just occurred to him. "You need a gun. I bet you need a damn gun to protect yourself. No problem, brother. I have guns. I have ammo. Shit, I even have a flame thrower."

CHAPTER NINE

Seated inside at a small kitchen table with only two chairs, I was struck by how clean and neat the place was kept. As a teenager he was disgustingly messy and disheveled. The military's training and insistence that service persons be orderly, clean and shipshape must've become a permanent part of my brother. The place was so uncluttered and tidy that you'd imagined Mrs. Cleaver lived there.

"Dogs?" Rick said, rubbing his chin with his thumb and pointer-finger as he considered this. "Dogs attacking you?" He paused. "Huh." He paused again. "Have you had a CAT scan recently?" He chuckled at his pun and I just shook my head and took out a cigarette from Rick's pack that lay on the table. Since entering his home, he had thrown on a pair of boxer shorts, but nothing more. Rick had lost some of his physique since active duty, but he was still more in-shape than most men. The scars from his combat wounds still raised on the skin like loud tattoos, lines and puncture scars cutting across his muscle-toned flesh from bullets and shrapnel taken in the desert of Afghanistan. No fanfare had been made when he returned home. Philadelphia was a big city with hundreds of recently wounded veterans. There was no small-town parade with flag-waving and all that "Welcoming Home Our Hero" bullshit. Not even any family greeted him. Our parents were dead of the usual diseases and Rick was a committed childless bachelor. When he stepped foot on American soil again, just an ambulance from the Veterans Administration greeted him at Dover Air Base and drove him for a long stint in Walter Reed to heal, both physically and mentally.

When I visited him at Walter Reed he'd become a prick, looking down on anyone who hadn't engaged in combat, talking to me as if I was some goddamn pussy for not enlisting and fighting after the terrible events of September 11. He would bitch about civilians and their cowardice and how we complained about "trivial everyday problems that were so insignificant" to the war-hardened. He made demeaning comments to the military doctors, calling them "the safely serving." I signed Rick out of Walter Reed one day on a four-hour pass to get some lunch at a local Hooters. After a few beers he couldn't resist telling some Navy guys who were there by happenstance that, "Only pussies enlist in an outfit that no longer fights. Since when have we had a great Naval battle? You think you can fight Al Qaeda from a ship?" I could only calm down the Navy guys by buying them a round of beer and wings. By the time he was permanently discharged from Walter Reed and asked me to help him move into his current residence, I could barely tolerate five minutes in his arrogant presence. Yet he was my brother and needed help moving so I relented (with Gwen's encouragement) and decided to help him get settled. That was the day he said to me, "It takes a brave man to wake up every day and face the nightmare of living. Since you're such a coward, I guess you're just sleep-walking through life."

That was the last day I spoke to him. Until this day.

"CAT scan," I said. "Cute. I hadn't thought of that one yet. Glad your sense of humor has returned."

"Returned?" Rick asked. "Did it ever leave?"

"I won't keep you longer than needed." I sighed. "I just need some protection. As you mentioned, a gun."

Rick looked at me for a hard and long second. "Damn, brother. I haven't seen you in months—years—and you are trying to skedaddle so quick? Talk to me. How's that wife of yours?"

"She's fine," I said, the embers of burning rage in my gut from the morning's argument now sparking into flame. "I really don't have time to get into all that. I need to …" my voice trailed off, and I realized that other than getting a gun, I didn't know what to do. I didn't have a plan or a solution. All I had was questions, which was half the reason I came here. "Rick, you served in that tribal area between Afghanistan and Pakistan, right? The mountainous area that really isn't a part of either country but ruled by tribes as old as Earth itself."

"I killed people all across that wasteland." His tone was flat, emotionless.

"Yeah but did you run into people with ancient, weird tribal beliefs?"

Rick lit a cigarette and took a deep drag. He smiled wide and let the smoke cascade out and upward from his beaming mouth. "You overeducated sonofabitch. You think dogs are chasing you because I had some voodoo freak from tribal Afghanistan curse you. Damn, that's cold. Even cold for someone like you who is burning with …" He thought for a second. "I don't know what you're burning with but something inside you is steaming and teeming, brother. It's palpable. I can almost feel the heat from you."

"What the hell are you talking about?"

"You, Lucas. You got something deep in your heart that is rising to the surface and it is lighting up your eyes and making your soul shine. It ain't light. Nope, more like heat. A furnace that is finally ignited but what is igniting it, I do not know."

I just shook my head side to side in annoyance. "Christ Almighty, Rick. Have *you* had a CAT scan recently?"

"I've never felt better," he said, smiling again, letting a small burp escape for good measure.

I leaned forward, squinting as if studying him. "Rick, I don't know about any fire in me or anything, but there is something different about you. You aren't the same person you were a year ago."

"I'm trying to be eccentric."

"What?"

"Did I stutter? I am trying to be eccentric." He sat back as if that statement explained everything with complete clarity. Seeing my confused look, he continued. "Listen, about three months ago I realized I had become a cliché. When I came home from the war I had become nothing more than a walking-wounded cliché. You know what I mean. You got a doctorate degree for Christ-sake, you should know this shit. When I got home I was all about bravado and busting heads. I thought I was king-shit 'cause I fought and was wounded, acting as if I single-handedly built and defended this country, all by my lonesome. I hated civilians because this was my country, I'd fought for it, and they were just my guests. I was Mister Military Veteran. Then one day I saw my future. I saw myself sitting at some VFW bar twenty years from now, wearing one of those loud baseball-style caps that says in military-looking letters, "Afghanistan War Veteran, United States Marine Corps." I'd be watching Fox News, applauding Fox's hatred against the damn liberals, on my third or fourth divorce, drinking my sixth or seventh bourbon, telling the bored old bartender the same damn war stories he's heard me tell a thousand times …" He just looked away. "You get the picture. I didn't want that picture."

I'll admit, I was stunned. "As a psychologist, allow me to say the epiphany you had is not only rare, it is downright supernatural. As your brother, allow me to say that I couldn't be happier, because you were a prick."

Rick waved a finger at me. "Don't think I've become a pussy, and you can lick my clit till I do your laundry."

"I didn't mean—"

"I'm still one badass warrior. I just decided that I want to do things on my own terms. I can be proud of my life without wearing my pride printed on a goddamn tee-shirt. I realized that being nutty, being the oddball, is so much more fun than being the angry meathead. Besides, being a wounded vet allows you to get away with doing nutty shit. Who the hell is going to question a Purple-Hearted veteran? So I'm trying to be eccentric. Different. Live a different style of living."

Liking this line of thought, I found myself nodding in agreement, smiling a bit. "Awesome. Eccentric! Like peeing outside stark naked in the early morning sunlight."

Rick looked perplexed. "What? No. Not like that at all. I just needed to take a piss and it's a beautiful morning. Are you listening to anything I'm saying?"

I stumbled for the right words but gave up, opting for just

a smile. Despite being confused, I thought maybe Rick had become someone I could like again. Shit, maybe he'd even become the brother I could love. I was confused but optimistic. I'd settle for optimistic.

Rick broke the silence. "So you seem to think you have a problem. A problem of dogs attacking you."

"I don't think I have a problem. I know I have a problem."

Rick was nodding in agreement now. "Okay. I'll help you. I'd be glad to. It fits in nicely with my new eccentric living, but I need proof. I may be eccentric but I'm not fucking crazy."

Almost as if on cue, a dog barked. I jumped. My body literally lifted off the seat of the chair two whole inches and landed again, shaking the chair. I startled my brother. "Whoa now, Lucas. That's just Cream. Calm down."

I can only imagine the fear raging in my eyes because my voice was thick with it. "Rick if you have guns, I'd get them out, loaded and cocked right now."

Rick stood and walked to a window, pulling the string to lift the vertical blinds. Looking out the window, he tried to calm me. "That is just Cream, the Captain's dog. The Captain walks him every morning at this time. He's a golden retriever. Beautiful dog. Light colored, almost the color of coffee with cream in it, hence the name. Friendly as pie and peaceful as a Quaker."

I was not satisfied. "Get the guns."

"Calm down. I bet he just walks by with Captain and maybe takes a piss. I usually go out and give him a treat."

Now I was at Rick's side and touched his arm. "Rick, if that dog knows I am here, it will attack. Not just attack, but charge with the ferocity of the devil himself."

"Jeez-us Cry-ist," Rick said. "Okay. I don't believe it, but I believe you believe it. I'll tell you what … we'll get prepared just in case you are correct."

Beneath Rick's mattress was a cache of weapons to make Rambo weep with joy. Rick selected a simple pistol, a .38 he told me, and checked to make sure it was loaded. It was, which made me thankful Rick had no children in the house.

He opened the front door, leaving only the screen door

between us and the soon-to-arrive Cream. Rick informed me that Cream, despite being a country dog, was still walking on a leash. It seems he was too fond of chasing squirrels and running off into the woods after his quarry. As an afterthought, Rick mentioned that when Cream did catch a squirrel, he didn't know how to kill it because he was a super-fucking-domesticated dog.

Despite all this good news about Cream's passivity, I still felt my bowels rumble in anticipation. As if reading my mind, sensing my fear, or smelling the shit moving in my intestines, Rick gave me the gun to hold and I was grateful. I expected the worst while I imagine Rick expected he'd be driving me to the Inpatient Behavioral Health Unit at Friends Hospital by the end of our experiment.

"Listen," he said. "The Captain ain't the type of guy you want to approach with a weapon. He's—" Rick searched for the right words. "Well, he's the fucking Captain. Enough said. So, you stay in here with the gun. If Cream goes crazy and charges in here, just raise the gun and plug two shots into his furry ass. The safety is off so be careful. I ain't giving you a quick shooting lesson because shooting isn't rocket science. Just point and pull the trigger. Simple."

"If I have to shoot Cream, won't the Captain go ape-shit?"

"Yeah, I considered that. If everything goes to hell and Cream pulls his leash free and gets past me, then I'm going to get behind the Captain in case I have to restrain him. That means I won't be able to help you fight Cream. So don't panic. Raise the gun, point and shoot."

"Right."

"If I'm behind the Captain, I can take him down easy and keep him pinned on the ground. When he hears you shooting at his dog, it won't be so easy to keep him pinned. So kill the pooch and get out here to help me."

"Right," I said.

"The Captain may be older but he is not a pussy. I will need you. Grab this rope as you come out. We'll have to tie him up till he calms down."

"Right."

"Right-right-right. That's all you keep saying. Right-right-right." Rick was waving a hand in front of my eyes. "Are you okay man? You hearing me?"

I realized I was in a trance and shook my head and snapped myself back into reality. "Yeah, I'm with you. Just taking it all in."

"Relax Lucas, nothing will happen. I'll give the dog his treat, he'll wag his little tail and go on his ass-sniffing way."

"Right."

"If it does go to hell, be ready."

I looked at Rick and saw a glimmer in his eye. "You are enjoying this aren't you?"

He let a small smirk crest on his mouth. "Well, it is damn more interesting than my normal, routine day." Rick started to walk toward the door. "Besides, look at us. We're fucking bonding." I smiled. The dog barked. I stopped smiling. "They're here," Rick continued. "Get ready."

Captain and Cream were on the property seconds later. Rick, still clad in just boxers, opened the screen door and stepped outside with a faux-bacon dog-treat in his hand. I remained in the house to the left of the door, pinned against the wall, staying out of sight. I heard muffled talking and the tags on Cream's neck jingling. What I didn't hear was what surprised me—no insane barking, no shouts of surprise from Rick or the Captain, no sound of the screen door being torn apart as a madly enraged dog burst through.

Nothing. Nada.

As Rick, Captain and Cream enjoyed their normal routine, I considered if I had become literally insane and had entered the providence of drooling-delusional psychosis. I could not understand why Cream wasn't attacking. Every dog I had encountered in the last eighteen hours had been intent on chewing me and digesting me and shitting me out as a brown turd on some friendly patch of green grass. Maybe my brother was onto something about the CAT scan. Maybe I had developed a brain tumor or, even worse, a galaxy of dispersed, small tumors throughout my brain. Maybe drool and diapers awaited me. Maybe this whole dog-attacking business was just a delusion.

Cream just sounded like a normal dog that, seeing a friendly neighbor with a dog-treat, was happily jumping around in excited anticipation. He sounded just like any other dog … and then it hit me—sound! Cream had not heard me, seen me or smelled me. The damn dog did not know I was there.

Or maybe Cream *was* acting strangely and I just could not hear him acting strangely. Rick's and the Captain's voices were so muffled by distance that they could have been discussing Cream's odd behavior and I wouldn't know. I needed to know. I needed to *see* what Cream was doing.

Taking a deep breath, I realized I was so tense I could shit two nickels if I swallowed a dime. I stretched open my hand, flexing fingers I had clenched into fists. My palms were damp. My forehead was sweaty. My muscles were twitching. I was nervous.

Mustering my bravado, I counted one-two-three in my head, and took the tiniest peek outside through the screen door. It was literally a moment's peek, just a flash of my eyes onto the scene outside.

It was enough. Cream, with the innate reflexes of a dog, caught the flashing movement of my head poking into the door frame for that briefest of instances. It was enough.

Whether or not Cream actually saw me, Lucas Miller, Ph.D., who had some maddening effect on dogs, or whether he just saw something flash in the doorway that aroused his confusion and concern … well, that question will never be answered. What is clear is that Cream went loco.

Before my head was back safely against the wall next to the doorway, perfectly hidden from view, I heard what I had originally expected. Cream, in all his furry cuteness, unleashed a torrent of furious barking.

I pinned myself against the wall so tightly I suspected I'd left an indentation in the drywall. I felt the weight of the gun in my hand. Rather than feel secure or empowered as my intellect reminded me that I should, I felt the gun was too small and insignificant to conquer the assault of an attacking beast.

Only a moment after the ravenous barking began, so too

did the panicked voices and frenzied responses of Rick and Captain. Overtop (or interlaced, to be more accurate) with the roars of Cream were the shouts of the Captain, his voice at first sounding surprised, then taking on a commanding tone. "Whoa Cream. Calm boy. What the—calm down boy."

Rick said, "hold him tight" or something to that effect, followed by the Captain giving direct orders. "Cream, heel. Now, goddamn it. Cream, heel."

The incessant barking only continued, and with Rick's constant, "Captain hold him, hold him," I imagine that Cream was pulling with all his force on the leash. His full intent and weight pressed onto the end of the leash and collar, demanding, begging to get inside the house and get his teeth around my neck.

I need to mention that despite all the dogs that had tried to kill me in the last three-quarters of a day, I still loved dogs. I valued them as creatures with kind, warm-hearted, and tender human emotions, capable of love and empathy. Best of all, they had child-like trust in their human owners. So when I heard a *whap-whap-whap*, followed by the high-pitched cry of a dog in pain, I felt bad. I knew at once that the Captain had taken soldierly control and had "disciplined" his dog. Poor Cream.

Suddenly remembering the gun in my hand, I felt a strong desire to use it, but on the Captain. It still had not completely registered in my thick head that dogs, even the cutest and most friendly dogs, had become my mortal enemies. While my intellect was beginning to accept dogs as destroyers of Lucas Miller, my heart was not. I was moved with compassion for Cream and anger at the Captain for hitting a defenseless animal. Even though I knew that with jaws and teeth made for hunting and tearing apart fleshy meat, dogs were anything but defenseless, I still wanted to defend Cream. I felt an urge to walk outside and raise the gun at the Captain, telling him if he hit that dog one more time, it'd be the Captain who would be yelping.

I never got the chance. Cream, despite getting what I could only imagine was a powerfully strong wallop from the Captain, continued his tirade of furious barking.

The Captain must have responded in-kind because the air became a mixture of roaring barks from Cream, *whap*s from the Captain and yells from Rick to "watch the leash" and "hold 'im."

I kept myself pinned against the wall, sweat dripping into my eyes, burning them. Using my empty hand to wipe away the sweat, I listened, my ears begging to gather every bit of information about what-the-fuck was happening out there.

The barking seemed to be growing, becoming louder and more frenzied, almost entirely drowning out the Captain's *whap*s on the dog's body and Rick's shouting. All three sounds seemed to reach a crescendo, consuming every molecule of the atmosphere until a sound broke through, the cry of a human voice in extreme pain.

Call it sibling intuition, but without conscious thought, my mind knew the person voicing the scream was my brother, my kin, Rick. My mind panicked. *Help Rick!* My body remained frozen, unsure. The debate between mind and body was moot, because a moment after the human scream, all the sound in the world was instantly deadened by the crisp, long-echoed retort of a gunshot.

I closed my eyes in the sudden silence, paralyzed by its harsh emptiness, but pleased the chaos of noise had stopped.

I was rigid against the wall, commanding my unmoving body to look outside and see what I could see. Counting again in my head to get my body moving, one-two-thr—I didn't complete the number three before I heard what must have been the Captain's voice, shouting despite the quiet. "You all right, Rick? I didn't getcha, did I?"

"Fine, Captain," Rick's voice boomed, loud enough so he could let his brother standing inside know that he was okay. "Just a dog bite. Been hurt worse. I'll be okay."

My heart dropped.

Again, the Captain was loud, this time with shock rising in

his voice. "I can't believe I just had to shoot my own dog. What the fuck? I just had to shoot my own damn dog," he repeated. "I'm sorry he bit you, Rick. You didn't do nothing to provoke him. I am so sorry he ..."

"Don't worry about it," Rick said. "No biggie. Just a scratch."

CHAPTER TEN

It was about forty-five minutes until Rick reappeared in the house. Through the window thirty-five minutes before, I saw the Captain carrying the corpse of his dog back toward the main house with Rick limping badly beside him, a small bloodied gashed on his leg. I knew Rick was probably intent on getting to the house to get his wound washed out and bandaged, but also to comfort the Captain, who strode holding his fallen pooch, stroking Cream's head, tears in his eyes, gun now again holstered on his hip.

When Rick came back to his bungalow, leg bandaged, his face held an indescribable look that combined disbelief, fear, and anger. "I'm fine, so don't ask. I got my leg away just in time. He didn't get a good hold, just a flimsy bite on the outer skin. No biggie."

"I'm sorry," was all I could muster.

"Did you peek outside?" he asked.

"Yes," I answered honestly.

"So that's why Cream lost his mind." Rick said this as more of a statement than a question. "He saw you and lost his mind. Lost it enough to go after me."

"No," I corrected, "he wanted me. You just got in the way."

Rick seemed to ponder this as he reached for a cigarette. He inhaled deeply and exhaled as he spoke. "If you are cursed and these dogs want to kill you, why is it that Cream attacked me? I have—had," he corrected himself, "a great relationship with that dog. Why on earth would he attack me?"

I was ready with my answer. "Because the faintest whiff of me made him so furious and so filled with rage that he could not control himself. He was overwhelmed with a desire to kill me, but since he was unable, he unleashed that rage on to you."

"No." Rick was pacing now, a small limp to his step that reminded me that my leg, despite its wound, was pain free. I chalked it up to the power of endorphins, nature's perfect pain killer. "It doesn't make sense. If the sight of you enraged Cream into an uncontrollable frenzy, then why did Cream not attack the Captain? The Captain was the more obvious choice. He was standing physically closer to Cream. You weren't out there. To get his teeth on my leg, Cream had to make a bounding leap to the end of his leash, nearly toppling the Captain. Why not just bite the Captain if his fury was so uncontained?"

It seemed obvious enough to me. "Because the Captain is his owner, his master, his Alpha. A dog doesn't attack his master."

"Really?" Rick asked, incredulous, "a dog in that state of complete insanity and he still has consciousness of mind not to attack his owner. It wanted off that leash and the Captain was holding it. Why not attack the person who has you bound? You talk about dominance. Between the Captain, Cream, and myself, both humans are clearly dominant. So that doesn't hold water."

I took a cigarette too. "So what are you saying?" I asked.

"I'm saying I stink of Lucas. I have stench. I have," Rich paused, searching for the right words. "Lucastench. I have Lucastench." He pronounced the combination of Lucas and stench as a two-syllable word, "Luca-stench."

"What?" I asked.

"I hugged you," Rick answered, looking at me like I was an idiot in a dunce cap. "I am covered in your scent. That is why it chose me as the target. Whoever has your scent on them is in danger. Let's just call it the Lucastench."

An almost operatic boom in my mind said GWEN. I reached for my cell phone, but before I could put it to my ear, Rick's hand rested on my forearm. "Yes, call your wife, warn her, but do it from the car. I could be wrong in my theory, so I need to test it. I want to perform an experiment." Rick started walking to the door. "Let's go."

"Are we going out in public?" I asked.

"Yeah, why?"

"Because you're only in your underwear."

CHAPTER ELEVEN

Despite having just been bitten by a dog, I have never seen anyone run so quickly. The old woman crossing the parking lot wearing a purple volunteer vest had probably never *ever* seen anyone running out of the front doors and across the parking lot of the SPCA.

While driving to the SPCA, Rick explained the methodology of his very uncontrolled experiment. It was a simple experiment, and in most cases, simple experiments are often those that yield the most information. I gave him due credit for keeping it basic. His methodology was thus: While I waited in the car, Rick would leisurely stroll through the SPCA dog-adoption wing and see if all the canines went bonkers in a murderous rage. Since all the dogs at the SPCA are caged at all times to protect the public, he figured he'd be safe from physical harm.

"If the dogs go crazy, then the Lucastench theory proves true," Rick said.

"Yes," I agreed, somewhat, wincing a bit at having my normal human odor being referred to as a stench. "Your little experiment will give a correlation between my scent and the attacks, but it is only a correlation, it does not prove certainty. Nor does it even begin to touch causality or duration. Then we need to consider the greater biological implication. Fuck Rick, I'm not applying for a science foundation grant, just trying to find out what we are dealing with here."

After we parked at the SPCA and before Rick began the experiment, he insisted on getting out of the car and hugging me again, wanting to be certain he was "well-scented with Lucastench." Of course, the newly eccentric Rick did not just hug me, but gave me a full body squeeze, rubbing his torso up and down against mine as he hugged me. I hoped no one was watching, but at least he had clothes on this time.

Well-scented, Rick walked into the SPCA. He was gone for only about three minutes till the door was thrown open and Rick ran toward the car like a steroid-fueled track star. A woman was crossing the parking lot wearing a purple volunteer vest with VOLUNTEER written in big white letters on the back. She was a thick, plump, countrified woman in her sixties. Spotting Rick, she stopped in her tracks, raised a hand to her now open, gaping mouth, and turned on her heels and power-waddled back toward her car. I imagine she thought she was running, but it was more like a walrus dancing on dry land. I had the car windows up so I heard nothing, but the contortion of her face told me she was screaming in fear.

Her fear was understandable. The sight of Rick running full-speed from the animal shelter probably conjured for her a terrible image of some great calamity, perhaps a terrorist attack on the SPCA by anti-PETA advocates. Or perhaps she imagined that people favoring animal cruelty had attacked the Bucks County SPCA for their humane treatment. Or animal smugglers with shotguns were heisting dogs to sell in Eastern Europe.

I was beginning to chuckle at the woman's waddle as Rick's body slammed into the car.

Rick's voice was muffled through the closed windows, but he was shouting as he pulled on the door handles. "Open the fucking door! Lucas, the fucking doors, open them." I hit the power-lock "open" switch but Rick was pulling on the handle at the same time, negating the locks from releasing. It became a Laurel and Hardy routine, with Rick and me shouting over each other, me yelling for Rick to let the handle go so I could open the door and Rick frantically pulling on the handle telling me to open the door. I finally sat still, not touching the "open" button. When Rick saw my sudden aborted effort, he looked stunned and froze.

He must've assumed I saw a dog and was paralyzed in fear because he turned around and looked behind him, slowly, as if he expected something to be waiting there to devour him.

I saw behind Rick so I knew he was okay. So as he turned to see if Armageddon was at his back, I hit the "open" button once, successfully releasing the lock. When Rick turned back around, I pointed at the car door handle and mouthed, "Get in."

As we drove away from the animal shelter, heading nowhere in particular, Rick didn't say a word. Panting from his sprint, he looked behind us a few times and then settled into his seat.

"So?" I asked, starting the car and pulling away.

Rick looked over at me as if I had asked if he'd ever fucked a transvestite. "What do you mean, so? Really? I just ran from that building like I was running from hell itself."

I made a turn, not knowing where I was driving, but needing to do something as I collected my thoughts. "So the dogs were …" I trailed off.

"Yes, the dogs wanted to eat me. The dogs looked at me like Rosie O'Donnell looks at a doughnut with a vagina attached." I must have looked confused because he clarified. "They wanted to eat me and nothing was going to stop them." I just drove, silently. Rick continued. "It is confirmed. You've been hexed or something. Or at least some freakish magical shit is happening here. So we need to figure out what the hell is happening."

I nodded in agreement. "I know."

"You asked about the hinterlands in Afghanistan. The mountainous regions between Pakistan and Afghanistan belong to neither nation, though they both claim ownership. The tribes there did practice hexes. Well, hexes mixed with Islam. Like how Haitians mix Catholicism with voodoo. The old and the new faiths mixed and blended. I'll be fucking honest, Lucas, I don't know shit about it. I was told they did it, but that's all I know."

I shook my head in acknowledgment. Of course he wouldn't know. Why would he? I should have known better. He was there to fight and maintain order, not make an anthropological or theological study of the tribal culture of mountainous peoples. He was probably briefed on basic customs and beliefs of the people, but that was all. A simple introductory course on the people they were invading. Rick was just a grunt, so he was given a grunt's education. "This is my problem, Rick. Not yours.

I'm going to take you home. You shower and get my stink off of you and then you ..." my voice trailed off. "Well, do whatever the fuck it is you do."

Rick smiled at my ignorance of his life with a smirk of both amusement and contempt. "You've got a big problem here. Bigger than I think you realize. You are in danger. You need help. You need guns." He paused. "Damn, this shit is exciting. It's so exciting that I'm going to quote the Rolling Stones and say wild horses couldn't drag me away."

I looked at him squarely. "It could be wild dogs dragging you away."

CHAPTER TWELVE

We returned to Rick's trailer and I had tried for the third time to reach Gwen on her cell, but I got only voicemail. I had sent her about ten text messages, all saying different variations of, "Stay home, lock the doors and call me. Avoid all dogs. Do it *now*." I got no reply to any of the texts or voicemails, so I was adamant about getting home. With Gwen working from home and the enormity of her pregnant state, there was no reason she should have left our apartment. Yet, there was also no reason her phone should have been turned off, nor did she avoid text messages. What gave me hope and kept me sane was that Gwen had a late night (we both had). With her over-concern for the welfare of our unborn child, she was adamant on getting adequate sleep and may have taken the morning off, opting to catch up on her sleep. Yes, I thought, that made the most sense. Gwen had simply gone back to sleep and turned her phone to silent before doing so.

I still wanted to drive straight home, but Rick agreed Gwen was probably "sleeping with the phone on silent." I protested, but only meekly. Rick made an excellent point when he suggested we first go back to his apartment and get more guns. All we had with us was the handgun I'd held while Cream bit his last bite. Rick reminded me of how badly this could escalate if we found ourselves in the proximity of numerous dogs at once. In essence, we needed firepower.

I consented, voicing that our next priority was to make sure Gwen was still tucked tightly and warmly into bed.

On the drive, Rick was acting like Sherlock Holmes on amphetamines. "Okay. We know a few things and we need to discover a few things. Dogs want to kill you. Cats do not."

"Wait," I said, suddenly concerned. "How do we know cats do not?"

"Because I walked through the kitty kennel before the dog kennel and the cats didn't even make a meow. They didn't even notice me. Even under normal circumstances, I usually have a greater effect on pussy." He smiled.

I was too preoccupied to even notice his little joke. I felt outside of existence, removed from reality, floating in some stratosphere of surreal madness. Was this really happening? Was I really under attack by domesticated dogs? It was too true and yet too silly for my mind to comprehend. The rational part of my brain processed, assessed and was convinced by the data it had gathered over the past eighteen hours. *Yes, I was under attack.* That same rational part of my brain searched the indexes of logic and reason to assert an equally powerful counterpoint. *I am not under attack. This does not occur. It cannot be. It is illogical. This is madness.*

Yet, can lunatics know their own insanity? If I was immersed in the squalor of psychotic reasoning, how could my brother and Lydia both agree with me? Could they too be delusions, conjured by my sick mind? Could Rick, sitting there right beside me, be nothing but a contrived apparition of mentally deranged brain matter with misfiring synapses?

"Ouch!" I screamed. "What the fuck was that?"

Rick had punched me in the arm as if we reverted to twelve-year-old brothers in the backseat of our father's Buick 8. I suddenly reached the conclusion that Rick was not an apparition as I felt the welt begin to rise on my arm.

"Are you listening to me? I ain't talking for my health," Rick said. "Pay fucking attention or it'll be your ass getting chewed in the mouth of some mangy inbred mutt."

I put my hands up in a sign of submission, my eyes telling Rick to continue.

"Okay," Rick began again, "so this is supernatural or super-human or Lucifer-induced or anything-other-than-normal reality," Rick had an unnerving edge to his voice as I navigated the back roads to his house. His speech was quick, terse and concerned. "These things don't just occur. This—the Lucastench—doesn't just occur, so it has a cause. That's where we need to start, the cause. You can't spend the rest of your life fighting off every dog you come across, so we need to eliminate the problem. Find the cause, find the cure."

I didn't like the sound of "cure." It made me sound diseased, sick, or otherwise unwell. As I possessed a hypochondriac's fear of disease-induced death to surpass even Woody Allen's obsession with terminality, I couldn't help but question my brother's prognosis.

"How do we know this is something that needs a cure? Maybe it'll just wear off or dissipate in a few days."

Rick looked me square in the eyes. "You'd be dead in a few days."

I looked at Rick with equal intensity, though only for a second since I was driving and the road required my eyes. "What does that mean? Are you saying I wouldn't survive? That I'm not tough enough? Well fuck you."

"Lucas," Rick tried to interject, but I stopped him.

"Listen, big fucking war-hero," I said, a wave of angry heat cascading across my mind and traveling down my neck, through my torso and over my heart, past my balls, and down my legs, seemingly emptying onto the car floor. "I may have come to you because I needed a gun. That is all I need. I can take care of myself. You understand me, tough guy. I can defend myself and my wife and whatever the fuck else I need to do, and I can do it alone. Just because I didn't volunteer to run around the desert in camouflage with a machine gun shooting at peasant farmers doesn't make me a pussy. You understand me. Killing poor desert-farming Afghans does not make you any fucking tougher than me."

Rick sat silently looking straight ahead. "Pull the car over, Lucas."

"Fuck you," I said, with a new wave of blood, heated in anger, pouring through me and over me. "I'm getting some guns then I am getting my wife. Period."

Rick didn't flinch from looking ahead. "Pull the car over, Lucas."

"No." I was resolute.

Rick grabbed the wheel and jerked it to the right. The car veered on a dime and instinctively I jammed the brakes with the full force of my foot and leg while also tensing on the wheel trying to regain control. I'd used so much force with my foot that Rick got what he wanted and the car stopped a few feet off the shoulder on a grassy easement. Rick thrust the center console shifter into the "P" slot and gave me a dead, unreadable look.

"I said, pull over," Rick mumbled when the car sat still, idling.

I took a deep breath, not of fear, but of acceptance, prepared for the worst and willing to face it. "You want to fight?" I asked. "Fine, but not now. I don't have the time. I need to get your guns and my wife. We can fight when this situation is ..." I searched for the word. "... when it is resolved."

Rick sat silently looking at me dead in the eyes with that same unreadable, unknowable look. His entire countenance and being seemed to pulse with something, but I could not determine exactly what. He should be pulsing with rage and anger at my comments, but I felt he wasn't. It should be resolution to kick my ass from Philadelphia to the sixth level of Hell and back again, but it wasn't that either. His aura, or what was radiating from his presence, was something else entirely and in an instant it hit me. It was blessed epiphany. Rick had reached a conclusion.

"What?" I asked, knowing that Rick now knew something. "What do you know?"

"You mentioned my career, as a soldier. It got me thinking about careers. You take children away from parents, right. For a living? That's what you do, right?"

I shuffled in my seat. "Not always. I just make sure children with questionable parents are being raised in a safe and secure environment conducive to—"

Rick interjected. "Spare me the resume. If you deem parents unfit to raise their children, you take the children away."

"Yes," I said, then corrected myself. "Well, no. A judge decides, in an emergency hearing, and then the police arrive and remove the children and take them to a foster care worker."

Rick's look was exacerbated. "Okay, but let's cut out the fucking schematic diagram of the legal system for a second. It is your decision, correct? You make an assessment and these family court judges know you and trust you and do whatever you say. So if you say 'snatch the children from the parents' then a judge signs the order. Correct?"

"They sign a thirty-day temporary removal order, yes. Well, it's more complicated than that. I actually have to show …" and I stopped for a moment, then started nodding. "Yes. The judges don't even read the reports I write. If I want the children pulled from the parents, the judges accept me on my reputation and they sign the order and the children are removed."

Rick smiled. "That is the cause. That is where we start. That is where your problem originated."

"I pissed off the wrong parent," I said, suddenly seeing his logic with complete clarity.

"Yup. One of these parents is knowledgeable and disciplined in the art of hexes or voodoo or some shit like that. They used that power on the man who is ultimately responsible for snatching their kids away. That person is you, Lucas."

I was nodding in agreement. "Let me think. Of all the parents recently who had children removed, I can—"

Again, Rick cut me off. "Lucas," he said, looking not at me but straight ahead, out of the front window, "one quick thing. If you ever mention the war again like you did, I will kill you. I mean that literally." Now he turned his head and looked at me, smiling. "Normally, if you'd made a comment like that about the war, I wouldn't have given you a second chance. You'd be bleeding-out in a slow death right now. I'm giving you a second chance because second chances are part of my new eccentric side."

I opened my mouth to begin to apologize when I was shocked into silence by the annoyingly techno-sounding ring of my cell phone. Maybe it was the weighted conversation occurring or maybe the events of the day had made us feel dislodged from normal, everyday functions. When the phone chirped both Rick and I looked at one another like we had never before heard a cell phone ringing. For a moment we both sat perfectly still. Rick broke the silence. "Answer it. It's probably Gwen."

I looked at the phone and almost didn't answer it. The screen's caller ID told me it was Lydia calling. When I had yet to talk to Gwen, it felt wrong answering a call from another woman, especially one who roused my sexual interests. I looked to Rick and back to the phone and then back to Rick. "Shit," I said aloud at my own revelation. "She's probably got the Lucastench." Rick looked confused. I tapped the "accept" button on the screen. A frightened, hectic voice greeted me.

I said into the phone, "Lydia, calm down. I can barely hear … What did you say?… Dogs?… When?… They attacked you?… Okay. Lydia, okay. Are you okay? Great. Good. Where are you? Okay, stay there."

CHAPTER THIRTEEN

While Rick was conducting his experiment at the SPCA and I waited patiently in the car, Lydia was attacked by two dogs. This is the story she related to me later that day.

To understand what Lydia was doing when she was attacked, an explanation may be warranted.

I always felt incredibly sad for Lydia. True, I enjoyed her company and found her conversation enjoyable, even amazingly honest and refreshing. It is also true that she presented well to the public. She was tall, thin (though thickening a bit with age), and had nice eyes and a flirtatious smile. She presented nicely as a lawyer for Philadelphia's Department of Children and Youth. She wore nice business attire in the latest fashion, accentuating her long legs, which were undoubtedly her best feature. Although she sported too much foundation on her face to mask her not uncommon hangovers, she generally looked good, professional, put together. She even owned a townhome in the city. Overall, she presented as a normal, everyday person.

As a man, I was attracted to Lydia for her sex appeal. As a psychologist, I knew she had narcissistic personality disorder, and as such, was cunning, self-serving, and remorseless. The biggest target of her narcissism was men (and sometimes women)—finding them, fucking them, and forgetting them. Her promiscuity stemmed from her mental illness and that promiscuity needed to be fed by an ever-revolving door of hard cock and wet pussy that she welcomed into her bed. Her true drug of choice was younger, thirty-something cock, such as myself, plus a longtime fascination with one steamy-hot woman in her twenties whom she routinely tried, but failed, to seduce.

Her age was a factor, too. Lydia was forty-five years old and her looks were beginning to show the speedy decline toward fifty, especially evident in fast-living women who never settled down.

Lydia's psychology was warped with confusion about sex and aging, and when you longed to be twenty-something again, it doesn't take a psychologist to understand why Lydia coveted a twenty-something woman.

Maybe ten years ago Lydia could have seduced her, but not now.

Lydia could not accept her age. She could not accept that twenty-five-year-old men thought of her as old. Even thirty-year-old men were beginning to see her as aged. The psychologist in me knew that as her sex appeal to men in their thirties and forties weakened, and when it disappeared entirely as she cleared fifty, her mental illness would spiral into an ugly, scary nightmare.

The future did not bode well for Lydia's sanity.

Sometimes she had moments of clarity about her fate. Her younger brother was formally diagnosed with borderline personality disorder and her older brother was a full-blown, day-drinking alcoholic. Lydia would say, in those moments of clarity, "Maybe I'm not so different from my siblings? If they are all genetically fucked-up, perhaps I'm doomed to the same fate." She tried not to dwell on the inevitable. "Eh, what can I do? Fuck it all, I guess," she'd often say.

Fuck, she did. Her promiscuity was a source of pride, which is common in narcissists. She even boasted that the only reason she got her position with the City was because she fucked a very-married higher-up in the City. She admitted he was gross and horribly inept in bed, but he got Lydia a good job and at a higher pay-rate than most people. In the end, getting the job was justified, as she once put it, "if it means letting him squirt his cum on me for a good job at higher pay."

She really had no other choice. Lydia went to the worst law school in the nation, whose admission criteria stood at a pathetic 2.6 undergraduate GPA (scary how easy it is to get into law school today). Post-graduation job placement at the school was less than 50 percent. After she barely graduated, it took her three tries to pass the bar exam. Since then her resume was a weak mash-up of glorified paralegal work. To get a good job, she used her only asset while she still had it—a tall, thin body. So she fucked the higher-up for a job and he became her boss. Occasionally, to keep him in her good graces, she still had to give the very-married boss a blowjob. As she was fond of saying, "it cums with the territory." (Her bad pun, not mine).

In fact, Lydia had just finished giving the boss a blowjob when she was attacked by the dog.

She had little actual work to do at work, so when her boss called she made an excuse to leave the office and met him. They met in the back of a crowded parking lot, parking in the last few empty rows. According to Lydia, this boss preferred getting car-head in the empty rows of crowded parking lots. He liked to watch people walking to their cars while he was cheating on his wife. It made him feel adventurous. He would be in constant panic that he was going to see one of his wife's friends, or, even worse, his wife. The threat of getting caught turned him on, so she relented. She figured no one could see her head bobbing up and down, or her fingers diddling in his rectum (fingering his ass was an oddity he often requested) unless they were directly next to the car, looking down into the window. That was unlikely to happen, so she often agreed to the childish parking lot fetish.

After three minutes and fifteen seconds (Lydia reported that this was a record in longevity for this guy), he was zipped-up and smoked a cigarette. His wife thought he'd given up smoking. He thought of this as "another fuck you to her," Lydia told me.

When Lydia relayed this story to me, I had bigger things on my mind than the fat man's little cock. I was trying to keep her focused on the dog attack. She finally got there.

After giving head, she exited the car and he pulled away. Her car was parked in the next spot, but she had no intention of going back to the office just yet. It was lunchtime but she didn't want to eat because she just swallowed semen and she didn't know how many calories semen contained. She figured because the guy was fat, his semen was more caloric. Like I said, it is scary how stupid much of our legal community is today.

So she decided to have a midday cocktail (or four), as was her custom. Besides, she needed a place to scrub clean her two fingers.

Across the street from the crowded parking lot was a typical Philly bar. She walked a few feet to the sidewalk and waited to cross the street toward Albert's Café while using her clean hand to rub and massage her sore jaw. She then remembered what I had told her that very morning about my "problem with dogs."

She leisurely scanned the parking lot behind her while she waited for a light to change, her mind absently thinking about my problem. She saw the higher-up guy's sedan idling still, waiting in the parking lot traffic as people backed out of spaces and others tried to pull in.

It was blindingly quick, she said. Two dogs, both black Labrador Retrievers, were at his car door in a flash. It was odd, she thought. They were sniffing the car, putting their snouts into the crack of the door jamb and appeared to be taking long, deep breaths. She thought, *Why are they smelling the door?*

Both dogs dragged limp leashes attached to their collars, and she saw a woman jogging across the asphalt with her mouth moving in big, exaggerated movements, presumably yelling the dogs' names, though Lydia couldn't make out the words.

Her mind made a quick observational assertion. *Dogs don't just sniff at cars. These must smell something. Are they smelling my boss? He must have a powerful damn smell. He didn't smell any different from usual. He always smells like sweat and Feta cheese and cigarettes.*

My own problem with dogs must still have been lingering in her mind, bouncing around unoccupied rooms upstairs because the connection hit her like a falling piano. *They are going to attack! Like Lucas is being attacked! They smell Lucas! Yes, they smell a whiff of Lucas. From when he hugged me this morning, I got his smell. Then I messed around with my boss and the scent transferred to him.*
To her audible exhale of relief, it ended that quickly for her boss.

Both dogs stepped back, the parking-traffic cleared and the car pulled away. Her boss probably didn't even realize they were there, since their height did not reach the window. Her mind eased a bit. *Okay, they didn't attack. Good. I was way-off. Maybe I'm just being paranoid. Maybe I'm a bit drunk on semen.*

That reminded her she'd dodged a bullet. Like any guilty person, relief swam through her thoughts. *Thank God they didn't attack. I'd have to help him and I would have a tough time explaining why I was here. This isn't my territory and he's so far from the office where he was supposed to be pinned to a desk all day. His wife knows he's a cheater and people at the office already suspected that we—*

The two black Labradors arched their heads back as high as they could, putting their snouts into the air, breathing. Simultaneously, both dropped their heads and scanned the parking lot, seeming to look for something. Snarls grew on their faces, and teeth slowly appeared beneath raised lips.

As with anyone, the expression of anger on the dogs' faces raised her alarms. *Dogs don't just get angry standing in a parking lot.* He mind scurried for plausible explanations. None came, until reality set in. *The scent transferred onto my boss was too weak,* Lydia surmised. *Lucas' scent is certainly stronger on me. I probably stink of—*

She didn't have time to finish the thought. The two dogs spotted Lydia and using that amazing canine hunting sense, they knew she was the source of the smell. Both bolted toward her.

For a second, she just froze, paralyzed and unsure if this was actually happening. It was only a second before her mind told her that yes, this was happening, and those long legs of hers moved her toward her car that sat only a few feet away.

The time it took to travel a few feet was all the time the dogs needed.

The parking lot was only about twenty-five rows long, and the dogs covered that distance in seconds. In those same seconds, Lydia was at her car door, fumbling for the keys. She hit the auto-unlock and swung open the door. Her timing was impeccable.

When the door swung open, it made a *THUMP* against something. The classic, high-pitched whine of a dog in distress came from the other side. Lydia jumped back from the wide-open car door and beneath she saw four black legs on the ground. A little yelp escaped her lips.

A bark came from the passenger side of the car. The second dog was on the other side. She saw a flash of its tail as it turned to go around the rear of the car and get to the side where she stood. It went toward the rear, so Lydia went toward the front.

The dog that hit the door regained its footing as its twin reached it. They both appeared from behind the still open door, and in unison both dogs growled. One licked its teeth with a long, pink tongue.

Lydia started backpedaling toward the passenger side of the car, keeping her eyes pinned on the dogs as she fumbled in her purse. Her hands worked feverishly inside the large faux-Kate Spade shoulder bag.

The dogs walked slowly toward her, methodically stepping forward, sizing her up. Lydia's feet too took careful steps backward, cautious not to trip on her high heels. They were all now on the passenger side of the car with Lydia backpedaling toward the trunk.

Both dogs lowered their heads toward the ground and Lydia knew that while all that stood between them was a straight line of open asphalt, they were going to charge at any moment.

Inside her purse, one of Lydia's hands finally grasped the target. She pulled out the can of pepper-spray, and held it out in front of her with both hands, pointing it at the dogs like a gun. This action caused the dogs to pause.

In fact, all paused. The dogs stopped moving forward and Lydia stopped walking backward. It was an old-fashioned stand-off, but Lydia knew it wouldn't last more than a few seconds.

Appearing as if she materialized from thin air, the woman who had been calling after these two dogs was instantly behind the Labradors, both hands reaching out, one hand grabbing hold of each collar. The dogs were so intent on Lydia they seemed not to sense their owner's advance. When she grabbed their collars, both dogs looked behind them and shuffled their feet in surprise.

Unfortunately, the suddenness of that woman's appearance caused Lydia to scream and hit the trigger on the pepper-spray, sending a long stream of eye and skin irritant into the air, hitting not the dogs as was intended, but the woman, directly in the face.

Reflexively, the woman released the dogs' collars as her hands flew up to her eyes, swiping at the fluid that had just hit them with an immediate, burning force.

The dogs startle-stepped as the stream of pepper spray launched through the air, and by doing so, realized they were not being held by the collar any longer. Turning to look at Lydia, they both sprang.

Lydia did too and was around the trunk and on the driver's side in a flash. The door still sat wide open and Lydia jumped feet first into the driver's seat. She reached for the door handle, found it, and pulled with endorphin-strength. As the door swung shut, one dog had just enough space in the swinging arch of the door to stick in its head.

The car door slammed the dog's head against the door frame with a loud *whap*, and a spray of blood flung across Lydia's face. The dog was stunned into stillness from the impact and its head leaned against the frame. The second dog was behind the one stunned in the door frame, barking furiously but unable to navigate a way to Lydia. The counterforce caused the door to bounce away from the dog's head, but Lydia held on tight and swung it shut again, hitting the dog's head a second time. Another spray of blood, but this time the impact forced the dog's head away from the frame a few inches, so when Lydia pulled the door yet again, it closed. The reassuring sound of the door connecting with its frame sent relief through her body and she hit the auto-lock button and stared out of the window.

The dog whose head got slammed in the door must've slumped to the ground because all Lydia saw were the head and teeth of one dog, which lunged at the window of the car trying to bite through the pane of glass. Lydia screamed and leaned toward the passenger seat.

Her hands now fumbled in her bag for her keys, found them quick and jammed the key into the ignition. She threw the car in reverse and hit the gas. The car lurched upward, into the air, and sagged suddenly downward followed by a loud CRUNCH sound.

Lydia knew she's crushed the injured dog's head and smiled. The other dog followed the car, barking and mirroring its movements. Her foot fell heavily on the accelerator and she almost made a complete circle in reverse until her foot hit the brake.

Once the shifter was in "D" she stomped the gas. Her tires let loose a small squeal as she pulled away. In her rearview, Lydia saw a woman on the ground rubbing at her eyes in obvious pain, a dog's body lying before a pile of red meat that used to be its head, and an insanely barking black Labrador getting smaller and smaller in the mirror as it lost a futile chase after Lydia's car.

Lydia decided then she was going home, locking her door, and crawling into bed. Little did she know then that her dog-day afternoon was just beginning.

CHAPTER FOURTEEN

While Lydia fortified herself in her apartment, my own day was progressing quickly.

"I gotta get to Gwen. This is taking too long." I was driving with intense speed and purpose now, my typically conservative driving habits abandoned in my panic. I was still heading to Rick's house after a brief debate determined our course of action. Rick surmised Lydia was safe for now, being battened down in her third-story apartment. While securing Gwen's safety was paramount, Rick convinced me that without proper firepower, we wouldn't be much help to Gwen if attacked by a rather large, vicious dog. Even a pack of little dogs could be fatal. Rick had detailed our plans as, "We get the guns, we get Gwen, we get Lydia and then …"

Then the plan trailed off. We still did not have the actual or exact cause of this problem. Nor did we know what would come next. As I drove, we sat in silence, both trying to figure out something—anything—from a bundle of nothing. It was like trying to see a black stain in a pitch-dark room.

We kept the radio tuned to the local news station, 1060 AM. The reporter babbled about the normal news, weather and traffic of the day, but nothing about dogs attacking anyone. So the problem remained singular to me and not widespread. I was relieved but frightened by the confirmation that I was the nucleus of the problem. I did not want to hear that large swaths of people were being mauled by dogs. That would be a horror of epic proportions. Yet, with the problem resting solely on my own shoulders, I felt alone, vulnerable and isolated.

Rick sometimes mused aloud, mostly with questions that

tried to pinpoint who might have hexed me. His questions were too broad and too generic to generate any real answers. Rick was basing his questions on grand assumptions. Assuming it was a disgruntled parent who had hexed me (and that was a large assumption to make) I had removed roughly 170 children from dangerous, unsafe, or parentally inadequate homes during my five-year tenure with the City's Department of Children and Youth. We also assumed that if we pinpointed the person who put on the hex (the hex itself was still nothing more than an assumption) then the hex could be removed.

Rick mused, "Maybe it was a parent from five years ago? We don't know the time constraints on these things."

"Or," I added, "maybe it wasn't a parent at all. Maybe we are talking about a child that I removed who has a special connection with dogs?"

"Now you're being ridiculous," Rick said, and I wasn't sure if he was poking sarcastic fun or was seriously dismissing the idea.

"If we believe a hex could cause this, then nothing, and I mean nothing, can be out of the realm of possibility."

Rick must have been seriously dismissing my claim because he seemed to reconsider. "Okay, so we widen the scope of our inquiry."

I slammed my open palm against the wheel with a ferocity that surprised me, both in its intensity and in the fact that it didn't break my hand. "Fuck this. We get the guns, we get the girls and get the fuck out of town." Rick started to protest but I cut him off. "Once we are out of town, we contact some authorities, police or SPCA cops or something, and we get other people on our side. Our priority—and I'm including you only if you still want to be a part of this—our priority is to protect the women, and if possible, ourselves. Then we get help."

We pulled onto Rick's long driveway and were quickly approaching his house as Rick waved his hand in dismissal. "Where the hell can we go in this world where we won't come across dogs? They are everywhere. They are like airborne bacteria. They are all around us. We don't even notice them most times but they are there. Everywhere. Fucking canines."

Rick said the word canine again, this time spreading the word out, stretching its pronunciation. "Kaaaayniiiines."

I slammed on the breaks because we both reached his house and I had reached an epiphany. "What did you just say?" I asked, rhetorically.

"What? Dogs? Yeah, they are everywhere. No escaping them."

I was shaking my head side-to-side. "No. The word canine. There was a family, the Kay family. They had nine children. I removed them. Well, I removed the ninth kid because the mom was going to work and leaving the kid locked in the bedroom. Said she couldn't afford a sitter. So I removed the ninth Kay child," I said. "Kay's nine." I repeated the phrase as I reached for the car door latch. "Kay nine. Canine."

Rick was nodding. "Kay nine indeed. Canine. Fucking dogs."

CHAPTER FIFTEEN

Rick's arsenal of weapons was even more impressive than what I saw earlier. My fucking brother had guns stashed everywhere, in his closet, his kitchen cabinets and even one little purse gun in the freezer. "Take that one out to let it thaw," he instructed. I didn't even ask the questions begging to be asked about that.

Within minutes we had guns and ammo. I do mean guns. An entire green army duffel bag full of revolvers, handguns, shotguns, rifles, and even an M-16 and an AK47. We didn't pack the flame thrower since it wouldn't fit into the duffel bag. Besides, Rick said, it really was too unwieldy in close combat. "We'd burn our own asses up," Rick said. I'll be damned, the sonofabitch had a flame thrower.

Rick suggested, and I accepted, a snub-nose .38 revolver with a hip holster. It was a standard-sized silver revolver, but with a short barrel only three inches long.

Rick outfitted himself with two 9mm Berretta pistols with a shoulder strap that allowed one gun to hang on each side of his chest. I put my holstered .38 at the small of my back, allowing my jacket to cover it. Rick was not so timid. "I got me a fucking license to carry and guess what…" Rick waved in the air what I suspect was the license. "Today I'm fucking carrying."

While we were getting the arsenal together, we mulled the possibility of the nine Kay children being the culprits behind my problem, my Lucastench. "So they weren't foreign," Ricks asked, rhetorically, since I just said they were not.

"Nope. As white as Ku Klux Klan members."

"Huh. Was the house full of weird voodoo religious shit?

Shrunken dolls and incense and little bottles of potions?"

"Do you have any idea what you are talking about or are you just pulling this crap from the movies?"

Rick paused as if in thought, a rifle dangling from his fist above the green duffel bag. "I have absolutely no idea what I am talking about. I'm just making this shit up as I go along."

I smiled for what felt like the first time in many hours. "Your honesty is refreshing," I said, "but it basically leaves us nowhere. This Kay woman with nine children is probably just a big fucking coincidence. If I approach her and ask her if she put a hex on me or some shit like that, she'll call the police and I'll lose my job for harassment and for sheer lunacy."

"Your job? Fuck the job. We're talking about your life here," Rick said.

"We gotta hurry up and get to Gwen." As if on cue, my cell phone rang with a ringtone that was programmed to play only when Gwen was calling. "Wind Beneath My Wings" by Bette Midler. I was in such a rush to answer that instead of hitting the "accept call" button I hit the "reject call." "Fuck me," I said. "I just hung up on Gwen." I started navigating through my phone to call her back.

"Bette Midler? Wow. You're the biggest pussy I've ever met," Rick said.

I quickly had my phone calling back Gwen. "Don't judge me. Bette is grossly underrated and many masculine men enjoy her lovely—"

Gwen answered without saying hello. "Why have you been calling and texting me so much? I was sleeping. What's all this about dogs? Have there been more? More dog problems?"

After assuring myself that she was okay and that the door was locked, I detailed everything to Gwen about my morning. In my haste, I forgot Gwen might find my morning coffee with Lydia a bit … well, troubling. "You piece of fucking shit," were her exact words.

"Gwen, she is just a friend and I needed a friend."

I saw Rick roll his eyes and shake his head.

"Lucas, are you having an affair?"

"Gwen, I promise you I am not having an affair." Rick took

a gun, pointed it to his head and pretended to shoot himself, falling on the floor in mock death.

"I'm bloated and eight months pregnant. We had a fight and you go call another woman and have coffee with her. How do you think that sounds?"

I had to admit, it sounded pretty despicable when she put it in that light. We had bigger fish to fry. "Gwen," I said, my voice more stern than I intended. "I've done nothing wrong and we are not having this conversation now." I detailed our plan of rescuing the women and getting out of dodge.

Gwen didn't take "women" too well. "You're going to take the other woman with us! The other woman! You fucker!"

I grimaced. Again, it sounded so much worse when she said it. "Gwen, she's under attack. So is Rick. It seems that anyone who has my stink on them is in danger. We're calling it Lucastench."

"Why would she have your stink on her? Huh?" Gwen's voice was thick with angry sarcasm. "She wouldn't get the, the—" she searched for the right word, "—Lucas Stink just sitting across a table from you at Starbucks."

"It's called the Lucastench, not stink," I said meekly.

"ERRRRR," was all I heard before what sounded like her throwing the phone across the room. I waited till she recovered it. "Lucas, I will ask you once. How did she get your smell on her?"

"I may have hugged her goodbye," I said. Rick shook his head from side to side in sympathy to how utterly fucked I had just made myself.

"Did you have sex with her?" she asked, her voice so wounded that I felt my heart sink.

"No, Gwen, I did not have sex with her."

In an instant, with the lightening quick speed that could only come from an older brother stealing a toy from his kid brother's grasp, Rick grabbed the phone from my hand. "Hi Gwen, it's Rick. Listen, I'm under attack too, which means I have the Lucastench and I certainly didn't have sex with Lucas. I'm not gay but even if I was gay and he wasn't my brother, I'd never do him. He's such a tight-ass I probably couldn't get it in." There was a pause and Rick nodded as if he was listening.

I was staring, dumbfounded. I was even more dumbfounded when Rick said to me, "Would you mind stepping outside to give Gwen and me a moment to talk." I started to protest but Rick cut me off. "Shush. Take the duffel bag and load it in the car. I'll be out in a minute." Rick reached over to the table and tossed me the pack of cigarettes and the lighter and waved for me to go outside.

I went outside with a duffel bag of guns and tossed them into the car. Feeling like a character from a Woody Allen comedy, I lit a cigarette as my estranged, newly eccentric brother talked to my pissed-off, pregnant wife about rescuing my almost-mistress from being attacked by dogs who wanted to maul anyone who smells like me. "Mister Woody Allen," I said aloud, "even you couldn't make this shit up."

A moment later Rick bounded out the front door, tossing me my smartphone as he walked toward the car. "Let's go," he said. "We get Lydia then Gwen then hide."

I stood frozen. "Wait, what? Gwen agreed to this?"

Rick had the car door open and was standing beside it waiting to get in. "Yeah, she's fine with it."

"How? What did you say?"

Rick smiled. "I got a gift." I shot him a confused look so he continued. "I got a gift for getting women to see things from my perspective."

"I don't understand. Is she still mad?"

Rick chuckled. "Nah. I smoothed it out. Now get in the damn car so we can rescue these women and save the day."

I walked over to the passenger seat and got in. As Rick started the car, I began to ask him what he said to Gwen but he cut me off before I could. "Dude, it isn't complicated. I told her that after we rescue them, Gwen and Lydia, that once we were safely hiding out somewhere I was going to fuck Lydia. Problem solved."

We were backing out of the driveway. "How does that solve the problem?"

Rick threw the car into drive and took off. "Because if I'm fucking her she's not going to have designs on you because she'll be infatuated with me."

"Oh," I said, not quite sure what to make of this. "If she does want me—and I'm not admitting she does—but if she does have a thing for me why do you think she'll suddenly choose you over me?"

Rick looked over at me and looked away. "Brother, do you really need to ask that? Gwen didn't." Before I could answer the insult, Rick added, "Oh and Gwen thinks we should go see this Kay woman. She believes it sounds too coincidental to be just a coincidence. I agree. She also said since you only make 50k it's worth risking your job. Dude, don't you have a doctorate? All you make is 50k? That's a shame."

"What the—?" was all I could manage to say.

CHAPTER SIXTEEN

I was festering in my indignity when the cops got us.

We were on the eight-lane Roosevelt Boulevard heading into the Torresdale section when a patrol car of Philly's finest threw on the flashing rack of lights and pulled to within inches of our bumper. Rick looked over at me. "Guess I got a lead foot."

Philadelphia's Roosevelt Boulevard is one of the deadliest roads in America. It is an eight-lane road that plows through miles and miles of heavily residential and retail sections of Philadelphia squalor. People constantly try to cross the mammoth road to get from one shopping center to another or one bus stop to another or (especially deadly) one bar to another. It is a prime example of poor city planning and since the road has no shoulders (and with the way people drive on it, no traditional driving laws), it is difficult to find a spot to stop. Rick, however, found a quick solution, slamming over the curb and hopping my delicate Kia sedan onto the grass median I imagined my little four-door sedan was not designed for hopping curbs and I imagined the repair bill I may soon see.

The patrol car followed suit without a pause, but of course if the officer broke the axle or killed the suspension in his patrol car what the fuck did he care? The taxpayers would fix it.

The two officers—a man and a woman—sat in their car for a few minutes, one talking on the walkie-talkie to dispatch, the other, I assume, running the plates. I almost felt the heat coming from Rick. "What's wrong with you?" I asked.

Rick's answer was an obvious one, yet I failed to think of it. "We have about twenty-five weapons in a duffel bag in the back seat, jackass."

Unbelievably, I was so caught up in my wounded pride over Gwen and Rick's conversation that I had utterly forgotten. "Are they all registered? Are they all legit?" Rick didn't answer and in so doing, he gave me the answer. No, they were not registered. "Fuck, we're going to the Roundhouse."

The Roundhouse in Philadelphia was literally a round-shaped building that held the City's temporary detention unit, or jail. It is where you sit for hours until you see a judge who determines bail. Well, bail for some people. Considering Philadelphia has about 400 homicides a year, not all detainees are awarded bail. Needless to say, the Roundhouse is not a fun place for an over-educated white guy.

"No we aren't going to the fucking Roundhouse," Rick said.

The two officers exited the patrol car and approached, one on each side. Rick already had his window down. Cars were speeding by on the Boulevard, only adding to my whirling mind. "Rick, don't do anything stupid. These are cops."

"We don't have time for this," he replied, his voice dripping in barely restrained anger. "We can't spend eight hours sitting in the Roundhouse waiting to see a judge. Besides with this amount of weaponry, we might not be able to afford the bail."

"Rick please," was all I could get out before the officer was at the window.

"Are you Lucas Miller?" the male cop at Rick's window asked.

Rick's answer was less polite than I would have liked. "Are you an over-paid ego-inflated asshole whose dick is so small he needs to wear a badge to feel like a real man?"

I looked down and shook my head, imagining the mess that awaited us.

I heard a little muffled grunt escape the lips of the cop. The female officer at my window didn't move a muscle. The male cop finally spoke. "Cute. Unoriginal, but cute. Nice guns," he said, pointing to the two guns dangling on either side of Rick's chest. "Unless you want me to check gun registrations, answer the goddamn question. Are you Lucas Miller?"

Rick was about to speak when I jumped in. "I'm Doctor Lucas Miller, officer."

The male cop leaned in a bit and looked at me. "You are to stay here until the sergeant arrives." Looking at Rick, he finished, "So turn the ignition off and hand me the keys."

Rick was again a tad impolite. "You smell like a syphilis-ridden whore birthed you from her stank c—"

"Rick," I cut him off, "shut the fuck up." I reached over and turned off the ignition and handed the keys to the cop. Rick sat back in a huff. "Officer, what did we get stopped for?"

The male cop was eyeballing Rick hard, almost seeming not to hear my question. I wasn't about to wait for Rick to explode.

"Uh, officer? Is there a reason we were stopped?"

The cop finally snapped his gaze from Rick and looked at me. "Yes, Doctor Miller, there is a reason. Sergeant Johnson put out an area-wide call to stop this car with these plate numbers if any officers happen to see it. I did, so I pulled you over. I told him we pulled you over and he said to leave you alone, no searches, no questions, just make sure you wait till he arrives, so you will wait. That's the only reason why I'm not running those guns through the system or asking to see in the trunk. So count your blessings."

"Thank you, officer, but one more question," I said, timidly. "Is it Sergeant John Johnson who wants us to wait?"

"The very same, yes."

"What," Rick laughed. "John Johnson? That is the stupidest, most redundant name I've ever heard."

In an instant, the cop had Rick's shirt in his fist and his other hand on the hilt of his gun. "You watch your fucking mouth, boy." The cop spat out the words through gritted teeth. I saw the female officer on my side had drawn her gun. The cop continued, "That man lost his partner today. You hear me. His partner was killed today. So no one is making fun of his redundant name. Not today at least. You got it?"

I didn't want to let Rick answer, though I could tell he wanted to, so I jumped in with a question. "You mean Officer McNally?" I asked. "He was killed?"

"Yeah."

"How'd he die?"

The cop let go of Rick's shirt and looked at me. "A dog. A

damn dog mauled him to death while he was jogging after his shift."

Rick and I looked at one another with knowing eyes.

"Here comes the sergeant now," the officer said. "Maybe he'll give me permission to beat your ass or run them guns through the system."

I put my hand on Rick's arm before he let loose a verbal tirade of foulness. "Rick, we don't have time for that." Rick looked me in the eyes and nodded in agreement and I felt the tension leave his arm.

CHAPTER SEVENTEEN

Sergeant John Johnson pulled onto the grassy medium of Roosevelt Boulevard. Coming from the opposite direction, he parked his car facing ours. With the squad car behind us and John Johnson's off-duty, long-boy, deep-auburn Buick sedan sitting in front of us with a little red light flashing on the dashboard, we created a small gaper delay on the always busy road.

John Johnson, the tall, lean, but strong black man in his forties, exited his car and walked toward us with the stiff-spine speed and determination of a Marine Corps drill sergeant on Parris Island. He was wearing an all-black outfit of dry-cleaned black slacks, ironed black shirt buttoned to the very top, sans tie, and a long black trench coat. When you added his black cowboy boots, his dark skin and his fierce face, he looked … well, fucking tough is the only way to say it.

"You know," Rick said to me, looking at John Johnson, "a black guy that dark skinned in complexion should not wear all-black clothing. At night you'd never be able to see him unless he smiles or holds up the palms of his hands. He's going to get hit by a car in a parking lot one night."

I looked over at Rick, who looked back at me and shrugged his shoulders. His expression was saying, "What, I'm just being honest." I was surprised. "Rick, are you some racist now?"

"Hell no," he said. "I served with dozens of black guys in that Afghan shithole. Damn fine soldiers, each and every one. I stay in contact with a few of them. I'm just saying, he's dark. In fact, in Afghanistan when we needed to send out a small night patrol, I always sent the black guys 'cause they were extra-camouflaged."

"Christ," I said, "You know how racist that sounds."

"I ain't racist and please don't take Christ's name in vain," Rick said. "I've become a Christian since last we met."

"Oh, let me guess, an eccentric Christian. Great, just what the world needs."

Rick ignored that comment as he watched John Johnson talking with the two uniformed cops. The male cop pointed at Rick and then made a jerking-off gesture with his hand. I felt Rick tensing up next to me. "Rick, let it go," I said. Then John Johnson nodded and seemed to be thanking the two officers who strolled past our car heading to their own. As the male cop got near Rick's window, he gave Rick the finger. Rick's hand reached for the door latch and I instantly envisioned sitting in the Roundhouse, having to take a shit in the sole, nasty toilet that sat in the corner of a large cell packed with 100 hoodlums. So I screamed out, panicked, "What would Jesus do?"

Rick's hand stopped in midair and he turned to face me. "Okay," he said. "You got me there, but that shit only goes so far, okay."

"Okay," I agreed.

Appearing almost like an apparition, John Johnson's tough face was in our window. "Doctor Miller, I can see by those guns your friend here is packing that you know we have a little problem so I won't waste time talking about the problem. What we need is a solution to that problem. I don't believe we should be deciding that solution on a median on mother-fucking Roosevelt Boulevard. A damn dog is liable to jump out a window and take a piece of my ass." He handed Rick the car keys that the officers had confiscated. I was so transfixed on the sternness of John Johnson's face that I didn't even see the squad car leave, but looking in the rearview, I saw it was gone. "Follow me. I'm heading over to Grant Plaza on Grant Avenue about a mile from here. It is customary to toast a drink to a fallen partner and I intend to do just that. Then we can figure out a plan to end this shit."

"We have our own plan," Rick said, "and we intend to follow it."

John Johnson made the same jerking-off gesture that the

uniformed cop made a few moments earlier. Rick didn't even show a hint of anger. I assumed Rick was too intimidated or mesmerized by John Johnson to do anything. "Follow me," John Johnson said.

He moved his head from the window and straightened up. I shouted, "I am sorry about Officer McNally."

John Johnson leaned back down into the window. "Me too," he said. "That boy could've been the Jackson Pollock of pottery and ceramics. Talented. He should've died at ninety years old on a stool at the pottery wheel doing what he loved. Damn shame." He straightened and walked to his car.

"Pottery?" Rick asked. I just dismissed the question with a wave of my hand. Rick started the car and we followed without a word.

CHAPTER EIGHTEEN

"Your brother," John Johnson said to me as I walked up, "was just telling me his theory about why a dark-skinned black man shouldn't wear all-black clothing. Especially at night, unless he is smiling or holding up his palms."

I froze mid-step, a brown bag containing one beer grasped in my hand. Rick was nodding, not at me but at the truth he saw in his theory of black clothing on black skin.

"You know," John Johnson continued, "he's damn right. I never thought of it till now but when I'm walking in a parking lot at night, people are always almost backing into me or turning their cars toward me like I wasn't even fucking there. I always thought it was because white folk just don't notice black people, in a sociological sense. What Rick said rings of truth. They can't see me. They physically cannot see my ass."

I smiled and looked from Rick to John Johnson, who spoke again. "It took balls—big fucking balls—for your brother to say it. Say that shit to the wrong black man, he's liable to rip your goddamn head off."

"He'd try," Rick said, and he patted John Johnson on the shoulder. "He'd certainly try. Oh, and don't take the Lord's name in vain."

"I hear that," John Johnson said, smiling.

I was pleasantly confused. "Okay," I muttered. Then more strongly, "I'm glad you two had time to bond, but I think we need to get this ritual over with and get to my wife." As an afterthought I added, "and Lydia."

"The ritual don't take long," John Johnson said, reaching for the single, 16oz can of Pabst Blue Ribbon beer I carried in a brown bag in my hand.

About thirty minutes before, we had followed John Johnson a mile or so to the strip mall called Grant Plaza on Grant Avenue. Much to our surprise, John Johnson didn't stop in front but pulled behind the conventional strip of stores (a beauty shop, laundry shop, coffee shop, a deli with takeout beer, etc.) and parked in the rear. Behind the strip mall shopping center there was nothing but doors that employees used to sneak outside for a quick smoke or to take the garbage to one of four dumpsters strategically placed at even intervals down the rear of the strip. Across from the rear of the strip mall was a small wooded area that separated the rear of the strip mall from an adjacent, undeveloped patch of grass the size of half a football field.

After we parked, we got out of our cars and John Johnson handed me a five-dollar bill. I took it with a quizzical look on my face, which he answered. "Go around front and get me one Pabst Blue Ribbon beer from that deli."

"Why are we back here?" Rick asked. "Someone could call the cops and—" He cut himself off, remembering we were with a sergeant.

"We are back here," John Johnson said, "because no people come back here, other than employees catching a smoke or something. Employees ain't likely to have a dog with 'em. Out front, well shit, there has got to be some dogs sitting in the backseat of some cars. I don't know if they can bust through the car windows or anything, but I am not about to find out. So go get my beer."

"Wait. Why am I getting your beer?" I said, dismayed, my voice betraying my fear.

"Because," John Johnson said, "this shit started with you. A person is dead because of you, at least one that we know of. So go around front and *fetch*." He accented the last word with both mockery and disdain. "Careful of Cujo while you're at it. I imagine you're armed?" I nodded. "Good. Use it if you need to."

"It isn't his fault," Rick said. "He was hexed. The person who put the hex on him, it is her fault."

"We will get into all that, after I toast my partner farewell. Now go get me that beer. Make sure it is Pabst Blue Ribbon."

I turned to do as commanded and stopped. "Pabst is cheap shit. Don't you want something more expensive for a solemn moment?"

John Johnson looked indignant. "They call you Doctor Miller? Pabst Blue Ribbon! My partner is a fallen cop. Cops wear blue. The blue ribbon. Pabst Blue Ribbon."

"Oh," I said, and did as I was told. It went smoothly enough. I did not see any dogs and I bought the can of beer without a problem. By the time I returned to the rear of the building, John Johnson and my brother had become chummy. Fucking fantastic.

"So let me do my ritual and then we talk," he said. John Johnson took the beer, opened it, and poured its contents onto the ground. He then crushed the can in his hand and put it on the roof of his car. "Okay let's talk."

"Wait," Rick said. "What the fuck kind of ritual was that? You didn't do anything."

"I most certainly did. I am supposed to drink a drink for a fallen partner. Well I don't drink. Booze makes people act stupid. So I poured it out for him. Ritual done. I added the Blue Ribbon thing as my own personal touch. Nice, ain't it." Rick and I looked at one another quizzically and John Johnson caught the look. He made an exasperated sound. "It's just a fucking ritual. It isn't magic or shit. What'd you think, I was going to pull a group of Irish bagpipers from my ass or something?"

We fumbled for words, but didn't find any. I did manage to move the conversation forward. "You said the ritual wasn't magic. We think this whole dog thing, we think it is black magic. A hex, actually."

"Yeah," John Johnson said. "I got that feeling too. This morning, around the time McNally got mauled into his grave, I was heading to my yoga class—" He stopped suddenly. From the expression on our faces, he must've realized Rick and I were trying to picture the tall, street-tough, stone-faced, scary-ass officer sitting in some new age yoga studio with soft Tibetan hymns playing, wearing skin-tight yoga pants, attempting to stretch himself into a Diving Swan position. "Alright," he continued, "you close-minded motherfuckers. Yeah, so I do yoga. Makes me better at love-making. I've gotten so goddamn flexible and limber and strong that my lady and I get into freaky positions you couldn't even imagine. So heed my advice. You want to fuck better, yoga better."

We both blushed and looked at our feet like innocent-eared school girls. I broke the silence. "Alright, sorry. Can we focus. You said you believe it's a hex. Why?"

"As I was saying..." John Johnson lifted his chin as he talked showing that it was his turn to be heard. "I was on my way to yoga class, walking down Olney Avenue near LaSalle University. Since I do this walk routinely, as usual I see this kid, Aaron. Aaron is autistic and he waits with his mother for the bus right near my yoga studio right about the time my class starts. We got a usual thing, Aaron and me. I say 'what's up Aaron,' and he does some weird thing with his hand that I suppose is his way of saying hello. Never looks at me. Never says a word. Going on six months now. I pass this kid three days a week and he never looks at me or says a word. I only know his name because his mother is a hot piece of ass and I chatted her up one day. She told me she turned dyke a few years back so I forgot about trying to bang that ass, but saying hello to the kid was my routine."

"Did something happen to the kid?" I asked, alarmed.

"No," Rick answered for John Johnson. "He spoke to you, didn't he."

"Rick," John Johnson said, admiringly, "you should be the one called Doctor Miller. Yeah, this morning, I say 'what's up' to Aaron and I'll be damned, the boy lifts his head and his eyes and looks at me square. It stopped me dead in my tracks. Couldn't believe it, and from the look on his mother's face, she couldn't fucking believe it either. So I say again, 'what's up Aaron,' and he says—this kid actually spoke—he says to me 'you smell.' Well, I'm just standing there shocked that this kid actually uttered a word. His mother, whom I suspect has rarely heard the boy talk, looked goddamn stunned."

"Using the Lord's name in vain again? Please," Rick reminded.

John Johnson put on a faux-apologetic voice. "Right, my

bad, Rick." His voice returned to normal. "Jesus Christ, let me tell the goddamn story how I choose to fucking tell it. So, I'm standing there shocked that he talked but then it hits me that he said, 'you smell.' So I say to him, 'What's that Aaron? What you say?' He looks at me and says, 'You got the stench on you.' I'm trying to figure out what the hell he is talking about, so—"

I had to cut him off. Gwen was waiting. "Okay, I got it. You don't know what to make of it but after hearing about your partner and thinking about my incident with the dog last night, you made the connection. You got my smell on you."

John Johnson looked annoyed but he relented. "Alright. You know, you cut my story short and normally, you'd be hurting right now for doing that shit. I pride myself on my storytelling. Since you got a wife needs seeing to, I'll let it go. Yeah, I deduced it. After your dog attacks and my partner being mauled by a dog, I must've gotten your smell on me and you must be cursed or something."

"Yup," Rick added, "we call it Lucastench."

"That's a clever fucking name," John Johnson agreed.

I wanted to move this forward. "Listen, we have an idea— just a far-flung idea—but we want to pursue it. Hear me out." So I detailed to John Johnson about my own morning encounter with the cocker while I sat in my car, about Captain and his now-deceased dog Cream, about our little experiment at the SPCA and about Lydia's own encounter with a pooch. John Johnson listened attentively but his blank-faced expression did not reveal if he thought we were completely incompetent idiots or on the right track. So I continued, detailing how my removal of the Kay woman's ninth child and "canine" were too coincidental and seemed worthy of an enquiry. I told him we were heavily armed and the women were safely locked away in their respective apartments. We intended to visit the Kay woman first to see if there was any connection, and after seeing if the Kay woman was involved, we planned to rescue the women and hide away until we could figure out how to undo the hex or wait till it wore off.

When I was done, John Johnson nodded, as if agreeing. "A pretty good plan," he said. Then he looked to Rick. "I'm assuming you came up with this plan."

Rick nodded in agreement. I contradicted. "We both devised it," I said.

"You cheating on your wife with this Lydia woman?" John Johnson asked.

"No!" I yelled. I said it so loud and emphatic that it sounded more like a lie because of the needless forcefulness.

John Johnson merely held up his hands, smiling. "Hey, I don't judge. Just wondering how she got the Lucastench on her, is all."

"I hugged her goodbye," I said. "That's all. Can we get back to the plan?"

"Sure," he said. "Your plan is fine and I'll go along. You're missing one key part though."

"Yeah," Rick asked, "what is that, Sergeant?"

John Johnson looked back and forth, taking a moment to look us each in the eyes. "Between here and hiding out, you are planning on doing a lot. Between here and that, there are a lot of fucking dogs. We all got the Lucastench. They say sharks can smell a drop of blood in the water one mile away. Well, how about three people drenched in Lucastench and all those goddamn dogs."

Rick was about to comment on the Lord's name being used in vain, but as if on cue, he was cut off by a series of muffled barks from the throats of different dogs that sounded much closer than was comfortable.

"See," John Johnson said. "Your plan is already turning to shit."

CHAPTER NINETEEN

In military engagements, they call it putting "eyes" on the enemy and it is rarer than people think. In today's warfare, drones and computer-guided satellites are usually the only things that actually see the enemy. When they do, a computer-jockey hits a few keys and, on command from a man of rank, uses long-distance pinpoint-precise bombs to eliminate that enemy. Even if one group in the conflict is low-budgeted and low-tech, they use roadside munitions to eliminate more modern warriors. When combat between soldiers does occur, the modern hand-held firearms are so accurate at great distances that soldiers rarely get a close encounter with the enemy. Instead, as Rick told me when he first came home from the war, the enemy looks like "ants scurrying between rocks." You could kill them with a nicely fired shot (and Rick won awards for doing so), but when they fell, mortally wounded, they just looked like ants that stopped moving. Just ants fighting ants to the human eye, though not to God's supreme eye, I suspect. On that cold October afternoon, sitting behind the Grant Plaza shopping center, my brother Rick, combat hero in Afghanistan, witnessed his first-ever close-combat encounter. In fine military fashion, Rick was the first to put "eyes" on the enemy.

When the first muffled barks were heard, the three of us looked at each other. It seems counterintuitive, I know. We should have been quickly scanning the immediate area, searching for the source of the barks. Our eyes should have been looking to put "eyes" on the enemy. Instead, I looked to Rick and then to John Johnson, and I saw them looking between themselves and me. We all carried a knowing, foreboding countenance and I can only guess that they, like me, were looking for some reassurance, for a collective solidarity to steady the fear that hit our minds like a roadside bomb. We looked to each other because we knew we were in for it now. True, it was only a few muffled barks, but it was enough. Those barks awoke in us the reality of what we faced, a reality filled with strong, fast, relentless dogs who wanted us dead as Dillinger. Being only animals ourselves—human animals, but animals nonetheless— we knew in the innermost recesses of our soul that this reality was about to voice its deadly intent. That voice was a bark and that intent was the shredding of the flesh from our bones.

All this was spoken without a word through the content of our eyes. It lasted only seconds before Rick and John Johnson stopped the pity party and started scanning the long emptiness behind the strip mall.

Despite the looks we'd just shared and despite how the gravity of the Earth seemed four times greater than normal and even despite the nausea filling my gut, I still held out hope. "Maybe we should just get in the cars and—" but I was cut off by Rick.

"No time!" Rick was pointing to the east, from the way we'd driven in.

It was Rick, the combat-hardened vet, and not John Johnson, our ad hoc leader, who readied us for our new reality. "All right boys," he said, crossing his arms and bringing forth the guns from his shoulder holster. "Time to burn, no time to learn."

Before I even saw where Rick had spotted the dogs, he darted to a squatting position behind my sedan and took aim. John Johnson reached behind his back and produced a black pistol, much like the guns uniformed police carry, and took position next to Rick. As I reached toward the small of my back and produced the compact .38 snub nose, I saw what Rick had seen seconds earlier.

A woman, who looked past her prime in that plump housewife way, lay face down in the mud in that small wooded area that separated the rear of the strip mall from an adjacent, undeveloped patch of grass the size of half a football field. The woman's right arm was extended at an oddly turned angle, in that inhuman, broken fashion. Her left arm lay limply next to her. She was writhing her waist and legs in that unmistakable look of human agony. Her twisted arms remained frozen, unmoving.

If it was old women that wanted to murder us, then we'd have been in better shape.

About fifty yards away and closing fast was a hodgepodge of canine pedigree composed of a Great Dane, a golden retriever, some grey and white mutt of medium build (smaller than a retriever) and a fucking tiny little toy poodle. Four dogs, each a different size and breed, running at full-tilt toward what I immediately thought of as our "defensive position." Each dog dragged behind it a leash, and I instantly knew what happened moments before.

The woman lying face down in the mud had her shoulders broken trying to restrain the dogs after they caught a whiff of Lucastench. She probably had the leashes wrapped around her fists. So when the dogs pulled without warning and with inhuman strength, even if she let go of the leashes, they remained wrapped around her hands. The damn dogs just pulled until her shoulder ligaments snapped, causing her arms to go instantly limp. The dogs probably dragged her till the leashes unwrapped themselves from around her flaccid hands, attached to now useless arms.

A thought flashed through my mind before the mayhem. *Who walks such a mismatched, stupid collective of dogs? Who walks four dogs? You can't control four dogs. That woman deserves the broken arms!*

"Big bitches first," Rick shouted and his voice moved my cemented feet. I took a kneeling position to Rick's left, John Johnson on his right, all of us behind the side of the car, arms on the car's hood, weapons at the ready. That quickly, the first hell hound was on us, the Great Dane.

The Great Dane was almost at the car, snarling teeth and barking. Foam and saliva dangled from its large jaw and I'll swear to it, the Dane had rage in its eyes. I was transfixed on this massive beast which, even on four legs, stood chest tall to most men. Fear and panic mixed seamlessly with an ongoing sense of disbelief that this was happening. It was a dreamlike feeling, as if I were a passive voyeur and it kept me suspended, unable to react. I just stared at the huge charging Dane, who through the sheer length of its stride led the ragtag pack of dogs by a good twenty yards. Two shots rang out and the Dane tumbled forward into the dirt, face first, skidding hard into the tire on the other side of the car. Rick's and John Johnson's guns were both smoking at the tips and moved to aim at the next target. Seeing the blue-grey smoke drifting from the tips of their guns lifted me from the dreamlike state and awoke me into consciousness.

While the Dane had taken the bullets, the golden retriever had gained ground and was just steps behind. It leapt onto the hood of the car and when its feet hit the hood, its momentum carried it right over like a bullet. It plowed directly into Rick with magnificent force. Rick tumbled backward, the golden rolled and landed on top of him, but the impact bounced the dog off of Rick and to his right.

The enemy had breached the defensive line.

Just that quickly, hell broke loose. Rick rolled and scurried to his feet. The golden had the same idea but was quicker at getting its footing and it lunged at Rick, plowing into him just as he got to his feet, hand raised to shoot.

I pointed my pistol at the goddamn golden retriever, but it was instantly entangled with Rick, snarling and pushing my brother backward. To shoot at the tangled mess would've been tantamount to shooting my brother. As my feet went toward Rick my mind thought, *Don't fall over, Rick. He'll win if you're on the ground.*

At the corner of my right eye, John Johnson unleashed a torrent of bullets toward the gray-haired mutt, which tried to scoot around the front end of the car and flank us. The mutt was cutting and weaving like a running-back, and hitting a moving target that small, fast, and agile was too great a challenge for John Johnson's gun.

As I was inches from reaching Rick and the golden, the mutt passed John Johnson and cut the path between Rick and me. It leapt for me. The mutt was so damn quick that it wasn't the force of the dog that knocked me over, but the surprise. I fell down for the same reason that people act like they are having a convulsion when a bee flies around their head. It is disconcerting, and even though your conscious mind knows staying still is the best course, we all flail about like epileptic dancers. For the same reasons, when the thirty-pound mutt leapt at me, I fell. I was in a bad spot, on the ground, on my back and the mutt's teeth were flying.

To say I knew what I was doing would be a bold-faced lie. I was just flinging my hands, swatting at the thing's face, my mind on autopilot. Teeth aren't a dog's only weapon. The fucking mutt's front paws were scurrying at a furious clip, like it was digging a hole in the ground. Except the ground was my shirt and the thin material of a business casual button-down does nothing to stop nails from scraping the actual skin beneath. I let out a scream as I felt the skin begin to open from his relentless scratching. I know I should have tried to roll over or thrust the mutt backward, but conscious, coherent thought had evaporated in the throes of panic. I just threw my arms at the dog's face and swatted and tussled. Somewhere, in the recesses of what remained of my conscious mind, I knew I was dog-meat.

Then like some black angel, John Johnson was above me and the mutt. He put his pistol to the savage mutt's head and *POP*, I was instantly awash in chunks of fur and flesh, and the dead-weight of the damn mutt fell on me like a brick.

I didn't even have a second to think before a loud thud erupted next to me, and John Johnson lay face down, with the Dane on his back. I surmise the thing had only been wounded and had reentered the fight. The dog looked more enraged than I thought a dog could look, as if getting shot pissed the Dane off worse than before.

Like the mutt, the Dane started digging with his paws as his mouth sought for flesh. The mouth found some, catching John Johnson on that strong flesh where the shoulder meets the neck. The dog bit and clamped and thrashed. John Johnson screamed bloody murder.

Without thought, I threw the corpse of the mutt off of me, found my gun in the dirt, and scampered clumsily to my feet. Attempting to copy what John Johnson had done for me, I raised my pistol and pointed it squarely at the Dane. As my finger was about to squeeze the trigger, my leg exploded in pain. It was a sharp, cutting pain that was enough to draw my hand into the air just as I pulled the trigger, releasing the shot into nothing but empty sky. I looked down to see this tiny fucking auburn-colored toy poodle had his little mouth locked onto my calf. I kicked out my leg with such force that the toy lost its hold for a second, and it was just enough time for me to point the .38 snub nose at the Dane. I fired a round and by its yelp I knew I hit the big dog though I had no time to see *where* I hit it. The poodle was on me again and bit and it hurt. I yelped and pointed the gun down at the little furry fucking thing attached to my leg.

I pulled the trigger.

What a snub-nose .38 does to a toy poodle at near point-blank range would make even the most avid fan of gore-movies cringe. All that was left was a pile of auburn fur and goopy intestine.

Looking away, my vision saw that my shot had not put down the Dane, only knocked it off John Johnson, who was quickly getting to his feet. The Dane was on the ground, trying to get up, but the shot caught it directly behind its front right leg, which now seemed immobile. The previous shot, when it was first charging, had also wounded a back leg on the opposite side. The Dane was furious, barking and showing its teeth in anger, but it couldn't stand. With two legs seriously wounded, it was trying to get up only to fall back down again in wasted effort.

Between the mutt, the toy and the Dane, I was paralyzed for a second in both space and time. My mind whirled, trying to interpret and understand the events that just occurred in a mindless flash. Guns, shots, dogs, blood, John Johnson, Rick …

Rick! I turned and my eyes befell a sight that still makes me quiver. Rick lay still, lifeless, covered in blood. Next to him lay the golden retriever, also still, lifeless and covered in blood. Fighting my own battle, I had missed Rick's epic struggle. I ran toward them knowing I would find two lifeless combatants who had fought bravely and fiercely, ending in a draw of mutual death.

Rick was so bloodied I couldn't immediately see his wounds. He looked like one big wound. His chest, neck, face, and arms were all splattered and cloaked in blood. I dropped to my knees beside him and looked closer. Behind his neck and head sat a pool of dark, thick liquid and the pool seemed to be growing. I could also make out long, bloody lines in his chest where the dog had used its nails to dig deep into the flesh of his chest. Four deep tears ran straight down the right side of his face, where the nails of a paw had hooked into Rick's flesh and pulled downward, taking lines of meat with it.

I couldn't look any more. I turned my head and my gaze fell onto the retriever. I hoped the beast was still breathing so I could choke the remaining life out of it with my bare hands. The retriever was dead, its fatal wound obvious. From its underbelly protruded the hilt of a standard issue military knife. Rick, God love 'im for being a weapon junkie, was carrying a knife. I should have known, but I didn't. I didn't think about it. Looking at the hilt of that knife in the retriever's underbelly, I realized that for the past decade or so, I hadn't thought much about Rick. I hadn't thought much *of* Rick, as a brother, as a human being. I looked up to the sky and my mind begged Rick for forgiveness, wherever he was.

"Ain't no dogs in the sky, douche-bag. Keep your eyes on the ground." The voice was Rick's and my head snapped to the tattered, torn and blood-painted face of my brother. He lay flat on his back, unmoving, not even lifting his head. His voice was strong, but thick with pain. "I hear barking. Why you sitting here with me? Fight."

The Dane was still rolling on the ground, barking, trying to get up. The shock of hearing Rick's voice was overwhelming. I didn't know what to do. I just stood over him, looking down at him. "Rick? Rick!"

"Don't blubber, I hear barking."

I looked over toward the Dane and saw it hadn't moved position much, hobbled on legs that couldn't get it to stand or move. "Don't worry," I said, "that fucker is down, just not dead."

A smile crossed Rick's face. "So we won, huh?" His voice was hoarse and weak, barely above a whisper.

"Rick—" I dropped to my knees beside him.

He cut me off. "Just listen. Stick to the plan. Get the Kay woman, get some answers, get our women and get the fuck outta here. Go to the mountains. Somewhere without people so there won't be any dogs."

I reached for my cell. "I'm calling an ambulance."

John Johnson approached and his shadow fell over a horrific picture … a brother kneeling beside his bloodied, dying sibling.

"You can call but it won't do no good," Rick said.

"I'll call," John Johnson said, "and tell them a soldier is down. Lucas, you talk to your brother. Make your peace." John Johnson strode away.

"Try to stay calm, Rick. They'll be here soon. Get you to the hospital."

Rick smiled a thin smile again. "If you say so, but I don't think so. I'm seeing you clouded in white light and your voice sounds like an echo down a long tunnel. That don't bode well."

"You've lost a lot of blood," I said with my most reassuring voice. "You'll be okay. You'll be okay," I repeated. "You will. They'll get you back into shape. Honest. You have to be okay."

"You sound about as sure as I am, which isn't very sure."

I didn't like the look in Rick's eyes. They had the glare of eyes that are half in this world, half in another. I looked away. Rick spoke, straining now to get the words out. "Thank you, Lucas. Thank you for coming to see me today."

"No. I shouldn't have come to see you. I didn't mean for this to happen. I shouldn't have dragged you into this. I am so sorry."

"No," Rick wheezed. "I am thanking you. You came to me for help. You asked for my help. No one has done that in a long time. It felt good."

"Rick, don't, it's all, just… be still," I stammered, unsure what to say.

Rick's voice gained some strength. It was the strength of pride, I believe. "I'm a soldier and I died fighting. That's how it is supposed to be. Soldiers shouldn't die of disease or old age. They should die fighting. Well, I am a soldier and I died fighting." A big smile crossed his face. "I died fighting an enraged dog because of some voodoo hex placed on my brother. It fits with my new eccentric motif. An eccentric soldier! It all came together."

With that, POOF! That was it. Rick's eyes lost that spark that living eyes possess and became the blank, vacant eyes of death. Coming from some hidden well of regret and despair, of love and hope, watery tears filled my eyes and I cried. It wasn't just a few tears rolling down my cheek. I wept and cried and moaned for a good minute. I felt John Johnson standing over me as I rocked back and forth and made all the babyish noises that pour out of a man when he cries. John Johnson said nothing. He just let me cry.

Just as quick as the tears came they stopped. I straightened my shoulder and rose to my feet. I felt the weight, suddenly, of the gun in my hand. Felt the sting of the scrapes on my chest from the mutt's nails. Most of all, I heard the barking of the "down but not dead" Dane.

I turned and walked toward the animal, raising my gun. John Johnson was a step behind me and put a hand on my shoulder. "Stop," he said. "Don't."

I turned and looked him in the eye. "I'm killing that fucking dog and nothing is going to stop me."

"Oh, that pooch is going to his grave today," John Johnson said. "I get to do it. He tussled with me, so me and him have some unfinished business. Oh, he's going to die but not before he feels my wrath."

Despite it all, I felt a sting of dismay. "You're going to torture it before you kill it? I don't know if that seems right."

"Normally, if anyone hurt an animal, I'd haul his ass to jail and give 'im a good thrashing before booking him," John Johnson said. "This dog here has my blood in his mouth. I'll never be able to use this arm properly again." He pointed with his left hand to his right arm where his jacket and shirt were torn and covered in blood. "I'm right-fucking-handed. Go figure."

"Oh," is all I could say.

"That dog having my blood in its mouth leaves a bad taste in mine, so yeah, I'm going to fuck with 'im before I put 'im down. You might not want to see it." His tone was so cold and callused I felt a chill. "Tell me the Kay woman's address. You take your car and I'll meet you there in mine. Don't get out of the car till I'm with you. You did all right in this fight but we are stronger together. We'll get this Kay woman, get some answers—"

"—yeah I got it. I know the plan. Alright. How long are you going to be?"

John Johnson turned and looked at the wounded Dane. "Just a few minutes." He looked back to me. "Besides, I want to be gone before my fellow boys in blue get here. They'll be following the ambulance."

"Yeah, with all this gunfire, I'm surprised they aren't here already."

"They are. Down the street, waiting. They are giving me a few minutes." I shot him a puzzled look. "I'm a sergeant. I radioed in for a short delay in the response. They listen. Once the ambulance is in sight, they'll come, no matter what I said. Now remember, don't stop for anything or get out of the car till I meet you at the Kay woman's house."

"I do have to make one stop," I said, raising a hand to stop John Johnson from protesting. I looked over at Rick's corpse. "I think I'm going to get another Pabst Blue Ribbon for a fallen partner. I'm drinking mine."

John Johnson smiled. "Good for you. Now where does this Kay bitch live?"

PART TWO

GET THE WOMEN

CHAPTER TWENTY

I took stock of my wounds. Sitting in my car in front of the Kay woman's house, I counted myself lucky. Not just because I was alive—Rick's death and the prospect that I too could have died was still just too surreal and too new to process and compute in my beehive mind. Instead, I looked at my right leg.

Ironic, I thought. One leg, two poodles, two different attacks.

The big poodle from the day before had sunk its teeth in good, but it didn't tear the flesh from my leg. It had caused some nasty puncture wounds where its teeth sank into my flesh, but it did not tear my meat into shreds. If fact, with the adrenaline of what was occurring that day, I had virtually forgotten about the pain. It was somehow masked by the energy of surviving. Thinking back, after meeting Lydia for drinks, I had even stopped limping. I was just too fueled by endorphins to feel those early wounds.

The little toy poodle had gotten me in nearly the same spot, and that little fucker's mouth had done some damage. His teeth had also sunk in, but when I jerked my leg in a kicking fashion to get the toy poodle off of me, its teeth had dragged across the top layer of my flesh, leaving a few long gashes that were two or three centimeters deep. That doesn't sound like much, until it is your own leg. It throbs and aches and stings, and what that toy poodle did would certainly make me limp for the next few days … if I survived a few days. I had a gym bag in the trunk, and I changed into a clean, black tee-shirt (it was a throwback to my favorite watering hole of youth with the *Knights of Philly Pub and Grill* printed over the heart beneath a white knight piece, like you'd find on a chess set). I took the tattered remains of the business shirt I had been wearing and tore it into a few strips. I then used one of the strips as a tourniquet on my leg, fastening it tight around my calf where the worst of the wounds were. It hurt when I tightened the strip and I wasn't even sure that what I was doing was worthwhile, medically speaking. I was simply mimicking what people in movies would do. It was done nonetheless and with my dirty, bloodied pants and this tourniquet on my leg, I looked like a deranged hobo. Seeing as my pants were pleated Jos. A. Bank's khakis, I looked like a deranged hobo who robbed a JC Penney's. Probably the smartest thing I did was exchange my business casual dress shoes for the sneakers from the gym bag. I would need to be mobile and quick and, as I would discover later, wearing sneakers would be helpful.

Waiting for John Johnson to arrive was the most tortured wait I ever had to endure. My mind was going in a thousand directions at once and I wanted John Johnson there. It is a difficult thing for a man to admit, but I wanted help from another man. Not just physical help in this battle either, but emotional help. I didn't want to go through this nightmare alone. I was scared. I felt unsure of myself. John Johnson was a man who did not seem easily scared and was always sure of himself. I wanted to feed off of his courage and certainty. Take his solidity and lean on it. Without it, I was a trembling mess of uncertainty and worry.

Despite my distracted mind, I had the forethought to call both Gwen and Lydia. They remained hunkered down in their respective apartments, doors bolted, and safe. I told them a brief, diluted version of our recent battle, leaving out the gore and definitely not mentioning my fallen brother. I felt no need to scare them now and I did not want to hear Gwen cry in grief until I was able to be there to hold her, reassure her, and comfort her. It would serve no purpose but to scare them and they were plenty scared enough. They would find out in short notice anyway, when we came for them.

I did tell Gwen that John Johnson had joined the fight and I tried to spin that fact as a huge victory in our favor. I miscalculated.

By telling her I was very pleased to have a warrior like John Johnson on our side, she misinterpreted this as *"Oh shit, we are in such trouble that we need a warrior! What the hell?"* So when I called Lydia, I presented John Johnson coming on board as just a good friend who is also a cop and offering to help. Presenting it this way was benign enough that Lydia barely acknowledged I'd said anything.

Lastly, I told them that since they were both safe, we were getting the Kay woman first in hopes of getting some answers. After seeing if the Kay woman had any influence in this, then we would decide what to do next. I mentioned nothing of fleeing to a cabin in the mountains. If Gwen remembered Rick mentioning this from an earlier conversation, she didn't bring it up.

So being bandaged, changed into sneakers, and the women called, I waited for John Johnson in my car three houses down from the Kay woman's house. She lived in North Philly, near Eighteenth and Diamond, smack in the thick of one of the most violent neighborhoods in the United States. Riddled with drugs, gangs and poverty, Eighteenth and Diamond was typical urban decay, complete with dilapidated row homes, many abandoned and used by the homeless as illegal drug dispensaries. Beaten, rotted-out cars were parked up and down the street, many, like the homes, abandoned like permanent litter. On each corner was a deli-market that sold more malt liquor than milk. Chinese food restaurants abounded, a few frightening bars, but not much else. Just urban American poverty.

I was far from intimidated by this neighborhood. Believe it or not, being an evaluation psychologist for the City's Department of Children and Youth often brought me into these neighborhoods. During the daytime, they were safe enough if you dressed like an overeducated social worker, carried a worn, leather briefcase and kept your ID badge dangling from a lanyard around your neck. The people out and about during the day were the victims of the drugs and gangs. The working-poor, I believe the Republicans call them, forced to live among the gun-toting gangbangers. When you looked like a social worker and kept to these neighborhoods only in broad daylight, they generally assumed you were there to help some family who was applying for some social service support and they left you alone. Believe it or not, I removed kids from less than 5 percent of families I evaluated. Most often, I told the families of resources and aid that was available to make their plight easier. Most families leaned on me, not hated me. So I generally had nothing to fear.

Besides, the gang bangers and dealers were not rousing from a drunken, weed- and crack-fueled night of illegal and violent activity till roughly two in the afternoon. I always made my visits to these neighborhoods before one, and was safely in my office in Center City by two.

Today, I was intimidated, but not by the people walking up and down "the block" (as the locals referred to the streets). No, I was nervous and fidgety because despite the poverty and decay, North Philly was home to many, many dogs. Since rap musicians and hip-hop moguls made them fashionable, the dog of choice in such neighborhoods was the pit bull. Before the Lucastench stole all affection I held for canines, I had come to accept that pit bulls were just misunderstood and I had actually lost most of my fear of them. Countless homes I entered had pit bulls, and after the normal "barking at someone knocking on the door," the pit bulls were just like any other dog. The owner would tell them to shut up, I'd come in, the pit bull would sniff me, then either bring me a toy because it wanted to play or simply curl up somewhere to nap.

Still, pit bulls had big damn jaws and they looked like powerful animals. An insightful woman who owned a pit bull (she lived not too far from this very neighborhood) once told me about her dog, a female. Paraphrasing: *She's a great dog. Very affectionate and obedient. It's a funny thing, though. That dog has no idea she has the power to rip me into a thousand pieces any time she wanted. Every time I tell her "no" or "get down" I always think that if she only knew she had the physical advantage, she'd enforce her own "no" with those massive jaws and teeth.*

Scanning my mirrors for any sign of pit bulls and thinking of what that woman said about dogs having the advantage in power, strength and agility, I jumped when John Johnson rapped his knuckles on the window. "Jeez-us!" I yelped, while trying to keep my boxer-briefs unsoiled.

John Johnson gestured for me to get out of the car. I did so. "You nearly made me shit myself," I said.

He had changed his clothes, but I only knew they were fresh clothes because these clothes had no rips, shreds, dirt or blood from our battle. Otherwise, it was the very same outfit he was wearing earlier. It was a clean, pristine version of the outfit he wore during the battle. Even the trench coat was too new to be what he was wearing only a short time before. It sort of made me feel like we traveled back in time. "Isn't that the same out—"

He didn't let me finish. "We gotta get inside this Kay woman's house. This is pit bull country. We don't want to face a pack of them. They are mean sons-of-bitches."

I was quick with my reply. "I was just thinking that about the pit bulls. Normally, they are okay. Technically, all dogs are sons-of-bitches."

John Johnson shot me a look that said I was a jackass.

"You still packing?" he asked.

I pulled the reloaded .38 snub nose from the small of my back. "Time to burn, no time to learn, as Rick would say." I instinctively looked to the ground, sadness flooding my mind.

"I'd give you a big pep talk and all that shit to help you stay focused despite what happened to your brother," John Johnson said, "but we ain't got time for shit like that. We really need to get off the street." I caught his eyes looking over my back. I turned and saw what he saw. About one block away, a young kid, thirteen or so (who ought to have been in school, my Department of Children and Youth mind said) was walking a… tah-dah… pit bull. If that dog whiffed the Lucastench, he'd be able to pull away from that kid in a flash.

I looked back to John Johnson and pointed to the Kay woman's house three houses down. "There. She lives there."

We started walking at a pace somewhere above brisk. "She got a dog?" John Johnson asked. It hadn't even occurred to me. "Shit, yes. I completely forgot about that. She does. Not a pit bull. Something big and fluffy. Real big, like a Saint Bernard, but not exactly that. A mountain dog or something. From somewhere in Asia."

"A Burmese Mountain Dog. Yup, I know 'em. Tall as my hip, bulky as a barrel, black fluffy hair mixed with white patches, huge jaws. Powerful fucking animals. Bred to handle wicked winters in the mountains of Burma. Hence the name. We only started to import them here in the seventies because they are fluffy and cute as hell when they are puppies."

I was taken aback by John Johnson's depth of canine knowledge. *This guy knows everything,* I thought. The look on my face must've given away my thoughts because he dismissed my question before I could even ask it. "Don't ask," he said, "just listen. We knock on this here door and any sign of that pooch, we put it down, no questions asked," John Johnson said, eerily calm. "I know the Burmese Mountain Dog is usually a docile family dog, but they are big. If it gets the Lucastench in its nostrils, it'll be bad."

My silence gave tacit approval. We approached the front stoop of the Kay woman's house. "How'd the Dane wind up, after I left?"

I saw a smile creep onto John Johnson's face. "It got lucky. I just put it down, painlessly. I realized I ain't no animal torturer, even though he may have deserved it."

I felt a smile creep onto my face.

CHAPTER TWENTY-ONE

The Kay woman, Miss Betty Kay to be precise, was less than thrilled when she looked out of the peephole on her front door and saw my ugly mug standing on her front porch next to the menacing John Johnson. I only know her feelings because John Johnson and I both heard her scream in bloodcurdling falsetto and then heard her feet running across the floor, retreating deeper into the house.

"She's heading out the back," John Johnson said, taking off down the stoop steps. "Stay here in case she comes back to the front."

Damn, John Johnson could run. He moved like a leopard. Since these were row homes, he couldn't just cut behind the houses. He needed to get behind the whole row of houses, which meant running to the corner, down a side street, and then into the alley behind the houses. If it was I who was doing it, it would've taken a few minutes, especially with my newly acquired limp. John Johnson was down the street and around the corner in a flash.

I stood on the porch, mouth open as if to reply to John Johnson that maybe it wasn't wise for me to stand on a front porch, considering I reeked of the Lucastench. He was off and running before my voice box kicked in.

Slowly, with a deliberate, subtle, smooth movement, I looked behind me onto the street, whispering a little prayer as my head turned. *God, let that kid with the pit bull not be coming down this street.*

I scanned where the boy had been. Nothing. I scanned the

remainder of the street. Nothing. I scanned what I could see of the –side streets. Nothing. I finally had some luck turning my way. Something!

I felt a bead of sweat tickle my scalp and then slowly crawl down my forehead, and then fall into a fast slide over the ridge of my eyebrow and onto my cheek. Conscious of the sweat, I wiped my head with the back of my hand. I scanned the street again and was caught off-guard when the front door slammed open and out tumbled an arms-flailing, sweaty, severely overweight, cream-colored woman named Betty Kay. She came flying onto the stoop and … "Outta my fucking—" was all I caught of Betty Kay's voice before what felt like a train hit me and I found myself flying backward and landing flat on my ass on the hard concrete. I didn't just fall on my ass … I fell completely flat on my back.

I saw bare feet shuffle past me at a speed I found surprising for a woman of Betty Kay's size. Seconds behind her I saw the blur of two black cowboy boots whiz by. I actually heard them more than saw them. All I actually saw was a black blur, but the boots made a distinct, crisp, *clink-clink* when each boot hit the pavement.

John Johnson yelled something at me and I only heard the first few words before his voice trailed off as his distance from me increased. "Get up, you worthless piece …" and then his voice faded.

I scampered to my feet as quickly as my body would allow, which was surprisingly slow. I felt not only the limp in my leg but the exhaustion in virtually every muscle in my body. The exertion of last night and today had taken its toll.

When I was finally upright, I turned to find John Johnson a few feet from me, holding big Betty Kay by her chubby arm, leading her toward the house. John Johnson said to me, rather curtly, "Can you manage following us into the house, pansy ass?" I was on their heels as John Johnson slammed open the screen door and led Betty Kay inside. "Shut and bolt the front door, Lucas."

I did as instructed and John Johnson led Betty Kay to a sofa in the tidy but small living room that was furnished with old, worn, mismatched furniture. Betty Kay sat down, obediently. She was about five foot three inches, and was round. She wore Capri-style pants and, despite it being only October, only a black tank-top, showing off her big, stretch-marked, flabby arms. Betty Kay was cream-colored, with hair that was somewhat kinked like a black person's hair but still draped onto her shoulders like a Caucasian's. I remembered my many conversations with her before removing her ninth child from the home (I removed only the ninth, while other caseworkers over many years removed the other eight). During one of those conversations, she told me she was a mixture of Puerto Rican, Haitian, Irish and Corsican. She commented once that she was an "odd mix." I, being a bastion of political correctness, told her that I too was an "odd mix" of English, German, Irish and Serbian. I remember saying, "I'm a mutt," to which she replied, teasingly, "Woof-woof." Though it was benign at the time, that teasing seems more ominous now.

John Johnson looked out of the peephole in the front door and returned to the room. "Okay, Miss Kay, you know why we are here. That is not a question."

Her voice was strong, loud and powerful, like a woman that has corralled rambunctious children for many years. "I ain't got no more kids for you to take," she said, looking at me.

John Johnson was not amused. "Cut the shit. You know what you did. Tell us. Tell us now."

"I didn't—" but she gave away the truth by looking down. She looked up again, and tried to return to her previous defense. "I swear I don't know why you are here."

John Johnson huffed. I jumped in. "Where is your dog?"

Her eyes opened wide and she inhaled deeply. "Why?"

John Johnson again. "Where?"

She looked down again with that guilty look. "Haven't seen her since yesterday. She ran away."

"Okay," John Johnson said, starting to pace around the small living room. "We don't have much time here before your neighbors start knocking to see why some big black dude— me—dragged you into your own house. So I'll make this brief. We aren't playing twenty fucking questions. I am a cop, but I ain't today. Lucas here is a psychologist for the City, but he ain't today. We both lost brothers today. His real brother and my brother in uniform. Both brothers were killed by dogs. Every dog that sees this man—" John Johnson pointed at me, "—and now, by extension, me too—wants our flesh for supper. So, Miss Kay, your eyes give it all away. We know you have something to do with this. Lie again or be elusive and I'll …" his voice trailed off. "Well, just remember, I am no cop today. Just a man at war with an army of mean fucking dogs. So, Miss Kay?"

"Betty," she said.

"What?" I asked.

"Call me Betty, please. I hate Miss Kay. Makes me sound like a mom and thanks to that fucker," pointing to me of course, "and cocksuckers like him, I ain't no mom anymore."

John Johnson checked the peephole once again, while saying, "Answers!"

Betty cleared her throat. "I didn't know it would work."

This time it was my own voice that was sterner than I intended. "What would work?"

"The curse," Betty said, shock and surprise in her tone. "My grandmom used to teach me this curse you could use against your enemies. I never believed in it. I'm a Catholic. I mean, I don't go to Mass or anything, but I pray to Mother Mary every night and Catholics don't believe in that voodoo shit. My grandma though, she always mixed the voodoo with the Catholic, but I think it's plain old wrong. I was pissed the other night and had some drinks and thought about that motherfucka—"

"Be specific," John Johnson said, cutting her off. "What did you do?"

"Well, my grandma used to say to me that I must got some dog in me since my last name was Kay and I had nine children. You know, Kay-nine."

"Yes," I said, more coolly now that we were getting somewhere. "That is how we figured out it was you. Kay and nine."

"She—my grandma—she always was sayin' that words got power. They got meaning in the voodoo. So when she taught me the curse years ago, you know, she said to make it more powerful and all, use words that have relation to me. So like I be saying, I was drinking and I was missing my kids—especially my baby Ricky, you fucker …" She looked me dead in the eyes. "Yeah, you. You're a cocksucker. Taking my baby boy from me."

I could not help but note the macabre coincidence that I removed her son, Ricky, and as a consequence, my brother, Rick, was dead. Ricky and Rick, two victims of the same story. If God spoke through symbolism, I wondered then, and still wonder now, what God was trying to tell me.

John Johnson peeked out of the peephole again. "Shit, we got a few people mingling out front. They are pointing at the house." He looked into the living room. "Tell us what you did and tell us now."

"Fine. Fine. You wanna know what I did? I grabbed my fucking dog by the scruff and looked into her eyes and cursed you," she said, pointing again at me. "I spoke the curse and added something about the vengeful power of Kay's nine and all things related to Kay-nine be brought down upon your head like hell fucking unleashed. See, I done used *canine* and *unleashed* in the same curse, and both must've added to the power."

"Wait," I said as I began pacing the room as John Johnson kept checking the peep hole. "You said 'canine' and 'unleashed' and you said it to your dog. Now your dog is missing."

"I finished by cursing your scent. Making it all powerful and shit. Enough to drive dogs fucking crazy." She now looked as if she was speaking to herself. "Still can't believe it fucking worked. Holy shit, Grandma was right. That shit worked."

Then she smiled. The smile was all glee and joy that her precious little curse actually worked. Counter to what she intended, or maybe exactly as she intended, that smile caused me to snap. I leapt across the coffee table and threw Betty down flat onto her back on the couch. I had her tank-top scrunched into my fist, while my other hand went around her throat. I felt blood fill my face. "You fucking bitch," I screamed. "You think this is funny. You're smiling, you degenerate whore. My brother is dead. *Dead!* That cop's partner is dead. Because of you, because of what you did." I let out a roar, like an animal enraged and I shook Betty, barely able to contain what felt like murderous rage.

Just as suddenly, my roar stopped and I stopped shaking her. My mind snapped back into the present, into my normal self, and I sat staring at a wide-eyed, ghost-white, frightened face of Betty Kay. She mumbled a phrase, softly, and kept repeating it. It took me a second or two to hear it. It was so low, I had to strain to catch the words. "I didn't think it would work. I didn't think it would work. I didn't think it would work."

I looked into those frightened eyes and heard the remorse and sorrow in her voice. It was that tinge of remorse that made me release my grip and jump off the couch, back to my feet. I looked at John Johnson who was looking back at me. He still stood by the door. He hadn't moved a muscle to restrain me or intervene. He must've just watched, thinking Betty's damn smile warranted such a reaction.

My face was blank as the rage drained away. John Johnson spoke up. "Plenty of neighbors out front now. All right, Betty, I'm going to handcuff you and walk you through this here crowd, my badge waving. You don't say a goddamn word. You ain't under arrest, but we are going to act like you are. Once we get to the car, we are heading to save some women who are caught up in your mess too." Betty still seemed stunned at my previous reaction, and she just nodded her head up and down in agreement. "Good," John Johnson said. "Once we get into the car, we need to know how to end this stupid fucking curse."

I was returning to rational thought. "Do you need to take any supplies to end this thing? Voodoo powder or black arts tools or occult shit or anything?"

Betty looked at me, fright still in her eyes. "I never thought it would work. I was just venting, is all."

My face gave its best reassuring look. "I believe you. We need to end it. Do you need anything to do that?"

"No," she said, "I don't think so. I just used words to create it. Words can't end it, I'm afraid. If what my grandma said is true, words certainly can't end it."

"Well," John Johnson said walking over with handcuffs in his hand. "You can tell us when we are in the car and on our way to rescue the women."

CHAPTER TWENTY-TWO

Getting to the car was not nearly as bad as it could have been if we had not had someone as intimidating, and experienced as John Johnson. With Betty handcuffed, he brought her to the front door inside the house and turned to me. "I was going to tell you to act cop-like," he said, looking up and down at my mismatched black tee-shirt and torn, blood-stained dress khakis, "but you look like a hobo who just had his ass beat by a pack of junior-high cheerleaders. So you just follow close behind and keep your mouth shut."

I didn't protest. John Johnson threw open the front door and with one hand held his badge high in the air. With the other hand, he held on to our prisoner and walked the handcuffed Betty through a pack of about thirty neighbors who had gathered out front. "Poe-lease!" John Johnson bellowed. "Poe-lease, so back the fuck up!" It wasn't his words that created a small seam in the crowd, a seam just large enough to inch our way through. No, instead it was John Johnson's fearlessness. He didn't give the crowd a chance to do anything but part down the middle and give us a path to the sidewalk. With one arm on the obeying Betty, he walked with a stern, brisk pace and the cockiness and certainty in his walk and demeanor naturally caused the crowd to part like a command from Moses himself.

I followed just inches away from them and tried to give my body and face a look of self-assured bravado. I must've looked like a fool trying to be something I am not (or at least wasn't then) because someone from the crowd shouted, *Goose da white fool! Slap that fool!* My heart skipped but John Johnson had heard it too and responded. "Mouth off and all y'all goin' to join her. Poe-lease! Stand back peoples."

The crowd followed us, but did little else. I heard rumbling and some less-than-kind comments, but we reached my car in one piece. Without looking back at me, John Johnson said, "We're taking my ride."

We progressed about twenty yards further down the street to John Johnson's big-ass Lincoln. He put his badge in his pocket, and must've hit his lock-release because the car made that annoying bah-beep-beep sound. Within seconds, Betty was in the backseat, I was in shotgun and we were pulling away from the block.

Once safely traveling, I looked over at John Johnson. "You think my car will survive being parked there all night? Maybe days, even?"

Betty answered instead, leaning forward. "What you mean, 'survive?' What, you think we be a bunch of scavengers down here where you white folk won't walk? Like once nightfall we going to strip any car that don't belong to someone from the block? That what you think?"

John Johnson and I answered in unison. "Yes."

Betty sat back in her seat with a huff. "Racist motherfuckas."

"Betty," I said, turning to look back at her. "You're half-white. John Johnson here is black. We are all one people. We live in a post-racial society."

"Post-racial my ass," John Johnson said.

"Wait," Betty said. "Your name is John Johnson? That is one redundant name. I hope your daddy ain't named John Johnson because that'd make you John Johnson the second." Betty chuckled loudly. "John Johnson the second. Now isn't that what they call—uh—what do they call that again?"

"Department of redundancy department," John Johnson said matter-of-factly. "I've heard all the fucking jokes before."

We all fell silent. I broke it. "We getting my wife first, then getting Lydia?"

"No," John Johnson said. "Lydia is closer. Then your wife. Then a mountain house."

"Mountain-what?" Betty said. "Fuck no I ain't going to no mountains."

"Oh really," I replied, smiling. "What, you don't think you'll be safe overnight in an area that black people won't walk?"

"Very fucking funny, Doctor Dickhead," Betty said, her voice rising. "I got shit to do. I got a job. You know, work, motherfuckers. I can't be going to no mountain house."

It was John Johnson's turn. "If I'm not mistaken, these dogs want to kill anyone who gets into close, direct contact with Lucas here. If they—anyone—gets his smell on them, then the dogs are after them, too."

The implications of this obviously hadn't occurred to Betty because her face slowly sank and faded into a look of dismay and fear. "Oh shit," she said, pounding her fist down into the seat. "Fuck me."

"That's right, Betty," John Johnson continued, "you are covered in the Lucastench and now have as much to lose as the rest of us. Canines, dogs, pooches, mutts, whatever, they are coming for you too, Betty Kay."

She was shaking her head, side to side, probably cursing her own curse. Then she looked forward, a sudden change in her face. "Luca-what?" she asked, actually sounding confused.

I answered. "That is what Rick called it, on account that my name is Lucas and any dog that gets a whiff of my stench wants me dead. We call the hex the Lucastench."

"Oh," Betty said. "That's a pretty clever name."

"Thanks," I said. "My dead brother was a clever guy."

Silence swept through the car as I let those words *dead* and *brother* hang in the air. Betty broke the silence. "I'm sorry about your brother. Like I said, never thought that shit was true. Just did it outta frustration. You took my goddamn youngest boy."

I turned to face her again. "Listen, I took your ninth kid. Others in my position took the other eight, so I had precedent. You worked two jobs but did not have adequate childcare. You left a five-year-old home alone, locked in his bedroom. That is grounds for removal. Lucky I didn't recommend filing charges for child endangerment."

"I left 'im locked in 'is room so I could go to my second fucking job, you cocksucka," she said, more sadness than anger in her voice. "I was trying to put food on the table and clothes on his back."

I turned back around. "Then you should've hired a babysitter."

"You know how much that shit costs!" she yelled. "I made eight dollars an hour. *Eight!* Know how much a sitter costs? Seven dollars an hour. *Seven!* You know how to do math, child-snatcher!"

"Enough," John Johnson said. "We can debate this the whole time we are driving to the mountains, but for now—"

Betty cut John Johnson off, which took guts. "I told you I ain't going to no mountains. You hear me. I ain't."

I was suddenly thrust forward into my seatbelt as John Johnson jerked the wheel while nailing the brake, bringing us to a dead stop on the side of the busy road. "Listen, Miss Kay. You either start talking and tell us how to end this fucking curse or I promise you, you'll be spending the night—at least one—in some shitty cabin in the lovely Pocono mountains." John Johnson paused, waiting for a response. Betty was quiet. So John Johnson added a little spice to the offer. "Many nights in some shitty cabin that is probably crawling with snakes and shit."

That did the trick instantly. "Snakes? Damn, snakes? Okay," Betty said, "drive and I'll talk."

CHAPTER TWENTY-THREE

Lydia lived only a few miles from my own apartment in the Northeast section of the city. The busy, weekday, noontime traffic, made the traveling slow-going from North Philly. John Johnson did not use his dash-mounted, red police light because he didn't want to attract any undue attention. He could keep the police at bay, but only to a certain point. If reports surfaced that he was traveling across large swaths of the City with his light flashing, blowing red lights and such, they'd think he'd really lost his marbles and they'd come. Yes, they'd come even for a sergeant with a legendary standing as a tough-ass, straight playing cop.

So this gave Betty plenty of time to talk. It was difficult to get Betty to focus. I suppose being pulled from your home and being told that a voodoo curse you uttered in drunken frustration had actually worked and taken two lives would cause anyone to lose focus. We eventually pinned her down to a few facts, none that boded well for me, Gwen, or the others dragged into this.

First, Betty could not undo the hex she had placed on me. She could not utter any words or prayers or whatever to undo what was done. Her Haitian grandmother had always warned her that the words—that is how she kept referring to them, *the words*—were powerful, dangerous tools, and once spoken in earnest against someone, they could not be withdrawn. Once uttered, they played themselves out.

"How do they play themselves out? What's the end of the game?" I asked, the desperation loud in my voice.

Betty feigned ignorance. It was a futile attempt. Her eyes told that she knew something, at the very least. It took only one more mention of the snake-infested cabin for Betty to forgo the ignorance and speak what she knew. I was tired of weeding through her hum-hawing, her getting sidetracked on tangents and her lack of focus, but John Johnson and I were able to glean some basic information.

The hex was not so much placed on *me* as placed on the *instrument* for enacting vengeance. When Betty placed the hex, her dog, and by extension all dogs in the greater Philadelphia area, were hexed with a deep-rooted, base desire to kill anything that had my scent. The dogs were cursed with a need—as potent as hunger or sex drive—to destroy whatever carried my scent. The dogs changed, not me.

On what to do next, Betty was very unwilling to spill her knowledge, but after some more coaxing with a description of slithering creatures in a cold cabin, she acquiesced. It seems that since the hex was uttered to one specific animal, the hex would instantly disappear if I destroyed the original dog which received the curse. In this case, Betty's Burmese mountain dog.

I was elated. "Wait, so if we track down your dog—wait, what is its name?"

"She's not an *it*. She's a female, you gender-biased asshole." Betty was nothing if not direct. "Her name is Licker."

"Okay," I said, mind racing, thinking fast. "So if we kill Licker, then the Lucastench goes away. The hex is broken."

"You ain't hurting my Licker. Haven't you taken enough from me?"

John Johnson "What kind of name is Licker? Is it Licker, like a tongue, or Liquor, like booze?"

Betty looked out the window. "I went to the shelter to pick her up. Someone abandoned her there and I was next on the waiting list for a big dog. So when I brought her home, I didn't know what to name her. After she sniffed the place, she spent the first hour licking my son Ricky's face. Yeah, the son you stole from me, you bastard. Anyway, so we named her Licker."

John Johnson cut in. "You sure it doesn't have something to do with drinking liquor, considering you put this deadly curse on him when you were drinking. You like hitting the bottle, don't you."

Betty was surprisingly calm. "Yeah, well, that was a bonus in the name."

I was almost giddy with anticipation. "Okay, I'm seeing light at the end of this sick fucking tunnel. We kill Licker, this ends. Period.

"Please don't kill Licker," Betty pleaded. "She didn't ask for the hex."

"Bitch," John Johnson said, looking into the rearview mirror. "You have the guts to ask us to spare that damn dog after this hex that you placed has cost two lives already. Two human lives. I oughta pull this car over and teach you a fucking lesson."

Betty's eyes locked onto his in the rearview, but she didn't utter a word. I couldn't tell if it was sadness or regret I saw in her eyes, but it was anything but pleasure.

I ended the stalemate, mostly because I wanted John Johnson's eyes off of the rearview and back on the road in front of us. "Okay, enough. I agree with you, Sergeant. Betty messed up. If she can help us end it, then I think we can call it even."

"It ain't even close to even," he shot back.

"I know," I said, consolingly. "It is the best we are going to get so we have to accept it. So let's accept it. Okay? For now." John Johnson said nothing, so I continued. "So Betty, how do we find this Licker?"

Betty was quick. "You don't have to find her. She'll find you. I'm surprised you haven't heard from her already."

"I don't understand."

"Man, I placed the hex on Licker to find *you*. According to my grandma, who has been correct so far, Licker is obsessed with finding you. Obsessed. All her other thoughts or desires or instincts or whatever-the-fuck, are dead. She only got one desire, one need, and that is finding your dumb ass and chewin' it up."

I turned around and looked at her. "So what does that mean

exactly?"

Betty leaned her face very close to mine and she spoke slowly, enunciating every word. "It means she's hunting you. It means she is tracking you. That's why she ran away from home. She's hunting. If you haven't met her already, all you gotta do is wait and she'll come to you, ready to fulfill the desire that's driving her mad."

I just looked at Betty. Her words were frighteningly poignant. I was transfixed on the idea that I was being hunted by a huge, angry and determined Burmese Mountain Dog.

John Johnson said, "You said she is hunting Lucas. Could she have found Lucas's house?"

I instantly knew what John Johnson was thinking. The dog from last night that had scratched apart the front door to my apartment was Licker. The dog whose lip I had caught on the hanger and torn apart was Licker. Then the worst hit me. Licker knew where I lived and Gwen was there.

I looked to John Johnson. "We need to get to my apartment. Now."

John Johnson slammed on the brakes, sending me again into my seatbelt. He threw the car into reverse and cut the wheel. He was parallel parking like a professional stunt-driver.

"Sergeant, we need to get to my apartment."

"Look around, Lucas. We are at Lydia's." I did look around and there was Lydia's building, twenty-five yards on the right. He continued, "Might as well grab Lydia now and then get your wife."

"Who the fuck is Lydia?" Betty asked.

CHAPTER TWENTY-FOUR

Much to her protest, we left Betty locked in the backseat of John Johnson's car while the two of us walked toward Lydia's building. I had my cell phone out and was calling Lydia when we both spotted it at the same time.

A medium sized dog, thirty pounds or so, with long black, silky hair, groomed to fanciful beauty. The damn dog was attached to a leash in the hand of a twenty-something woman. She was dressed in tight, expensive jeans and an even tighter shirt that showed just a hint of her flat stomach. Her knee-high boots were expensive and with her perfectly done makeup and hair, she was all sex appeal. As soon as we spotted the dog, it spotted us and started barking its little ass off, showing its teeth and pulling on its leash, stretching its body out toward us. The woman holding the leash was taken off guard, and the pull of the dog on the leash made her stumble a step or two. The dog was not big enough to be more than a nuisance to her. She had a Bluetooth headset in her ear and was chatting away. When the dog pulled again, she shouted at it. "Peanut, stop! Stop Peanut!"

We were within a few feet of the dog and its owner, who didn't seem too concerned that her little dog on the end of its leash was going ballistic. She continued to look absently around as she talked on her blue-tooth. Quickly approaching the dog, John Johnson spoke without looking at me. "We don't have time for Peanut."

Almost as soon as the words were out of his mouth, a handgun was in his palm and he pointed and fired one round, splattering pieces of Peanut all over the woman's expensive, knee-high boots.

I was just as shocked as the woman and surprisingly, neither of us made a sound. I didn't even miss a step and dutifully continued in stride next to John Johnson. The woman's jaw dropped open as we strode past and her eyes were frozen down at the gory mess at her feet.

We were just a foot or two past her when I heard her mutter, "My boots. My boots."

In my shock, I had forgotten that I had the cell-phone to my ear. I was thrown back into reality by Lydia's voice on the other end, saying, "Lucas. Lucas! Christ was that a gunshot?"

"Uh, Lydia, yeah, we are here," I muttered.

John Johnson pulled open the door to the lobby. "Tell her to leave her apartment now and take the back stairs down to the lobby. We will be waiting for her. No elevator. If it stops at a floor and someone brings a dog into a small elevator, she's toast."

"Lydia, did you hear him? Okay, good, do as he says."

John Johnson added, "Tell her to hurry."

Hurry she did. I don't know if it was the gunshot she heard over the other end of the phone, or if it was just the damn nuttiness of this day-unlike-all-others, but she was in the lobby in moments, looking a frazzled, hurried version of her normally lovely self. She had changed into jeans and sneakers, attire I did not often see her wear. She looked good and I felt a twinge of guilt even thinking that, considering Gwen was still trapped at home. Contrarily, I knew I *didn't* look good, which was confirmed by Lydia's reaction to me. "Christ Almighty Lucas, what happened to you? Are you—jeez, are you okay?"

"No time," John Johnson said, and he turned and rushed to the lobby door, opening it for us to follow.

I limped as fast I could to the door, Lydia behind me. "I'll explain more in the car. Just hurry."

When we reached Peanut, he still lay splattered on sidewalk. When the woman saw us, she took in a deep breath and became rigid, frozen. As we shuffled past, I looked at her and put on my best apologetic face. "Sorry," I uttered. Lydia too smiled at her, grimaced at the mess that had been Peanut, and meekly said, "Sorry."

When we were at least twenty feet past, John Johnson seemed to have a last-moment thought. He turned around and shouted to her, "Sorry too."

Lydia didn't say a thing until we reached the car and John Johnson unlocked the doors with the requisite "bah beep-beep" sound.

I opened the car door for Lydia to get in next to Betty and Lydia asked, "Who the hell is that?"

"I'm Betty, bitch. Who the hell are you?"

"She," I said to Lydia but pointing to Betty, "is the cause and answer to our problem."

John Johnson was behind the wheel and had the car fired-up in no time. Lydia got in next to Betty and I hopped into shotgun. "To Gwen. As fast as you can."

John Johnson looked at me and flipped on his dashboard red light. "Oh yeah," was all he said, and we were off. As we sped past the woman with Peanut on her shoes, she looked even more stunned as the red police light flashed. Betty waved at her through the window and mouthed the word, "Sorry."

I imagine all Peanut's owner would be able to tell police was that a big black guy in a trench coat, a bloody, tattered white guy, an attractive middle-aged white woman, and a fat cream-colored woman had all apologized for killing her dog. The police would probably think she was in shock.

John Johnson liked to do everything fast, and driving was no exception. He weaved and maneuvered around traffic as if he were in a Hollywood car chase. The red light just seemed to add to his focus, his determination, his agility. His driving through the streets of Philadelphia reminded me of a mouse escaping a predator, darting around, finding any tiny crevice to avoid any impediment to our movement. John Johnson didn't need to stop for anything. Blowing red lights, cutting-and-weaving between cars, hardly pausing at stop signs, I closed my eyes and said a tiny Hail Mary.

"You keep driving like this and we going to end up looking like dat poor dog you just shot," Betty said.

"You shot that dog?" Lydia said, astonished.

"It was a preemptive strike," John Johnson said, eyes never

leaving the road, speed not decreased even one MPH.

"A what?" Lydia said.

"You know, like Bush with Iraq," John Johnson replied. "That dog was going to cause us big problems if it got off that leash, so I preempted."

"Ever since that fucking war," Betty said, "people feel they can do anything in their lives and say it was preemptive. That is what that cracker president gave this country—an excuse to do shit to people who haven't done shit yet, and to feel okay about it because it was preemptive. A load of shit."

I peeled my eyes from the road and looked into the back seat. "Lydia, meet Betty Kay, our eminent political scientist and sociologist."

Lydia shot me a confused look, so I explained. "This is the woman who caused the hex."

Lydia looked over at Betty. They were two women who couldn't look more different. Lydia was a tall, skinny, white, demure, quietly manipulative, emotionally fucked-up city lawyer. Next to her was Betty, the short, creamy-colored, chunky, shabbily dressed, outspoken, voodoo-Catholic. They looked like Abbot and Costello. While Lydia took in Betty's imposing figure, Betty said, "Hey, nice to meet you. I didn't know the hex would actually work."

"Hey," Lydia said. "You're a sociologist? Really?"

"Well, I'm social if that's what you mean."

"Hang tight," John Johnson said as he took a sharp bend in the road a bit too fast, sending us all flying to the left side of the car. If I didn't have my seatbelt on, I'd have been on top of John Johnson. Lydia did not have her seatbelt on and flew into Betty and was wrapped around her as the car leaned into the bend. When the car evened out, Lydia was practically bear-hugging Betty. Lydia looked into Betty's eyes and said, "Sorry."

"Ain't nothing," Betty said. "I think you can get off now."

"Sorry," Lydia said, pushing herself off Betty.

After John Johnson told Lydia to put on her "goddamn seatbelt before you end up inside Betty," Lydia complied and asked what the hell was happening. I gave her the Cliff Notes version as we were within minutes of my, and Gwen's, home.

"Yeah, but you left out something," Betty said.

"No he didn't," John Johnson defended. "He covered it all."

"Nah, man. He left out the other way of getting rid of the hex."

I looked at John Johnson who shot me a quick look back, before returning his eyes to the road. "I'm not going to like this," I said.

"Probably not," Betty said, loudly, "because the other way the hex ends is when your ass is dead. The very second you're dead, this all ends. The dogs become just regular ass-sniffers again. It's supposed to happen instantly."

The implications of what Betty said immediately registered in my mind, so I said nothing in reply.

I could kill myself, and in so doing end this whole mess and protect John Johnson, Lydia, Betty, and especially Gwen. Ending one life could save four. It had already cost two lives, could I let it cost four more? By taking my own life I would offer a noble, chivalrous way to save the lives of my wife and the others. Would I have the courage to do it if the time came? If we were squeezed, surrounded, and only doom was waiting for us all, would I have the strength, the sheer will, to end my own life … end my life to give life?

John Johnson peeled his eyes from the road for another second and looked at me. It was like he was reading my mind because he said, "Don't even think it, Lucas. It won't come to that."

I hoped he was right.

CHAPTER TWENTY-FIVE

Parking on my crowded, narrow block was always a bitch. John Johnson didn't seem to notice. He zipped his big-ass car right up to my apartment and threw that big-ass car into park, double parking on the tiny street.

I reached for the handle to open my car door and I caught a glimpse of John Johnson's face. His deep-brown complexion had instantly turned ashen as his eyes looked past me toward my ground-floor apartment. His jaw dropped open a little. Before I could turn to look at what he had seen, I heard Lydia, "Oh no."

My head zipped around and pinned on the apartment door. Other than the wood damage from the night before, the door was shut and looked secure, and the porch looked like it always did. My eyes just didn't see anything, so I looked back to John Johnson, who was still ashen. He looked at me and said, "Give me your keys."

I simply handed them over in a daze, unsure of what his demeanor, or Lydia's exclamation of shock, referenced. As soon as the keys hit John Johnson's hand, he had the car door open and was barreling toward my apartment. I turned and looked again, and then I saw it.

On the right side of the front porch (which was really just a slab of cement ten-feet by ten-feet) was a window. That window, my eyes saw in horror, was lifted open, exposing the screen. The screen was torn into tatters.

My mind raced as John Johnson raced to the front door, pounding on it with his fist a few times, then trying each of the three keys on the key ring.

Lydia was out of the car too, and Betty moved her considerable girth across the car's bench seats to get herself out, too.

I sat frozen, thinking, *she opened the window*. To let in some air, *she opened the window*. Since Gwen's pregnancy, she was always getting warm. *She opened the window*. Gwen's body was always overheating since it was carrying the extra weight of our unborn child. *She opened the window*. It was a cool October day and Gwen was warm. *She opened the window*. She probably did it without thinking. *She opened the window*. A cool breeze swept inside and Gwen felt better, felt the heat of her body dissipate. *She opened the window*. A stray dog caught a whiff of Gwen's scent through the open window. *She opened the window*. No, a stray dog caught the whiff of my scent... my scent... my scent...

While my mind raced my body remained seated, motionless in panicked thought. I saw John Johnson find the right key to open the door and enter the apartment, followed by Lydia and Betty. I heard a yelp that was almost a scream. Still, my body could not move. It was as if my body understood what my mind was unwilling to comprehend—Gwen opened the window and a dog had gotten inside.

My body seemed to thaw a bit so I reached for the car handle as John Johnson emerged from my apartment. He looked at me from the patio, his eyes locking on mine. He shook his head from side to side, very slowly, as if saying "no." What he was really saying was said in his eyes. He was saying, *I'm sorry*. His eyes were saying, *I am so damn sorry*. As I looked into those eyes, I saw them well with watery tears for the briefest of seconds, and then the tears receded to wherever they originated. Then John Johnson squatted down and put his head into his hand, still shaking his head side to side.

Lydia and Betty were on the porch a second later, and Lydia ran to the edge of the concrete slab and puked. After a large burst of vomit, strings of bile remained dangling from her lips. Betty was behind her now, whispering comforting words and rubbing her back.

On auto-pilot, I opened the car door and got out. One foot

moved in front of the other and dream-like, not actually feeling my feet, I walked toward my apartment. John Johnson saw me coming. He stood from his squatting position and still shaking his head, he articulated what the side-to-side motion was indicating. "No. You hear me, Lucas. No. Do not go in there."

I heard his voice, but it sounded as if it was being spoken through a thick filter of cotton. His voice, usually so firm and demanding, was muffled and soft on the edges, with each word stepping on the end of the previous word.

"Lucas, do not go in there," his odd voice said, standing before me to block my entrance. "Trust me, Lucas, don't."

Under normal conditions, the thought of pulling a gun on someone as intimidating and menacing as John Johnson would never have entered my mind. At that moment, I don't think I was in my mind. I existed somewhere *other*—that *other* place our minds go at moments of life's extremes. I felt this once before immediately following a car accident and have heard that people go to the *other* as the doctor tells them their cancer is untreatable. I was in the *other*, the place where the mind works but is not on this earth.

So when John Johnson was blocking my path and telling me I didn't want to go into my apartment—my home where my wife lived with my unborn baby—I reached into the small of my back and pulled out the .38 snub nose revolver and pointed it square into the center of John Johnson's face. He shook his head again, and those tears welled again in his eyes, and he stepped aside. As I walked past, he patted me on the back and I heard him say in a fog, "God be with you."

I paused for a second before crossing the threshold from the patio into the apartment. I felt time stop, if just for a moment. I felt the eyes of John Johnson and Lydia and Betty on my back. I felt the cool October air that Gwen wanted to feel on her overheated body. However, even though John Johnson prayed it, I could not feel God with me.

I crossed into the apartment, my senses absorbing everything in slow, deep motion. I smelled and tasted the metallic odor of blood. My eyes first caught sight of the living room wall.

Droplets of blood splattered across it in an arc. I followed the arc, oddly in the shape of a rainbow, down to the carpet. There, no droplets of blood. Instead, a swimming pool of it. In the center of the pool, on her back, lay Gwen. Her head lay toward me, her feet toward the back of the apartment. I focused on her open eyes. They had rolled back in her sockets as if she was looking behind her, and as such, were looking directly at me. Those eyes communicated a lifetime of loves, hopes, dreams and other things that would take more books than the world can hold to tell properly. Those eyes will never leave me.

Conflicting emotions swelled in me. Sadness. *My dear, dear Gwen.* Pain. *My unborn baby, never given a chance.* Anger. *Gwen, why would you open the fucking window!*

I wanted to run to Gwen and wanted to run away from her. I wanted to hold her and I wanted never to see her again. I wanted to cry and scream. I wanted to collapse and run.

Then I was startled. A sound filled the room. The sound was not a sound you would expect to hear in this situation, in this setting. Standing there in the entrance way to my apartment, looking into the dead, lost eyes of my wife, wind coming in from the *fucking open window*, I heard a repulsive sound.

Chewing.

I scanned the room, trying to avoid looking at Gwen's body. I saw nothing. I looked again, hoping to discover the genesis of the noise. Nothing. The sound continued, the mushy, mouth slobbering sound of someone—something—sloppily gnawing and licking and swallowing.

Squaring my feet, steadying myself, I took in the full view of Gwen. Flat on her back, she was surrounded by a large circle of blood. Her throat was torn open on her left side, exactly where the jugular now lay still, not pumping anymore. The tear left bits of skin and flesh sticking out in spiky, odd angles. There was too much blood, now coagulating, to see into her neck, instead showing only a dark, thickened maroon wall of that most precious bodily fluid.

Lying flat on her back, Gwen's eight-month-pregnant

stomach protruded into the air like a mountain on a prairie. I used to tease her about it, her mountain-stomach. Once she'd lain down on the couch to take a nap and I quoted the Bible, "Faith to move mountains." She looked over at me with a smirk. "You keep calling me a mountain," she'd said, "and you'll need more than faith to protect you." I smiled at her quick comeback, and got her a blanket for her nap.

As I looked at her now, flat on the hardwood floor, her stomach did appear as a mountain, or rather, a volcano. Her maternity shirt had been torn open and the top of her stomach was torn open too, flesh and skin opened like a flower that had bloomed. *Her stomach looks like a volcano.* Blood and flesh lay down the sides of her stomach. *Her stomach looks like a volcano that had erupted.*

Chewing. I heard the sound again. I took a step and the hardwood floors creaked a tiny bit.

That tiny creak must have caught the attention of the chewer because the sound instantly stopped. I froze with the silence, unsure, too afraid to guess what was happening.

I didn't have to wait long. From inside the volcano, out popped the tiny, blood covered head of a little, petite dog. Its eyes looked at me, those buggy eyes that look like they might pop from its tiny head. Those eyes were unmistakable. They belonged to a Chihuahua. From the diminutive size of this particular Chihuahua, it was either a young puppy or a teacup Chihuahua.

Its eyes looked at me and it raised its nose, sniffing the air. It caught a whiff of me, the originator of the Lucastench, and it raised its upper lip in a snarl and began to growl at me. In its teeth was flesh. The flesh of my unborn child it was feasting on.

I felt the presence of John Johnson, Lydia, and Betty behind me. I heard a gasp and someone trying to choke back a heaving stomach.

With only its little head sticking out of my wife's belly, the fucking dog started to squirm and claw, trying to get itself out of my wife. Despite enjoying the feast of my family's flesh, it was dominated by one more powerful impulse, an impulse it could not reason with or fight—the need to kill me.

It was having difficulty getting out of my wife's belly. I heard the sloshing of its legs as it tried to get a firm grip to rip itself free of the body. It could not get a firm hold. It continued barking and snarling, eyes fixed on me.

I felt the weight of the gun in my hand and I dropped it, purposefully. It thudded to the floor. In two long strides I was across the room, and dropped down to my knees before my wife's stomach. The dog was a whirlwind of frenzied barking and clawing, still unable to get footing to get out of my wife. The instant my knees hit the floor, my hands reached for the dog's throat. When my hands shot through the air, the dog's teeth took a nick from my right hand.

My hands remained undeterred and didn't flinch as I wrapped them around its throat. I squeezed with a strength and power I didn't know I possessed. As my hands applied a superhuman pressure I threw back my head and wailed a scream so loud and agonized and animalistic that I suspect even the devil covered his ears in hell. I squeezed and squeezed and screamed until I felt a spray of moisture hit my neck and arms.

I had squeezed so hard, the Chihuahua's beady, buggy eyes had burst.

With the mist of the eye-matter and goop hitting me, I unclenched my fist and dropped the dog. I didn't see where it landed.

I sat there kneeling before the corpse of my wife, my half-eaten unborn child and a tiny little dog who would never get the chance to digest my family. I wept. I wept with the weeping of madness.

From that moment on, the madness has never left me.

My mind was fading to darkness when I heard Betty say, "Damn, I'm never ever eating Taco Bell again." I wanted to chuckle, but the blackness was taking over.

CHAPTER TWENTY-SIX

How I got from my apartment to my car was a blur. I remember little and what I do remember is like trying to recall your earliest memories of childhood. You have flashes and images of what occurred, but you cannot be certain if they are real memories or imagined.

I recall John Johnson was behind me and guiding me to my feet. He then led me toward the door but my eyes were pinned to my feet, looking at my sneakers covered in thick, deep-red blood. I was shuffling my feet like a psychotic patient on too many meds when I walked past Betty.

I looked up at her and she seemed suddenly scared, at least my memory recalls it that way. Betty was probably scared that I'd be angry at her for the off-color Taco Bell comment. As I looked at her I felt conflicting emotions. For bringing this hex into my life, I wanted to choke her like I did that Chihuahua. I knew then I could kill Betty Kay. I was capable of it and had some deep-rooted desire to remove the life from her eyes. Yet, what she said was funny, too. I had seen the Taco Bell commercials with the little Chihuahua dog promoting the products and it was damn funny. I appreciated a good joke and I especially appreciated a good joke with great timing.

So between two opposing desires—to murder and laugh—I laughed. I stood there, now covered in a thick coating of blood on my hands, arms, pants and shoes, looking at the woman who hexed me who stood beside the woman I was dangerously close to cheating on my now-dead wife with, and I laughed. Not just a chuckle or smirk, but a full-bellied, out-loud laughter.

John Johnson must've thought I had just lost my last tenuous hold on sanity, but I heard him say, again through a cloudy fog, "Lydia, take Betty and get in the car and lock the doors. We'll be out soon."

The rest is quite a blur. I have memories—images really—of me at the kitchen sink and John Johnson washing my hands for me with soap and warm water as he massaged the blood off of my hands ... John Johnson with a warm, wet rag, wiping my face... In the bedroom, John Johnson rifling through my closet and bureau, throwing clothes onto the bed... Me sitting on the bed, fresh clothes on, John Johnson putting socks on my feet, followed by a different pair of sneakers, these not covered with blood... John Johnson's hand over my eyes, shielding me from the sight of my wife as I was walked through the living room... Me sitting in the car... The car moving... all a big, cloudy blur.

I didn't drift back to reality, but rather was thrown back into reality. A tractor trailer drifted into my field of vision, but it drifted too close, too suddenly and the part of my brain that still insisted on survival was awake and alert and slapped the remaining portion of my mind into action. I was instantly in the present just as John Johnson muttered an expletive, the women let out a unified squeal of fright and the tractor trailer that was just inches from my window jumped back into the other lane. "What the fuck!" I yelled.

My sudden ability to speak must've shocked the car's occupants as much as the tractor trailer did because Lydia let out another little squeal, this time with a twinge of happy surprise. John Johnson looked over at me. "Welcome back, Lucas," he said, a broad smile forming on his face.

"You almost killed us," I uttered with a shaky voice.

"No my brother, that was the tractor trailer's fault," John Johnson said as placidly as if he was ordering a hamburger at a drive-thru. "Dumbass trying to get into my lane like fucking Dukes of Hazard. Man, if we didn't have more pressing issues, I'd pull his ass over and give him one goddamn big ticket. Some people just shouldn't be driving."

I looked down at myself and saw I was in jeans and sneakers, a sweater with a tee-shirt underneath, and a black pea-coat jacket. My hands were clean, though bits of dried blood still remained in the cuticles. I touched my clothes as if they were completely alien to me, though I recognized each item since they were from my own closet and bureau. "Yup, brother," John Johnson said, "I had to throw some new clothes on you. You were a bloody fucking mess."

"You, ah ..." my voice trailed a bit as I searched for the least humiliating word, "... you *changed* me."

"Well," John Johnson replied, passing a slower car, "I didn't change you like a baby. The boxers you had on this morning are the boxers you are wearing now, though I threw a few clean ones in the bag I packed for you."

"Bag?" I muttered.

"I did change your clothes for you," John Johnson said, ignoring my bag question. "I can say with absolute certainty that I never stripped a man down to his skivvies before. I never dressed a nearly naked man before. That's a first and a last time for me, my brother. You were in a daze, like you had yourself a lobotomy or something. Glad you're back, brother. Oh, and if you are wondering why I'm calling you brother it is because I decided that we've been through enough shit together in the last day that we are no longer just acquaintances but brothers, in every way but blood."

"I'm glad to hear that," I said, peering into the back seat. Both Lydia and Betty smiled at me, looking much the same as I remembered them, with the same look of fear and dread in their eyes. I faced forward again and looked at the road. We were on a four-lane road that wasn't the turnpike, but looked like an arterial road into the country from the City. I didn't know exactly where we were, but the road felt familiar.

My eyes were heavy with exhaustion and it was only accentuated by the comforting warmth of the pea-coat and the smell of my clean, fresh clothes. I suddenly understood exactly what John Johnson had done for me, and I was grateful. I looked over at him. "Thank you, Sergeant. Thank you for taking care of me like that."

John Johnson did not return the look but kept his eyes straight ahead as he spoke. "Don't need to call me Sergeant anymore. Either call me brother, or call me what my friends call me. They call me John Johnson."

I knew that for a man as tough and smart and worldly as John Johnson, that was the most tender thing he could ever say. I accepted it as such, and not wanting to embarrass him more, I just remained silent.

Betty broke the silence. "Your friends call you by your full name? John Johnson? That's weird."

John Johnson looked into the rearview and said to Betty, "You can call me Sergeant." His eyes then moved over in the mirror to Lydia. "You too Lydia, but only because I hardly know *you*."

If Betty registered the insult, she didn't respond to it. I had questions. "Where are we? Heading to the mountains, I suspect. How far up the turnpike are we?"

Lydia spoke up for the first time. "He's been trying to explain it and I guess I understand the logic, but it just doesn't seem right. Something tells me it doesn't seem right."

"Yeah," Betty agreed, "and you promised me if I helped, I wouldn't have to go to no snake-infested mountains. John Johnson here—yeah, that's right Sergeant, I called you John Johnson—he says we are all going anyway. Like he be my master or something."

John Johnson let out a long breath of air in exhaustion. "I've been over this with them while you were in your funk."

"Was I sleeping?" I asked.

"No," Lydia answered for him. "Your eyes were open. Then again, you were so out of it, it might have been tantamount to sleep. You looked strange, to be truthful."

"Anyway," John Johnson said returning to the issue at hand. "Where we are is half the fucking distance to nowhere. Why we are going there seems straight-fucking-forward to me, but these women don't seem to agree."

"I just think," Lydia said, timidly, "that we ought to go to the police or something. Hole up somewhere and let them track down and kill Betty's dog, Licker. Then we are okay."

John Johnson said, "I told Lydia, as nicely as she makes her case, that her plan is fucking—" John Johnson stopped himself and backtracked. "Well, her plan is full of problems."

"The sergeant here doesn't think the police will believe us," Lydia answered. "He doesn't believe they will offer us any protection or hunt down Licker. He says they will think we are nuts and tell us to call the SPCA."

Though I knew the power of Lydia's instincts and ability to manipulate, I had to agree with John Johnson on this one. "Well, I think John Johnson is correct. I think we are nuts and I've lived through this shit. Imagine trying to tell the police about this. They'd just laugh at us. He's a cop so he'd know."

"That's what she keeps saying," John Johnson said. "She keeps saying that because I'm a cop and know people that they will listen. I told her that even I couldn't sell them on this fucking craziness. They'd probably ask for my badge and gun and order a psych eval."

"All the evidence of these damn dogs being after us should be enough," Lydia pleaded. "Like Lucas getting bitten yesterday, his call last night about a dog trying to break in, the dead dogs behind the supermarket, the dog you shot outside my apartment, the dead dog at your apart …" and Lydia's voice fell silent.

I put my head down and felt my eyes warm with impending tears, which I fought back and pushed away into the deepest part of my mind where I hoped they could be caged by my defenses until this whole mess was over. Then I had a momentary flash of Gwen standing in the kitchen on a warm spring day last year, before she was pregnant, the sun shining in through the kitchen window onto her chestnut hair. Beautiful Gwen, young, vibrant, intelligent, with the whole world ready to blossom before her. Her smile like sunrise, wearing her favorite pair of yoga pants whose sheer tightness exposed her sexy, long legs. How I walked over to her and kissed her, slipping my hands down the front of her stomach over her pants and massaged between her legs, lightly, gingerly. How she gasped in the small pleasure of both my hand and in anticipation of our lovemaking. How she looked at me and smiled, then kissed my neck, putting her hand over my jeans, feeling my swollen cock waiting for her, wanting her.

I shook my head and demanded that my mind stop

replaying such memories. This was not the time, I told myself. Later maybe, but not now. I had to focus.

"No," I said aloud, both to my mind that wanted to raise memories of Gwen and weep about them, and to Lydia's argument. "That evidence would only show that we are a group of people who are killing dogs. As soon as we told them that this ever-increasing pile of dead dogs was done by us, we'd probably all be arrested, or at least held."

"Besides," John Johnson added, "and I hadn't thought of this till now. If we go to the police station and there is a K9 unit, or multiple K9 units in the building, well, we'd be toast. Only I could bring a gun into a police station. You'd have to disarm. You'd have no weapons to fight back against highly trained, agile, strong police dogs. Shit, we'd be done. We might as well give up at that point."

"I hate those fucking police dogs," Betty added. "Mean sons-of-bitches."

I turned rather suddenly. "Betty, you are the reason we are in the mess. So we can do without the commentary." I sat facing forward again in a huff.

"Hey," she replied, leaning forward, completely not intimidated. "I got the stench on me, too. So I'm in this just as much as you. I didn't think the goddamn hex was real."

"Enough," Lydia jumped in. "She didn't believe in the hex, but just did it to release some frustration. I don't blame her. I wouldn't have believed it and might have uttered it myself if I was her. I mean, when I was a kid, I did the Bloody Mary thing."

"Bloody what?" Betty asked.

"It's a legend. You say Bloody Mary three times while looking in the mirror and she'll appear. She might even hurt you. Scary stuff when you're a kid."

"I don't get it? Why would she appear?" Betty asked.

"Probably bullshit, but a few centuries ago a woman named Mary Worth claimed her child was stolen, never to be seen again. People didn't believe her and she was always under suspicion. In her grief at losing her kid, she committed suicide, but before dying placed a curse on the world based on her name. Something like that."

"Oh," Betty said, and I felt her eyes digging into my back. "So this woman had a child taken from her and was so fucked-up over it that she killed herself. I can imagine that. I've felt that pain."

Betty's sincerity was evident in her voice and as such, I couldn't muster the courage to comment or respond. I felt justified in removing her ninth child, but I couldn't face the pain that I'm sure was weighted in her eyes just then. So I kept looking at the road.

"That wasn't my point," Lydia said. "When I was a kid, I knew of a supposed curse and I tried it, probably out of boredom. Fortunately nothing happened but I see what Betty did with this hex as nothing different than kids saying Bloody Mary in front of a mirror."

I couldn't help but agree. I too had tried some of those urban-legend games when I was a kid. Like Betty with the hex, while trying them allowed me some satisfaction by proving to myself and my friends that I wasn't scared, that deep down inside I knew those games would never actually work. Then again, Betty's did work.

I turned again to face her. "Okay. Okay, I agree. I tried that shit too when I was a teenager. I guess what Betty did was no different. I won't mention again that this is your fault. You didn't know, Betty. You were just like a teenager before a mirror."

"Agreed," John Johnson said. "Besides we need to be focusing on the plan."

"Can we clarify the plan?" I asked. "I know we are heading to the mountains because few people means few dogs. Where in the mountains?"

"Well," John Johnson said, "not the mountains anymore. The woods, yes. See, a buddy of mine once let me borrow this bare-bones cabin he has. It's way out in the fucking woods but not too far from the City. In northern Bucks County. The undeveloped part. Nothing around the cabin for miles. No people anyway. Since my buddy is in the midst of getting chemotherapy, I don't think he's there. Considering the circumstances, I say we just break in and make a defensive camp at that mother-fucker."

"How does that help us end this?" I asked. "We can't stay there forever."

"Oh, well, we've been handling that shit," John Johnson said. "Lydia, show him." From the back seat, down by her feet, Lydia lifted up a garbage bag that was bulbous with content.

"I don't get it," I said.

"Man, we are leaving a scent," Betty said. I just looked at each of them, confused.

Lydia clarified. "This is a bag of your dirty clothes, taken from the hamper in your room before we left. The sergeant's idea. Every few miles, we throw an article of clothing out of the window. We figure Licker is looking for your scent and will continue to check your apartment."

I finally understood but wasn't sure I was convinced. "So," I said, "from my apartment, through the City and along this highway, you are scenting the path, leading Licker to us. When she attacks at the cabin, we kill her and end the hex." Lydia and John Johnson and Betty nodded in agreement. "Okay," I continued, still skeptical. "So even if the dog follows the trail of breadcrumbs we are leaving, it'll take her weeks to travel this distance. What are we going to do for weeks?"

"Actually," John Johnson said, "the cabin is only about thirty-five miles from this godforsaken City. If Licker is the crazy, enraged dog that we suspect and she is determined and doesn't stop much for breaks, she could travel that in a day or two. So we only gotta make do with the cabin for a day or two."

I was still unconvinced. "There are many 'ifs' in this plan. Too many."

Lydia seemed to be getting more convinced of the plan. "I think this Licker is so consumed by the hex that in order to kill you it would travel a thousand miles if it needed to. You always hear these stories on the news about dogs traveling hundreds of miles on their own and walking up to their owners' front doors like nothing ever happened. No one understands exactly how they do it, but they do. They find where they want to go."

John Johnson added, "We are leaving one hell of a nice trail for her. Which reminds me, Lydia, toss out another piece of clothing. Something really scented this time. Like dirty underwear or some shit like that."

"Allow me," I said, reaching into the back seat and grabbing the bag. "I think I'll be handling my own dirty clothes from now on."

Lydia chuckled. "I especially liked your bikini briefs with the Superman logo."

"What!" John Johnson said laughingly. "Shit, that's funny."

"I don't … what? You made that up," I replied, face flushed in embarrassment.

"Yes, I made it up," Lydia said smiling.

"I think Superman bikini briefs would be sexy," Betty said, big smile on her face. "Wanna sit back here with me, Lucas?"

I smiled back. I looked at John Johnson, who was also smiling. Lydia was beaming too. It occurred to me that in all of this madness, murder, death, hexes, and being hunted by Licker, we still had the ability to smile and laugh. It was a remarkable thing when human beings laugh despite the circumstances, as if when the brain has taken as much shock and strain as it can take it just laughs because it doesn't know what else to do.

So here we were, four people from different walks of life, hardly knowing one another, having witnessed unspeakable horrors, barreling together toward a future filled with crazy uncertainty, and ready to make a stand to defend our lives, together, as a team. I could never have dreamed such a thing was possible and my mind said a tiny prayer of thanksgiving for not having to do this alone.

Lydia broke the laughter and my silent prayer. "Is there running water at the cabin?" she asked. "I didn't pack anything."

"I ain't shitting in no outhouse. No fucking way," Betty added.

John Johnson was calm. "Yes, there is well-water that is pumped into the cabin. It isn't the dark ages. There is an indoor shitter and a shower, a small kitchenette, a few bunk beds, without mattresses though. It is rustic but livable."

"I should've packed a bag," Lydia said remorsefully.

"We pass a Walmart soon. After that, there is nothing. So we'll stop there and you ladies can buy what you need. I packed a bag for Lucas and I always have a bag in my trunk."

"I ain't got no money to buy nothing," Betty said, a bit of embarrassment in her voice. "It's all right though. I'll survive. Always have."

As if the gesture was my way of telling Betty that I had forgiven her for the hex and that she was now part of the team, I turned and looked at her. "I'll buy you what you need. Don't worry, okay? We are in this together."

Betty smiled and nodded her head in thanks.

PART THREE

PUNCH THROUGH THE FACE TIL' YOU HIT THE BACK OF THE SKULL

CHAPTER TWENTY-SEVEN

We decided to split into two groups for protection. We knew that Walmart didn't allow dogs inside, but they did allow seeing-eye dogs. That meant a potential killer could be in any aisle walking beside some blind person. So checking that my snub nose .38 was in my jacket pocket and John Johnson assuring me his 9mm was ready, we split up, me with Lydia and John Johnson with Betty.

I did note that socioeconomic class structures were never more evident than in the shopping habits of Lydia and Betty at Walmart.

Lydia had a shopping cart full of jeans, shirts, sweaters, sweatshirts, socks, sneakers, boots, underwear, deodorant, toothbrush, floss, mouthwash, hairspray, etc, etc. A whole goddamn cart full of stuff.

Betty only grabbed a package of underwear, a Penn State sweatshirt (heavily discounted since the child sex scandal at the prestigious University) and a toothbrush/toothpaste combo pack.

When we met at checkout, John Johnson looked at Lydia's cart and just shook his head in dismay. When I saw what little Betty had grabbed, I shook my head in frustration.

I told Betty she'd need more things and that I didn't mind paying for more. She didn't agree, saying she had on pants, a shirt, sneakers and a jacket, and that would last her for days. "If we are at that cabin longer than a couple days," she said, "I'll kill you all in frustration and take your shit." I couldn't disagree with her logic there.

John Johnson ordered me to get toiletries and food while he

bought what he called "miscellaneous supplies." Those turned out to be mostly camping gear, including four sleeping bags, a propane grill with a tiny propane tank attached, two crank-powered lanterns, four big-ass, high-powered flashlights, a portable radio (also crank-powered), a case of fireplace starter logs, a Rambo-style hunting knife, and a Danielle Steele novel.

Seeing the novel, Lydia reached into the cart and picked it up, strumming through it. "Oh, great idea, I haven't read this one."

John Johnson snatched it from her hands. "That's for me. You can shop for your own damn entertainment." Hearing that, I looked away to hide my awkward smirk.

Having paid for our survival items and lugged them to the car, we were off and on our way.

Our destination was actually just about thirty-five miles from Philadelphia, east of Richlandtown and west of Kintnersville, north of Nockamixon State Park. It was a remote part of Bucks County that liked to call itself a suburb of Philadelphia, though it looked nothing like a suburb. It was all rural woodlands, with an occasional cabin or rustic-style home thrown in here and there. As we turned off the nearly vacant highway that was mainly used to carry tractor trailers from distant factories to the City, we traveled another five miles on a stone, dirt path that I supposed could be called a road, though a desolate cow-path would be more accurate.

As we drove John Johnson's big-ass car across this bumpy, bare-earth, meandering road, I saw nothing but trees and undergrowth. It is surprising how you can drive only thirty-five miles from a huge urban city and see nothing but nature and empty woodland. As we progressed up the path and continued seeing nothing after nothing, I felt a weight being lifted from my chest. We were alone back here in these woods. It would be just us and the trees. No people. No doggies.

Sure, there were animals, deer and raccoons and possums, but as basic common sense told each of us in that car, Pennsylvania does not have wild dogs. As for stray animals, they mostly stick to areas populated with people so they can scavenge from trash cans and litter. Stray dogs don't go walking aimlessly into woods surrounded by nothing but mere trees.

No, we were safe. Well, at least until Licker arrived. I was sure Licker would arrive, sooner rather than later. Every mile or two we tossed out my dirty, though well-scented, clothes for that dog to follow. Seeing how marathon runners could cover 26.2 miles in a few hours, I assumed that Licker could do 35 miles in 12 hours at the most, 6 hours at the least.

If she caught the scent soon after we left the general area of my apartment, she'd be well on her way. Considering our substantial stop-time at Walmart, I wouldn't be surprised if Licker covered a good ten miles of the thirty-five by the time we even reached the cabin.

As I threw another piece of laundry out of the window, I was comforted by the thought that Licker might not survive the journey. We were leaving clothes along a highway-style road, which meant Licker would be following the road to keep the scent. As such, she could be hit by a car or reported as a stray and nabbed by animal control. This latter thought troubled me because I did not wish for any person, animal control officer or not, to have to face a dog that was rancid with a burning hex that could only be sated by death—my death. So in my head I prayed for a car to hit Licker and splatter her across the road.

I knew that too was unlikely. Licker would be coming and despite expending so much energy on her travels, she would be ready, eager, and fit for battle. I don't know how I knew this. Maybe it was everything I'd seen during the last twenty-four hours. Maybe it was seeing the Cocker Spaniel that attacked me while I sat in my car very early that morning. Even though when I sped off in the car and broke its back legs, it still tried to come after me. The pain and shock of having its back legs crushed wasn't enough to stop it. Knowing that, I knew a mere thirty-five-mile trot would do nothing to hamper Licker from being ready for war.

We were ready for war too. We still had Rick's arsenal of weapons in the trunk and we had the added advantage of knowing Licker was coming. She had lost the element of surprise. Also, she was a big dog, massive really. This, too, worked in our favor. While big dogs are powerful, their size makes them less agile and a bit slower. Plus, her largeness made her a bigger target and as such, easier to shoot. All to our advantage.

If she attacked at night, the darkness would favor Licker. I don't know much about a dog's vision, but I do know it is reported that they can see better in darkness than humans. Looking at the sky as we drove down that rocky, dirt road to our cabin, I realized how late in the day it was. The sun had turned the sky a golden orange and outlined the clouds with the pink edges of an October sunset. It was really a beautiful sight, but also a reminder that darkness was fast approaching. Looking at my wrist to get the exact time, I noticed my watch was missing, probably so caked in blood that John Johnson had simply removed it and discarded it while he redressed me. I checked the dashboard, and there was a small digital clock that read 5:15. The sun would soon give way to the blackness of night.

If Licker attacked at night, she'd gain some advantage. I could only hope the damn dog was still dog-enough to be diverted along the way by scents of other animals, stopping frequently to take in the smells, slowing her pace. If Licker was diverted enough, it might take her till morning to get to the cabin. Something told me nothing was diverting Licker. She was a bitch on a mission and she was intent on fulfilling it. Hell hath no fury like a woman scorned, or hexed, as the case may be.

Suddenly, a gravel driveway appeared, seemingly out of nowhere, from amidst the miles and miles of trees. John Johnson pulled the car in and I tossed the last piece of my dirty clothing out the window at the edge of the driveway. I looked up and studied the cabin, our defensive base.

If the word "cabin" was originally intended to denote something simple, rustic and made of logs, then this cabin was true to the original definition. The driveway was not long, maybe twenty yards from road to cabin, and ended next to a square structure made of logs with a slanted roof coated with large cedar shingles. These logs were not local trees cut down and milled on site, but were trees that were pre-fabricated at a factory, treated, measured and cut to perfect size, making the structure more modern than it looked. Still, it certainly was just a cabin in the woods, and if the logs were modern manufacturing, the interior was anything but modern.

The cabin was locked with a deadbolt, as we knew it would be. As John Johnson assured us before we arrived, within three minutes and using an Allen-wrench type tool, he had the lock opened.

The cabin, much like Rick's home, was just one large room, with one separate, off-shoot room that held the toilet and shower. Unlike Rick's, this cabin was designed to be left unoccupied for months at a time, and therefore, equipped with only the bare-bone necessities. The floors were made of plywood and the furniture was scarce. Along one wall was a bunk bed, which was also made of wood and lacked mattresses. Along another wall sat another bunk bed in the same style. Next to the front door was a kitchenette. In a semi-circle around the fireplace were two rocking chairs and a two-seater wooden bench. That was it.

"I get the top bunk," Betty said, rushing into the cabin, arms around one of the sleeping bags John Johnson had purchased.

Lydia shot me a look of panic and I just shrugged, giving my best, *what do you want me to do about it?* looks.

John Johnson was not so demure. "Woman, are you crazy?" he said. "You think those damn beds are made of steel. You're liable to make that thing tumble into toothpicks." Betty looked hurt, so John Johnson added, "I'd probably break it up too. All right, here's what's what. Betty, you sleep on the bottom of one and I sleep on the bottom of the other. The two small people can sleep up top."

"I don't think I'll be sleeping much tonight," Lydia added.

"You are on adrenaline now," I said. "It dissipates quickly and when it does, you're going to feel exhausted. I bet you'll sleep like the dead."

"Well," John Johnson said, "if we don't want to be dead, we need to get everything from the car into the cabin and set up our defenses. That's the first thing. Then we eat supper 'cause I'm fucking starved and then we decide on shifts for sleep. Two people awake at a time. That way, one can keep the other awake and vice-versa. Agreed?"

We all nodded and began unloading the car.

CHAPTER TWENTY-EIGHT

John Johnson's defensive plan was simple, tidy and efficient. He felt, and I agreed, that the more simple a plan the more effective they usually were. John Johnson got right to work. He loaded every gun, safeties off, ready to fire. He gave each woman a small handgun and a simple tutorial on reloading and firing. He placed each of the bigger guns at a strategic point around the cabin, saying that once hell broke loose we would be scattered around so we should have guns everywhere waiting, at the ready, for us to grab. He then gave us all a quick tutorial, John Johnson style, on how to shoot each larger weapon. "I got each one ready to shoot. Rifle-sized guns are shot with the butt in the crook of the shoulder. No hip-shooting shit. Keep your feet planted, be ready for the gun to kick-back, and keep your damn eyes open. Otherwise, all you have to do is point, aim, and squeeze the trigger. When the gun clicks, it is empty. Drop it and find another. God knows we have enough."

Simple.

We all agreed it sounded like a good plan, and decided to get moving on unloading the car.

Once the car was unloaded we got the fireplace lit, the lanterns cranked and shining, and ate a meal of canned beef stew with some whole-wheat dinner rolls. As we sat and ate, everyone was quiet. I don't know what made me think of Danforth of the Isle of Man, but the story just spilled out. Everyone quietly listened as I told the tale.

"There was a 16th century warrior named Danforth of the Isle of Man," I began, talking slowly, calm, and flat throughout. "He hailed from England but joined the crusades at a young age and spent much of his adult life in the Mediterranean area, fighting for the Christian God against the Muslim God. During many campaigns and battles, sieges, and defenses, Danforth made quite a name for himself as one of the fiercest and most skilled warriors of his day. On both sides of the world, Christian and Muslim, Danforth's reputation as a soldier became legendary. It was said that young Christian soldiers would step aside as he strode through camp, out of respect and awe. It was also said that around the enemy Muslim campfires, they spoke of Danforth as almost something superhuman. All the young Muslim soldiers were warned that if they encountered someone on the battlefield who fitted his description, it was wiser to flee than fight.

"So, as these things go, Danforth of the Isle of Man's legend swelled to infamy though no one in modern history knows if his conduct on the battlefield warranted such admiration and fear. Well, like all soldiers, Danforth reached his peak in strength and endurance and after spending ten years in almost constant war, he decided to retire somewhere in the Mediterranean, though history does not say exactly where.

"He took an Arab wife who converted to Christianity. They had a baby daughter and as luck would have it, just weeks after his daughter was born the Muslims overtook the small village where Danforth lived. Well, once it was known among the Muslims that the infamous Danforth was living in this village, they sent 200 soldiers to arrest him. Two hundred armed men to arrest a single, aging, ex-soldier.

"The soldiers surrounded his home one warm summer day. When Danforth emerged from his little home to greet the 200 soldiers, the amassed men all went down to one knee to pay homage to the great warrior. They then proceeded to arrest him, and Danforth, believing his fame would ultimately give him freedom and safe passage back to Christendom, did not put up a fight. He surrendered to the arrest, believing it would be brief. Besides, they let his wife and newborn remain in the home and assured him they would be provided food and other sundries."

"Sundries?" Betty chirped in, interrupting my story. "Who

the hell uses that word? Sundries? If you mean living supplies and household shit, then just say it, damn."

I continued without acknowledging her. "Anyway, he was placed in a tiny, dank, dark cell in the basement of a rich man whose home was seized by the Muslim invaders. Danforth spent days in his cell, but he remained confident that he was just too famous for prison and as such, his release was eminent. He was pleasant to his captors, who only entered his cell to bring him food and drink. They were equally pleasant to him, offering the respect due to a proved warrior. Danforth was not at all surprised when one of the guards brought a cask of fine ale to his cell, leaving it and a mug for Danforth to enjoy as he waited for his release.

"The cask was a ten-gallon drum and had a corked tap at the bottom. It was placed on the only table in his cell and Danforth spent his days greedily enjoying its contents, often drinking himself drunk, only to awaken and do the same again. On the third day, much to his dismay, the cask was nearly empty, providing only two mugs of ale. Knowing as all good drinkers do that if you tilt the cask forward you can almost certainly get yourself one or two more mugs before it is truly empty, he did just that.

"As Danforth of the Isle of Man tilted the nearly drained cask forward, he felt something inside of it thump against the side. Startled, he returned the cask to its upright position and stared at it, wondering what could have made such a thump from inside. Curious, he picked up the cask and shook it, and sure enough, something plopped and thumped around inside.

"As he learned in war, hesitation was cowardice, so Danforth began pounding on the cask with his fist, looking for a weakness in the wood. Finding none, he hoisted the cask above his head and threw it onto the ground. A small crack formed, leaking out the remaining trickle of ale. He kicked at the small crack until it gave way, and one plank of the cask snapped open. He reached his hand inside and felt something small, the size of a grapefruit, and mushy to the touch. Assuming it was exactly what it felt like, a piece of fruit thrown into the cask for taste or fermentation or some other such purpose, he was at ease when he removed the object through the cracked plank.

"What Danforth of the Isle of Man held in his hand was not fruit from the earth, but the fruit of his loins. He looked in shock at the pickled head of his baby daughter. For a second, he did nothing but stare, looking into the vacant eyes of his one and only progeny. Then he threw the head across the room in fright and shock, a sudden "urrr" escaping his mouth, his face twisted in horror.

"Then he heard the faintest chuckle muffled beneath a hand, coming from outside the cell. He knew at once that his jailers, probably a bevy of them, were watching through small cracks and fissures in the oak door, watching to gauge his reaction to this fantastical horror.

"He looked toward the door where the chuckle emanated and stared, the rage he felt in battle pulsing through his body. He thought to charge the door, to beat on it until it broke open so he could massacre his jailers one by one, painfully ending each life. The better part of his mind knew that the door, despite its fissures and cracks of age, was solid, thick oak and would never succumb despite his desperate strength.

"He never took his eyes off the door as he walked backward to the corner of his cell where his child's head lay in a corner, muddied from the filth of the cell's floor. He picked up the child's head in one hand and walked toward the door, keeping his eyes pinned on where he knew his jailers' eyes watched, trying to gauge the great Danforth's reaction to the sadistic joke they'd played on him.

"Danforth realized his ego had blinded him. These invaders saw him as less than human because of his Christian faith. The homage they paid him was all a ruse to arrest him without loss of life, specifically their lives. He also knew now that his wife had been killed, too, and probably brutally raped by a hundred men before being murdered.

"Danforth of the Isle of Man would not cry or scream or grieve. He wouldn't give them the satisfaction. Instead, he held his child's head up high and showed it to the eyes behind the door, displaying it like a trophy. Danforth then bit a chunk of flesh from the child's cheek, twisting the head side to side as he bit, trying to free a chunk of meat from the skull. When the bite of meat tore free from his baby's skull, he chewed the meat in a slow, methodical manner, never once removing his eyes from his cell door.

"Danforth heard someone retch and vomit as they watched Danforth swallow the meat and put the head to his mouth for another bite.

"He ate the head clean of loose flesh and tossed the meat-cleaned skull into the corner of the cell. He then lay down and went to sleep, never once gagging on the meal he had consumed, his own child.

"History says that Danforth was never released from the cell and was never again given food or drink. He died the death of thirst and starvation, resting peacefully, knowing no one ever got the best of him."

The cabin was quiet when I finished telling the tale, either from the shocking content or because Lydia, Betty, and John Johnson weren't sure if that was the end of the story. So I added, "The end."

"Man," Betty spoke first, "that was messed-up. Why would you tell us that."

"Shit, brother," John Johnson said. "That's some dark shit."

Betty continued, "They let you work with children?"

Lydia just looked two shades of disgusted.

"I didn't make the story up. It's history. Or legend, more accurately," I defended.

"Why did you feel the need to tell it to us?" Lydia asked.

"I thought it was a good story about a warrior never letting his enemies see his fear or horror. They sought a reaction but did not get the reaction they wanted. We need to do that with Licker. She has fear on her side. Her barking is designed to invoke fear and dread in us, causing us to act foolishly, but we need to hold ourselves together. Control our emotions. That was the point."

I think everyone wanted to forget about Danforth from the Isle of Man because we all started to talk at once about the problem we faced with Licker and what we could expect from that bitch.

We continued to talk about the problem. Then we talked some more.

I felt the tension in my neck and the beginning of a headache forming. Except for John Johnson who was sternly silent, the other three of us were repeating the same facts we already knew and spending way too much time speculating about what might happen, when it might happen, and how it might happen. It was a dizzying litany of guesswork and assumptions that I was equally guilty of indulging. When I realized how tight my jaw had become from the tension of all this speculation and how hoarse my voice was from all of this conversation, I stood up. "Enough," I said. "Enough of all this talk. I can't take any more. I just can't. I need a break. I need to just be silent."

My eyes filled with tears. Gwen and Rick, my wife and brother, were dead. I turned my head and tried to fight the tears down, but they were too powerful and overflowed onto my cheeks. I walked away from the fire to the other side of the cabin, ashamed at my tears but also wanting some distance between myself and other human beings. Grief, I learned as a psychologist, can be a deeply intimate experience and not something everyone wants to share.

As if understanding the gravity of what I was going through, the two other chatterboxes remained quiet as my sobs filled the silent cabin. I must've sobbed for a good three or four minutes, and while I did so, no one said a word or moved a muscle, and I was appreciative for it. If someone tried to hug me or offer words of encouragement, I might have punched them in the face. Sadness and rage are close cousins.

It suddenly occurred to me that I had trouble getting the sobbing to stop. It felt as if the tears were in control and they planned on staying in control for a long time, perhaps the entire night. I made an attempt to stop them, even forcing myself to fake a smile, but they overpowered me and continued as a sob escaped my mouth. I tried again, wiping my eyes on my sleeves and standing up straight, but again, I lost the battle and the sobbing returned.

John Johnson interrupted the silence that surrounded my

sobs. I like to think he knew the fight I was waging within myself to control my emotions. He knew I could only win that fight and regain my wits if I was shocked back into reality. I didn't expect John Johnson to say what he said. "We need to pack up these guns and put them back in the duffle bag."

That did the trick. As quickly and as powerfully as the tears and sobbing had overtaken me, they left, leaving me dry-eyed and focused. "What did you say?" I asked, my voice crackling a little from the sobbing but regaining its strength.

John Johnson stood and walked over to a shotgun leaning against the wall. "The guns need to go back into the duffle bag. We have too many guns. I made a mistake in my planning. We have too many guns out."

"What the fuck?" Betty said.

"Too many guns?" Lydia's voice was full of confusion. "How can we have too many guns? That doesn't make sense."

"You ever hear of friendly fire?" John Johnson picked up a shotgun leaning against a far wall and walked it over to the duffle bag and placed it inside. "Think about it. Let's say that Licker gets in here. Jumps through the window or some shit like that. She'll cause all sorts of wild confusion. This shit will turn chaotic quickly. So we scatter around the room and each grab one of these guns lying all around. We start shooting. Fear takes over. Noise and smoke and a snarling dog. All hell breaks loose. We are all firing in different directions at a dog that is charging us, scattering us. We'd only manage to kill one another. Friendly fire is a very real thing." John Johnson reached another weapon, some military looking rifle type thing, and placed it into the duffle bag. "Friendly fire is the mistake."

"I see your point," I said, "but what choice do we have? You can't ask any of us to stand here unarmed. If we each have only one gun, what difference does it make? We could shoot each other with one gun as easily as from ten guns."

"I agree," Betty chimed in. "The handgun you gave me..." she reached into her considerable waistband and produced a generic looking pistol. "It ain't leaving my hand till this whole fucking mess is over or I am dead and cold. Whichever comes first."

"I agree," Lydia said. John Johnson had outfitted her with a small pistol and she instinctively touched the jacket pocket where she kept the gun.

"I would never ask anyone to surrender a weapon," John Johnson said, looking to each us, "especially considering what we are up against. Shit, you'd have to kill me to get my gun."

"Then what are you saying?" Lydia asked.

"Our plan—my plan—is too dependent on firepower. We figured Licker would show up, find a way in, and we'd be so heavily armed that we'd be ready for her. We'd unload so much firepower on her ass, she'd be nothing but a pile that vaguely resembles Alpo."

"That doesn't sound like too bad a plan to me," I said, not masking my contempt for changing that plan.

"I'm so tired, I must not have been thinking straight," John Johnson chided himself. "If that happened, shit, the confusion, the gunshots, the smoke! Well, I've explained it already. It'd be chaos, and while we might kill that fucking Licker, I bet at least one of us will be dead along with her. Maybe more than one of us."

"So we do what? Huh? What?" Lydia asked.

"We keep our handguns, fine. We put away the rest of these guns. We don't need 'em," John Johnson said while collecting the assortment of rifles from around the room. "What we need is to set a trap. Lure her to a spot and one of us just *boom*, cracks a single shot in her ass."

"I see what you mean," I said. "Control the chaos."

"Exactly, my brother," John Johnson said. "We control the playing field, we control the weaponry, we control the chaos. Almost poetic."

"Yeah, until it goes to shit, as plans always do," I added.

"Well, then we still got our handguns," John Johnson replied. "Handguns should be enough against one dog. If we plan correctly, lure her to a spot, then we can end this with one bullet, one shot fired." As he spoke, John Johnson collected the last rifle and placed it into the duffle bag. He walked into the bathroom and laid the duffle bag of guns in the tub. When he walked back out, he looked at us. "If anyone disagrees with me, well, you know where the damn guns are. Help yourself. Just don't accidentally shoot my ass 'cause if you do, it'll be your own ass that pays for it."

"Okay." Lydia walked toward John Johnson. "What trap, or lure, or whatever, are we going to set for this bitch Licker?"

All three of us snickered when Lydia said "bitch Licker." It took her a second to realize what we were laughing at, but once she did, she smiled too.

"I've been waiting all day for someone to make a pussy-licker joke," I said, a little laughter in my voice.

"Me too," John Johnson said, smiling widely, lips upturned in a half-laugh.

"Shit, I needed to laugh a little," Betty said. "Fucking bitch-licker!" Betty laughed harder, out loud, even slapping her thigh. "That cunt-licker, Licker," she continued, laughing even more.

"All right, all right," Lydia said. "I think using the c-word ended the joke for me. Plus I'm a little anxious about this plan to trap Licker. It seems to be a non-existent plan. Can someone explain it to me, please?"

"Shit, I said we need a plan to trap that fucker, I didn't say I had one," John Johnson replied.

The laughter in the room evaporated in an instant.

"Wait, what?" I asked, shock in my voice. "You said—"

John Johnson cut me off. "—No-no. Correction. I said what we shouldn't have is a chaotic shootout at the O.K. Corral. I didn't say I had any plan."

"Christ Almighty," Lydia said. "We need to make a plan and do it quickly."

That's when we heard a growl.

CHAPTER TWENTY-NINE

The growl drew all of our attention to the front door. The growl was deep, throaty and was followed by a series of snorts as if the dog (and we all knew it was a dog) was getting a good scent.

"How the fuck could Licker get here so goddamn quick?" I said aloud.

Then we heard a similar growl and snort from the beneath the window on the opposite wall. *More than one dog?* my mind asked. *Impossible!* my mind reasoned.

As if reading my mind, Lydia put a hand to her mouth, removed it and said, "There is more than one."

"Did Licker recruit some friends?" I asked aloud, to no one in particular.

"Licker don't like other dogs," Betty chimed in. "She don't get along well wit 'em."

A bark came from outside the wall behind the fireplace, and then a series of barks outside another wall. We heard footsteps in front of the front door, and the snorting was audible from the fourth wall. "I'm counting at least four," John Johnson said.

"Surrounding the cabin," I added.

Another bark came from the right, and you could tell this dog was moving northward. It barked again, this time moving southward.

"They are pacing up and down the walls," Lydia said.

"John Johnson," I said, "Listen to that bark. What does that sound like to you?"

"I don't know. Fucking dogs, man," he answered.

"No-no. Not just any dogs. Bloodhounds. They got a deep, throaty, almost howling bark."

"Bloodhounds?" Betty said, holding the gun up in front of her chest. "Fuckin' bloodhounds!" Betty had good reason for her fright. A bloodhound is a long, tall, short-haired, brown-colored dog with long ears and droopy skin on its long face. Those long faces are really just extra-long noses, multiplying the olfactory receptors along the length of the nose. Known for scenting, bloodhounds are used by law enforcement to track scents across great distances. It is their scenting skills that often overshadow the fact that they have long, deep, powerful jaws. Their sheer length and height make them formidable in all instances. Betty was right in her exclamation of fear—*fucking bloodhounds!*

"We made another mistake," I said. "There are people in these woods. Hunters. This is hunting season and those are hunting dogs."

"Yeah, but we didn't see a cabin for miles around this place," John Johnson said, defensively.

"This is wilderness country with many unmarked roads," I answered. "Shit, there could be another road a few hundred yards up this road that leads to another cabin like this one. Bloodhounds can pick up a scent for miles. How could we have forgotten hunting season!"

"None of that shit matters. They're here now." Lydia's voice was full of fear and dread. "What's the goddamn plan?"

Lydia and I looked to the bathroom with the guns, with the same idea I imagine. John Johnson was slowly spinning, looking at each of the four walls. "They haven't tried to get in yet. Maybe they can't figure out how to get in."

"Jesus Christ!" Betty was shaking. "Four damn dogs. How are we going to fight four? Man this is bad. Four dogs! Bloodhounds!"

I told Betty she needed to remain focused and walked over to her and put my arm around her. "John Johnson is right. Maybe they can't figure out how to get in. Maybe they'll just circle the cabin until…" My voice trailed off.

A few barks came from outside, as if the damn dogs wanted to remind us they were still there.

"They'll just circle the cabin until when? Until what? So we're prisoners?" Lydia asked.

"Or they will circle until Licker comes and breaks down the fucking door?" John Johnson added. I wouldn't have believed it unless I was there, but I heard a bit of fear in his voice. "Or they figure out how they might be able to jump through a window to get in."

I looked at John Johnson and nodded. "All right, we need to put shit in front of the windows, on the window sills. We don't have any hammer or nails or wood to board them up, another piece of our poor planning, but we need to give the windows the appearance that they are solid. Maybe then they won't be so apt to try to break through them."

"I don't know," Lydia said. "I don't think dogs think like that. Logically-like. They don't think like we do."

John Johnson's voice had regained its strength, its confidence. Thank God because I felt my own confidence slipping. "Correct," he said. "Normal dogs don't think logically. What I've seen from dogs with the Lucastench in their nostrils, they do think aggressively. Anything is better than nothing. We put whatever we can in front of the windows."

We all nodded in agreement but stood frozen. "Move, people," John Johnson said.

The south-facing window was easy. The emptied and flattened box of starter logs fitted nicely into the window frame and filled out almost the entire window. If a dog burst through the window, it could easily knock the box out, but we were simply going for the illusion of solidity, not actual solidity.

The three other windows took a bit more work, but once John Johnson suggested we cut up and somehow secure pieces of the sleeping bag onto each window and then jam things behind them, it moved quickly. We used the Rambo-style knife to cut pieces of sleeping bag and then placed them on the window. Having nothing to secure them to the actual windows, we jammed cans of food, different-sized flattened boxes and even a few fireplace starter-logs behind them to keep them in place. Again, it was an illusion of boarding up a window, but just an illusion.

The front door had a bolt lock from the inside, so that felt secure.

We each walked around and looked at our supplies to find other miscellaneous items we could jam into the window sills. As we did it, it felt like a religious gesture that helped our psyches understand we were doing something, even if only symbolic, to protect ourselves. It was an act of hope and we needed it.

Once the ritual was done, we all just stood there, looking at the walls as if they might suddenly fall down and let in the swarm of devils waiting outside. In the sudden silence, we heard the dogs' feet on the earth outside, running up and down the exterior of the walls, with the occasional snort of deep breath as a dog checked our scent, making sure the quarry was still contained.

It felt like hours, though I'm sure it was only minutes, as the four of us stood completely quiet, listening to the patter of paws prancing all around us. We didn't look at one another but kept our eyes on the walls.

The thick sense of foreboding, anxiety, and fear seemed to suffocate the room. My mind was as silent as the air, and I thought of nothing. When death surrounds you, hunting you, waiting for you, trying to figure out how to get at you, your mind becomes quiet for once, acutely aware of your surroundings. In fact the tiniest things overwhelm your senses. I felt my heartbeat but was also conscious of my hurried, deep breathing. I felt the cold that had taken over my fingertips and nose and the ache in my bitten and scratched leg. I also sensed the feelings of Lydia, Betty, and John Johnson. I felt their nerves tingle as if they were my own nerves. I felt the worry in their minds. I felt the tension in their muscles.

Like all silence, it needed breaking. "Should we douse the lanterns? Go dark?" Lydia said, always the manipulative pragmatist.

John Johnson snapped from his rigidity and walked toward the fire, sticking his hands over the flames, rubbing warmth into them. "It doesn't much matter now. They know we're here. We'll need the light for the fight."

"That rhymes," Betty said, a nervous smile creeping onto her face.

"When do you think they'll make their move and, you know, attack?" Lydia asked to everyone.

"Who knows," I said. "I don't think logic applies anymore, if it ever did."

"They'll wait till Licker gets here," John Johnson said. "These dogs here now, they got the hex, but they only got the regular hex. They don't got it like Licker does. I saw what she did to your front door. That dog is determined. She'll find a way in and the bloodhounds will follow."

The gravity of the situation was not lost on any of us, especially when Licker arrived. Five dogs. Five big dogs. Four humans.

We were at a great disadvantage and the chances of victory seemed dismal, at best. John Johnson and I saw what multiple dogs could do in a battle and how quickly a situation can deteriorate. Even worse, how quickly a situation can turn deadly. My brother Rick was a seasoned warrior who saw actual combat in Afghanistan and he lost his life fighting dogs. John Johnson was a seasoned street-cop in a violent city and he nearly lost his life. That battle was against two big dogs and two small ones.

Our little army now consisted of a wounded and exhausted street-cop, an overeducated yuppie psychologist (who was also wounded), an emotionally sadistic ditzy lawyer, and an obese mother.

As our army looked weak, the enemy looked strong with four large bloodhounds (hunting dogs for Christ-sake), and an enraged Burmese Mountain Dog expected soon. Without saying it, we all knew surviving the night was unlikely.

I looked at my three companions and felt an almost loving bond toward them. None of them wanted this and none of them deserved this. Even Betty was just venting some frustration when she unleashed the hex. She never wanted this. Lydia, despite my extramarital sexual flirtations with her, never would have wanted anything to happen to Gwen. She certainly didn't expect meeting me for coffee would lead to this terror. John Johnson was just a simple street-cop who answered a call while on duty last night. He was just performing his sworn duty, nobly and honorably, and he too didn't deserve this ending. Looking at each of them, I knew none of them deserved to fight this fight. None of them should have to die in the jaws of a dog.

I smiled as I looked around at them, and I realized that since losing Rick and Gwen, they had become my family. If only for today, or only until the hex was ended, they were my family. A man should be willing to do anything for his family. "There is one line of defense that we haven't considered yet," I said as I removed the .38 snub nose from my waistband and put the muzzle against my temple. A gasp escaped Lydia's mouth. I looked at each of them as I spoke. "If I die, the hex ends. The bloodhounds leave, Licker goes back to being a normal dog, and everyone gets to go home."

"No," Betty whispered, pleading in her voice.

"Noble, Lucas, very noble," John Johnson said. "Also very cowardly. You do that, and they win. The dogs win."

"No," I said, gun still at my own head. "You win. All three of you can pack up the car and head home. Have lives."

"Don't, man," Betty pleaded. "I don't want your death on my conscience."

"It won't be," I said, my voice confident and strong for a man who was about to kill himself. "I absolve each of you from any guilt or regret or responsibility for this. I do this of my own free will and I do it not just to protect you, but to be with Gwen and Rick and my unborn child. I choose this. None of you asked for it."

"Gwen. You said Gwen," John Johnson's voice rose as he spoke. "You think this is what Gwen would tell you to do? You think Gwen would want this?"

"She might," Lydia said.

John Johnson and Betty snapped their attention to Lydia, faces full of shock and outrage. "What the fuck did you just say?" John Johnson asked, anger building on the edge of his voice.

"Well." Lydia looked away toward the ground. "It would end the hex. It would save us three."

"Bitch, shut the hell up," Betty yelled to Lydia. Then to me,

"Don't listen to her, Lucas. Suicide is never the answer, all right."

"If those dogs got in here," Lydia continued, this time with more power, conviction, looking at each of us in turn, "we could all be dead. Four dead people. They will get in, and when they do we won't survive. Lucas could end this, this whole thing, with just one life lost in this cabin."

"She's right," I said and I cocked the gun.

"No!" John Johnson yelled so loud that I jumped and almost pulled the trigger. "Christ Almighty, don't listen to her! She's a manipulative whore. Besides, suicide is what cowards do. Think about it, think …" his voice stumbled, his mind searching for some logic that would prevent me from taking my own life. "If you do this, Gwen and Rick get no justice." John Johnson must've seen a flicker of something in my eye that told him he hit a nerve because his look of heightened concern morphed into the look of a man selling his point. "That's right," he continued. "You do this, and Licker wins. That damn dog just stops, sniffs her own ass, and walks away. You get no justice for your wife and brother."

"Justice?" Lydia pleaded, her voice not even attempting to mask her contempt for this argument. "How would killing Licker be justice? That dog didn't hurt anyone. Her anger and desire to kill isn't even in her control."

"You are wrong there, Lydia," John Johnson said as I stood there, gun at my head, listening, feeling as yet unmoved by John Johnson's argument. "Lucas, it isn't just about killing Licker but about saving your own life. Fighting for your life, damnit. If either Gwen or Rick were here, they'd say fight, *fight!*" John Johnson shouted that last word, his rhetorical flare shining bright. "Gwen and Rick and my partner, McNally, would say they wished they still had their lives because life is worth living. It is worth fighting for. I'm fighting for myself and for them. All of them."

"Me too," Betty jumped in.

John Johnson continued in his proselytizing. "Gwen and Rick and McNally fought for their lives and, sadly, lost. They fought, *fought*, and they'd be furious if you so freely ended your life when they fought so hard to protect their own. Worse, Gwen and Rick would be sad if you didn't stand up and fight for your life. It would be like spitting on their graves."

It was that last statement, about spitting on the graves of my wife and brother that broke the back of my resolve. Well, it almost broke the back of my resolve. John Johnson was correct, in part, but so was I, in part. I could save the lives of my compatriots then and there, but if they wanted to fight alongside me, then I owed it to Gwen and Rick to fight for my life. I knew John Johnson and Betty both said they wanted to fight, but Lydia just wanted to protect herself. Lydia took care of Lydia, others be damned. Can't say I blame her in all instances.

"Okay," I said, still holding the snub nose to my skull, "I see your point. I'd agree if everyone here was of the same mind and was willing to fight for both ourselves and all who died today." I looked at Lydia who looked directly back. "Not everyone here is of the mindset, though."

John Johnson looked at Lydia with an utterly blank face. "Lydia?" was all he asked, and I understood then that John Johnson had followed my logic and realized that not killing myself to end this nightmare only worked if everyone—all of us—agreed that fighting was the honorable thing. Without Lydia, John Johnson knew what I must do.

Lydia looked around the room and her eyes told me that she didn't want this decision placed on her conscience. She also didn't want to fight these dogs. I saw her eyes weighing the options. Oddly, one option was for me to put a bullet through my own head.

In the end, I think peer pressure got to her. Lydia was a creature who sought to manipulate others for her own advantage, but when that was no longer possible her mind was too childish to make a real decision. In those instances, she followed the crowd. Peer pressure even affects the greatest narcissist, apparently. Seeing the resolve in the faces of John Johnson and Betty, Lydia looked down, relenting, and with a crackle in her voice, said, "Let's fight."

I lowered the gun from my head. John Johnson and Betty both nodded their own heads in solidarity. "Good," John

Johnson said. "No more of that bullshit, right, Lydia? We're a team. You too, Lucas, okay?"

Before I could agree, we heard a window break.

CHAPTER THIRTY

When the glass shattered, I heard the crash of safety and peace evaporating.

All of us scanned the four windows around the room. While we had the windows faux-fortified, they all looked undisturbed. "Fuck me," John Johnson said, his voice carrying a twinge of disappointment. "The bathroom! We forgot the bathroom. It has a window."

Fortunately, when my eyes hit the bathroom door, a door is exactly what I saw. A closed door. I started to breathe a sigh of relief that the door was closed when it violently rocked and jolted. Barking came from the other side. As the barking continued, the door thumped again.

"Fortify that door," I yelled.

Betty shocked me with her speed. Before I could even think of what to grab, she had one of the single wooden chairs from in front of the fireplace in her hands and was already halfway across the room. She shoved the chair at an angle so the back was wedged beneath the doorknob, bracing it closed. "Forta-fucking-fied," Betty said aloud.

A loud thump hit the door. Very loud. We all realized without saying it that the dog was ramming the door. Betty had "forta-fucking-fied" it just in time. "Is that Licker?" Lydia asked, not even trying to mask the fear in her voice.

"I don't know," John Johnson said, "but you heard that barking. That ain't from no bloodhound."

The bloodhounds too had not relented in their menacing patrol of the outside. In fact, the appearance of this fifth dog only seemed to encourage them, and they escalated their barks and snorts as they paced around the perimeter of the cabin.

Despite the bloodhounds, all human eyes looked at the bathroom door. The door started to rattle again and we all heard the canine's claws scratching at the wood.

It wasn't bravery or curiosity, but instead was the dog's clawing at the door that made me walk over and knock. I wasn't surprised what I heard in reply.

A deep, throaty growl came from the other side. I instantly recognized it from the night before, when I lay on my belly in my apartment with coat hangers as weapons. Just one night before, when Gwen and Rick were still alive and I had no idea about the godforsaken Lucastench. That growl belonged to only one dog: a 150-pound Burmese Mountain Dog named Licker. She had come for me, and rather than wait and pace outside like the bloodhounds, Licker found the one window we left decoy-free, and she made her move. Again, she was stopped by a solid-wood door. Thank God for old-fashioned craftsmanship.

"What the fuck you knock on the door for?" Betty asked.

"To see if the door is solid or one of those cheap hollow doors. It's solid."

Lydia's eyes were full of worry. "What do we do now?" she asked.

"Well," Betty answered, "Hold our shit in our bodies because we ain't got no toilet now."

Lydia was not in the mood for humor, however true the humor. "I meant in general, Betty. What do we do? We were going to make a plan to, you know, to kill Licker without all the friendly fire."

My certainty that Licker was behind that door was a fact that I decided to keep to myself. No need to add to the anxiety of this already intense ragtag crew. It dawned on me that our duffle bag of extra guns was now trapped in the bathroom with Licker. We each had a handgun, and that would need to suffice. Besides, I was developing my own plan for dealing with Licker.

"A plan, right," Betty said. "Any suggestions?"

"Well, we might consider—" John Johnson started to say but never finished. The window on the east wall blew open and easily knocked out our decoy-fortification, which was only a flattened box. There, with eyes and ears and teeth and snout was the head of a snarling, barking bloodhound, filled with rage.

Lydia was closest to that window and she screamed and jumped away at the same time. John Johnson took a step forward and let two shots off at the window. The dog dropped from view without any clear indication if it was hit.

We didn't get a chance to check. The sound of shattering glass filled the small cabin and our faux-fortifications tumbled onto the ground in a shower of miscellaneous gear. The pieces of sleeping bag that covered the windows sagged limply, shards of glass strewn around them. The only window that remained untouched was by the front door, and we soon found out why.

A thud hit the door with such gravity that I assumed whatever dog hit that door had broken its neck. Of course, I was wrong. After only a brief pause, a thud of equal power hit the door again. In the back window a bloodhound made a daring leap and half his body was in the cabin, the other half outside, leaving the dog teetering on the sill of broken glass. Like the poodle that attacked me yesterday and had ripped open its underbelly while trying to clear the fence, this bloodhound too was tearing open its underbelly on the shards of broken glass as it thrashed and wiggled about, in an effort to make it through the window.

Instinctively, I raised my gun to shoot at the pooch but John Johnson beat me to the punch. He fired a round that hit the dog square in the head, leaving a massive hole in its skull, exposing brain and clotty blood. The dog lay limp, suspended and dangling on the window sill, half inside, half outside, but entirely dead. *One down,* I thought.

A bloodhound's head appeared in another window. "Shoot, goddamn it," John Johnson screamed at the rest of us as he turned and opened fire, missing his target.

His aim was clearly distracted by another of our bloodhound guests, who must've taken a running start because he flew through the window, clearing the sill by half a foot. He landed inside the cabin, almost in the center of the floor. He lost his footing, falling to the right and skidding into the center of the cabin.

This dog had done exactly what John Johnson warned us might happen. He landed in the center of four gun-toting, scared-shitless people. Considering how we were each positioned in the cabin, the dog landed in the center of a square with each of us as a point on the square.

Betty didn't scream, yell or even gasp. She didn't even flinch. When the bloodhound hit the floor she just raised the hand holding her gun and squeezed the trigger again and again and again, bursting off loud, powerful rounds, until her little pistol finally emptied, making only a *click-click-click* sound as the hammer hit an empty chamber.

Apparently, no one had ever taught Betty how to aim. From the shock of the sonic blast from the multiple rounds of gunfire, we all winced and took a step back. As soon as her gunfire ended and only the *click-click-click* sound filled the cabin, the bloodhound was on its feet, unharmed and charging the closest person, Betty.

It seemed to fly to Betty, reaching her in one leaping stretch of its long body. Its front paws left the ground and landed on Betty's chest, but she didn't budge. For the briefest second, it looked like Betty and the dog were dancing, until I saw the dog's jaw snapping at her face. Betty had dropped the gun as she grabbed its front legs with her hands and was wrestling to keep the dog's teeth away from her face.

From my left I saw Lydia raise her own small pistol and point it toward the dog that had Betty in a tussle. I shouted, "No Lydia," as I reached across the few feet that separated us and grabbed the gun and pushed it down. Lydia must not have had a firm grasp because as I touched the gun, it fell from her hand and flopped on the floor.

I heard shots and turned to see John Johnson firing at the window where the dead dog lay dangling. For a moment, I wondered why he was shooting at a dead dog, but then realized another bloodhound was trying to climb into the cabin on the back of its dead compatriot.

Another thud hit the front door, but the door held. I turned my attention back toward Betty, who was still brawling with the dog, still holding her ground by holding the dog's front paws in that dancing-like position. I was across the room in a few steps and pointing my gun toward the ground, I shot the dog in its back legs, in what I thought would be the dog's hip.

The back legs instantly gave way and the dog tumbled down. At first, Betty did not let go of her grip on the dog's front paws and she started going down too, but instinct loosened her hand a second before she toppled over. The dog dropped to the cabin floor.

Despite just being shot, the dog didn't hesitate. It had barely reached the ground when it craned its neck and locked its jaw on Betty's right ankle. She let out a scream of ungodly pain as the bloodhound sank a full-powered, locking bite. She dropped to the ground in a heap and blood appeared everywhere like magic.

I readjusted my aim and let loose another shot, this time hitting the dog in the rib cage. It released Betty's ankle to yelp and look at me, rage and pain in its eyes. I let another shot go in roughly the same area but this time the dog didn't yelp as its head hit the floor in a dead drop. I suppose I hit its heart with that third shot, but I don't know for certain.

I was about to crouch to check on Betty in that natural human tendency to help another wounded person, but I stopped when I heard Lydia cry out from behind me. From the sound of the cry, I knew what I would find even before I turned to see it. A dog had gotten Lydia.

John Johnson continued to fire, but I didn't see at what or where. I turned to Lydia and she was on her back and the bloodhound had her at the throat. It clamped on her neck and thrashed, splattering Lydia's blood around the cabin. Then it was still and seemed to readjust its bite, only to take a big pull with its head and yank backward. It turned to look at me and a large piece of Lydia's throat dangled from its mouth.

I raised my gun, a grimace of anger and fury on my face. The big bloodhound turned to charge me, its floppy ears swinging with the movement of its body. Its movements were not as agile or quick because of its long body, so I had a chance to smirk as I pulled the trigger, knowing I was about to avenge Lydia.

All I heard was a tiny *click*. My eyes left the target and looked at the gun, and in that instant my mind said, *I got two shots left. It fucking misfired.*

That was all I had time to think about before the big bastard barreled me over. When it hit me, my eyes were, for the briefest of seconds, on the gun, so I wasn't prepared for the impact. It was a blessing in disguise.

The force knocked me back two feet—two feet away from the bloodhound. It lost a step too from the impact, giving me a moment to roll sideways and get to my knees. With a growling huff and a pump of its legs it was on me.

I reached my arms out to full length and it kept the dog's teeth from reaching my throat, but not my arm. The sonofabitch got a good grip on my right forearm and sank his jaws down. I wasn't aware that I was capable of screaming such an inhuman sounding scream, but what I heard I would've guessed came from an alien if it hadn't come from me.

I rolled to my side, forgetting my own advice about… *don't fall down… it'll have you if you fall down.* The pain was blinding and my eyes bugged out of my head. I heard the dog growling, but worse, I felt him tugging on my arm, trying to get a good thrashing going. I tensed and squeezed every muscle in my arm to keep it still and with help of the adrenaline, I was fighting the good fight. My other arm was wildly punching and slapping at the dog's face, in a futile attempt at a counterattack.

In that instant, my eyes caught a sight over and around dog's body. It was Betty, lying on her side next to the dead dog, cocking her pistol (I assumed she had just reloaded it) and beginning to aim at the dog that had my arm.

Even though my rational, cognitive thought had given over control of my body to pure survival instinct, I had a moment of clarity. *Betty has the worst aim ever. She'll end up shooting me.*

I tried to yell, "Betty, no!" but the dog had decided to get a better grip at that very moment, releasing its bite for a millisec-
ond only to bite down again in a fresh spot. So my "Betty, no!"
scream turned into a "Bet—ah, fucker! *Aaahhh!*"

My free hand, acting independently of my mind, started
to beat on the dog's snout. Each punch caused a sharp, clear,
excruciating pain in the arm that was attached to the dog's
snout via its jaws. As I beat on the dog's snout, blistering stabs of
white-hot pain shot up my arm and into my pain-soaked brain.

I heard two shots, almost fired on top of one another, but the
dog that had my arm continued trying to thrash, still on its feet.
I let up the punching for a second and distantly heard a voice
say something with "Betty" in the words.

I didn't realize what happened, but the dog that had
possession of my arm made a "yelp" in its throat and let loose a
long stream of hot piss from its dick. The piss hit my chest and
began to soak my shirt. The dog stopped trying to thrash, but it
still held a tight grip on my arm, though something in its eyes
had changed.

Then I saw a big black figure, John Johnson, straddle the
dog, standing over it as if he might ride it like a horse. The dog's
eyes rolled backward as far as they could go, trying to look at
who was behind it, though it was not ready to relinquish my
arm. John Johnson reached down and I saw the Rambo-style
knife in his hands that he lowered beneath the dog's neck. With
one deliberate, slow and strong stroke, he drew the blade across
the skin and through the tissue and tendons. A gush of blood
poured from the dog's neck as if a bag of water had broken open.

The dog did not collapse immediately, but kept its feet, still
holding onto my arm. I felt the tension drain from its grasp as it
died. The dog stood there for a few seconds, its blood draining
in fast drips and spurts from its open neck, and I was happy I
got to watch the life leave its eyes, slowly, perceptibly.

Finally its legs gave out and it dropped to the ground, eyes
entirely lifeless.

John Johnson was standing above me and the dog, his legs
still straddled on either side of the dead pooch. He was sweating

and had dark, moist spots of blood on his black shirt. Looking up at him from the ground, he looked like the tallest, biggest man in the world. A giant of another world. He also looked like an angel, albeit a giant angel. "My giant black angel," I said.

John Johnson didn't respond at first, then he let his big wide grin show, but only for a second. His smile drifted back into its normal stern, stone countenance. His voice was calm, business-like. "Lydia's dead. I count four dead bloodhounds. There is still a dog trapped in the bathroom. Is that her? Licker, I suppose?"

The dog's teeth were still in my arm and I was still in terrible pain, so my voice was less steady. "Yeah," I said. "That's Licker. No one gets to kill her but me."

CHAPTER THIRTY-ONE

John Johnson tried his damnedest to be tender when he removed the bloodhound's teeth from my arm but the dog's jaw had locked when he died. I grimaced and moaned as John Johnson pried the dog's jaw open just enough for me to slip my arm out. Considering the length of a bloodhound's incisors, it wasn't as easy as it seemed. Before he began, he put on his leather driving gloves and lifted the dog's flabby flesh that covered his jaws, exposing teeth buried into the torn, blood covered flesh of my arm. He got a few fingers under some of the smaller teeth—which caused me considerable pain—and once he got a good grip on the top and bottom jaws, he used his immense strength to pry the mouth open. When my arm was free, he let the dog's head drop to the ground as if it was burning hot.

I lay there for a second, catching my breath and catching my sanity. I heard Betty moaning, presumably at the pain in her ankle. I also heard the incessant scratching and clawing at the bathroom door as Licker tried in futility to get through the solid wooden obstacle. The scratching sound suddenly stopped, and a loud thump bellowed against the door. Still lying on my side, I looked over at the door.

"Yeah," John Johnson said. "It seems that bitch switches between scratching and ramming the door. The bathroom is small. I assume it doesn't have enough room to get itself back out of the window to the outside. The window in there is higher than the ones out here, on account of the toilet and all. Probably took a nice running leap to get in, but don't got enough room to get out. It's essentially trapped."

I tried to smile. I could picture the large, bulky, tall,

black-haired dog in that little bathroom, barely enough room for it to turn around, let alone hoist itself through a high window. "See, we didn't even need to plan a trap. It did it for us."

John Johnson didn't respond, just extended an outstretched hand. I took it with my good arm, and he helped bring me to my feet. I reached down and picked up the .38 snub nose I had discarded after the misfire. I made a mental note that the misfired bullet already passed the firing hammer and the chance of a second dead-round was statistically next to impossible. Mentally counting all the shots I fired, I concluded one good round remained. If needed, the next round would work.

I looked at the carnage of the room. It was chaos defined by pools of blood, jagged pieces of cartilage and flesh, dead dogs, a wounded Betty, and one dead woman. I looked at her body, but kept my eyes from even glimpsing at her face, especially her throat. "Oh Lydia," I said quietly. "I'm so sorry."

John Johnson caught my eyes and looked directly into them. "There ain't nothing to say about that, okay. No time for sorry. Not now, not ever. What happened, well, it happened. Period."

"What did happen?" I asked John Johnson. I glanced at a dog in the corner that I never got the chance to see during the fighting. It must've been the one that got into the cabin by climbing over the body of the dog dangling in the window. It was impossible to tell what killed it because it was shot, stabbed, and bludgeoned. "Christ, John Johnson," I said not masking my surprise at the wounds the dog sustained. "I guess you had one hell of a battle! You okay?"

"He was a tough fucker, that's all I can say."

Betty chimed in. "I'm just fine, Lucas, thanks for fucking asking." She still lay on the ground, propped on one elbow, the other hand rubbing her calf above her wounded ankle.

I walked over to her and squatted down. "Betty, you're such a tough bitch, I didn't even think I needed to ask. You did great. You fought great."

"I'm old school, okay," she said between grimaces. "This wasn't my first rumble."

"It must've been your first fight with a gun because you can't shoot for shit," I said, smiling. "Were you trying to shoot the dog or just put holes in the floor?"

Betty played angry, but really wasn't. Even she saw she was a horrible shot. "Man, fuck you. That damn gun doesn't shoot straight. Someone could have warned me the gun was all cockeyed."

I smiled and stood up. When I turned around, John Johnson had used the remnants of two sleeping bags to cover Lydia in a makeshift shroud. My chin dropped to my chest in sadness.

"I know it hurts and all, losing our friend, but considering what just happened, we was lucky," John Johnson said. "It could be all four of us. Easily could have been all four of us."

"It is sad, damn sad," Betty said. "We ain't done yet. We got that one in the bathroom. Is that Licker?"

I looked to the bathroom door and felt my pulse begin to quicken, my muscles begin to twitch and my mind begin to focus. I was preparing myself for Licker. "Yeah, Betty, that's Licker."

"Well, let's all reload, open that door and just unleash a hurricane of bullets on her ass," she said, trying to straighten up and get to her feet.

John Johnson was waving her down. "Stay down. Don't put weight on that ankle. This is something me and Lucas can do on our own."

"No," I said, still staring at the door.

John Johnson misinterpreted what I was saying. "Yes, we can. She's right. We load up, stand in front of that door, pop it open and unleash our guns into her. It's tiny in that bathroom. We can't miss."

"It can be done, but I will be the one who does it. Alone. Myself. I have to do this myself. For Gwen and Rick and…" I said, nodding toward the corpse of Lydia, "… and for her." Then I added as an afterthought. "For Officer McNally and my unborn child."

"Oh, I see," John Johnson's voice was thick with irony. "I see now. You want to go solo against this Licker, huh. Just you and her, twelve rounds, heavyweight bout. You think that'll fulfill something inside you. You think that'll make you feel better."

"Yes," I said. "That's what I think."

"Well I think that is stupid, asinine thinking. I think we fight her together. That's what I think."

I turned and looked at John Johnson. "Since we are speaking what we think, I think I am going to do this on my own, and I think you are going to let me." I reached into my belt and pulled out the revolver. I didn't point it at John Johnson, just held it at my side.

He looked at the gun and smiled. "Oh, I see. It's like that. Well let me tell you something—"

I cut him off. "We don't have time for more discussion. Don't forget, the hex remains. It remains on all dogs as long as Licker is alive. If another hunting dog or a pack of 'em is around… well, we won't survive another attack."

"Lucas, no," Betty said. "Do this with the sergeant."

John Johnson didn't take his eyes off of me as he addressed Betty. "You, Betty, can now call me John Johnson."

I wasn't in the mood for pleasantries. All I felt was the haunting weight of the five people that had died since yesterday. I felt their memories, their fear when they were attacked, and their pain when they died. I felt them watching me now, waiting, as if their souls were trapped around me until this hex was removed. I was acutely aware of each of them and was determined in what I had to do. "No more lives will be lost because of me or Licker," I said, my voice strong and determined. "This ends now. I will fight Licker. One of us will win. It doesn't matter which one because either way, the hex ends. Either my death ends the hex or her death ends the hex. Don't be mistaken, it will just be the two of us fighting it out. No one else."

John Johnson started to protest, but stopped himself and just looked at the ground. He knew what I wanted to do, why I wanted to do it, and why it made sense. The hex would end when I fought Licker, no matter what. So that wasn't the issue. Betty was in no condition to walk, let alone fight. Someone needed to help her back to the car and drive her into the City for medical care. John Johnson realized as I did that if we fought Licker together and our plan fell to pieces, we could all die. If anything, it wasn't fair to put the severely wounded Betty in harm's way.

John Johnson knew all this when he looked up. He was still going to challenge me, though his challenge had lost some steam. "You are badly wounded. You only have one good leg and one good arm. You'll lose."

"I'm not so sure. I have Gwen, Rick, my unborn child, Lydia, and Officer McNally on my side. I'm not one person, I'm six."

John Johnson just nodded. Betty said, "No he can't," but John Johnson just stared at me. "Okay, Lucas. Okay. I get it. Let me get Betty out of here, then you do what you must."

I smiled a crooked half-smile at him and put my gun back in my waistband. "If I don't make it," I said, "drink a Pabst Blue Ribbon for me, okay."

John Johnson nodded.

CHAPTER THIRTY-TWO

Licker continued her scratching and thumping at the door. I was pleased by this, hoping it would deplete her energy, though I knew the overwhelming power of the Lucastench would be all the fuel she needed.

I searched through my overnight bag and took out two clean tee-shirts. I placed one over the bite as a dressing and tied the other tight around the wound. The arm was definitely sore, but numb more than painful. Numbness wasn't a bad thing, unless the dog had done nerve damage. That might not bode well for the long-term. In the short-term however, it was better to have a numb arm when going into battle than an arm ravaged by pain. I counted it as a good sign.

Betty continued to protest against my one-to-one fight with Licker. As John Johnson and I helped her off of the floor (which was no easy feat considering her girth), she protested and questioned my sanity. "I think the wheel is spinning but the hamster is dead." When John Johnson and I each supported one side of her as she hobbled to the car, she said I would be eaten alive. "I'll look through piles of Licker's dog shit tomorrow to find you." When we were putting her into the car, she questioned my logic. "No matter how many times you slap a chicken, you can't make it moo." Those were the nicer comments.

I said nothing, only sneaked smirks and grins at John Johnson, who grinned in return. After she was carefully inside the car, I shut the car door and turned to John Johnson to say my goodbyes.

John Johnson spoke before I could. "I don't want you thinking about anything but killing that fucking Licker. When

I get back to the City, I'll square everything with the police. It won't be easy, but I'll do my best. They still might drag us all in for questioning, but I'll pave the road so it is a bit smoother."

"Right, I almost forgot about that. You think they will charge us with crimes?" I asked.

"Well, I'll make sure they keep it to misdemeanors," John Johnson said with a conviction that allowed me to believe him despite my doubts. "All the dead people have been killed by dogs. All the dogs have been killed by people. They'll see that. Just don't expect them to believe Lucastench. They'll believe me that we were victims of..." He searched for the right words, and said, "... of some odd crazy shit. As long as I can convince 'em that we were the victims, we might be all right."

"I'll make sure the fight is done before you get to the City so you won't have to worry about dogs. Just don't stop along the way," I said, trying to make it sound like my contribution.

"Yeah, you got a fight coming. I know you got the hunting knife and you got the .38, though I suspect you don't plan on using it."

"No," I agreed, "I think I need to do this down and dirty, up close and personal."

"Hunting knife is a good weapon," he said.

Betty opened the door and shouted, "Lucas." I turned around. "You listen to me, Lucas. If you are going to do this, then do it. Don't be half-assed about it. Fight like nothing else matters 'cause it don't." I nodded and smiled. She continued. "Listen, again, 'cause this is good goddamn advice. I once took a karate course and the instructor said that when you punch someone, you don't try to punch their face but punch the back of their skull." I was confused and she could tell, so she explained. "Your goal is to punch so hard that you punch *through* their face till your fist hits the back of their skull. That's how you win."

John Johnson let loose a chuckle. Then another escaped his lips, followed by a series of chuckles. This rolled into outright laughter and John Johnson leaned against the car and laughed, even putting a hand to his stomach where his laughter was born. I did not join in the laughter. While I was determined to face Licker alone, I was still downright frightened about the prospect of facing her. I was not in a laughing mood.

Betty wasn't laughing either. "What? You mocking me, John Johnson?"

John Johnson heard Betty and must've caught the serious look on my face, so he controlled his laughter just enough for him to speak. "I know, this shit ain't funny. I know that. You could get hurt," laughter still hung on the edge of his voice, "or even get yourself killed. I don't know why I'm laughing." I could tell he was forcefully trying to get the remnants of laughter out of his voice, but it was a fight. Something caused John Johnson to get into this laughing fit, and once those fits start they are tough to end.

It occurred to me that I am a doctoral-level psychologist, and even though I had forgotten about that during this last forty-eight hours, I should have an explanation for John Johnson about an unusual emotional response. "Don't worry, Betty. He isn't mocking you. John Johnson is beginning the process of shock, which can cause unusual responses to stimuli."

This helped John Johnson tuck away the few remaining chuckles, though a hint of it still remained in his thick voice. "It ain't shock, Lucas" he said.

"Oh, I beg to differ," I said. "Remember, it's Doctor Lucas. After all this shit we went through, yeah, you're in shock."

John Johnson was all serious now. "A psychologist should know that you need to ask a psychological history before making any diagnosis. If you had, I'd have told you that when I get really tired, I tend to laugh. Shit, I've worked thirty-six hours straight when I was a plain clothes cop. By the end of the shift, I was so damn tired I was laughing my ass off as I handcuffed somebody. Right now, I'm fucking exhausted. Case closed."

I nodded at him, acknowledging that he was right, of course. His explanation, coupled with the history, was equally, if not more, plausible than my own explanation. It seemed befitting that as I was preparing to say goodbye to John Johnson, he bested me. He had been besting me since I met him, and I realized with heartfelt gratitude that one of the greatest things that ever happened to me was having John Johnson answer the call to my house when Licker scratched up my door. Perhaps it was selfish to feel this way, considering Officer McNally was dead because he too answered the call, but I couldn't help the overwhelming thankfulness I felt in my heart for having John Johnson with me during this horror of Lucastench. "John Johnson," I said, strength in my voice. "I just want to say that without Rick and you, I—"

I shouldn't have been surprised that he cut me off. "—Eh, no need for all that. I understand and I appreciate you trying to say it." John Johnson started walking around the car to the driver's seat.

"You know," I said, as John Johnson walked around the car, "my wife thought when it came to moments like this, moments of conflict, I was a coward. She didn't use that word, but that's what she meant. I would've disagreed with her then, but she was right. I been scared shitless the entire time."

Betty still had the car door open. "Ah, that's some bullshit. You did alright."

"Naw, Betty," I answered. "The only reason I didn't find a corner to hide in and cry was because I had Rick and John Johnson with me. I drew the strength from them."

John Johnson stopped in his tracks and looked at me. "You know, your wife was right. You are a coward," he began. "You're a coward because you don't have the courage to feel proud of how you handled yourself with bravery. You know why you don't have the courage to recognize that bravery?" I shrugged, unsure. "Because," John Johnson continued, "once you prove you can be brave in one moment, then you are duty-bound to be brave in all the moments that require bravery. That, my friend, is really scary."

I could only grin at the man. He opened the door to climb into the car. "John Johnson," I said, stopping him before he dropped into the seat. "An act of bravery is defined as sitting in the Emergency Room for hours upon hours with Miss Betty Kay."

Betty smiled and said, half joking, half serious, "Yeah, I hate those fucking places, man."

John Johnson grinned a big grin and then looked serious. "What makes you think I'm waiting with her? I'm dropping her ass off than going home to bed."

Betty shot him a pissed-off and anxious look, and as John Johnson slid into the driver's seat of his big-ass car, I heard Betty starting a verbal assault against John Johnson for saying he was going to leave her. As John Johnson closed his door, Betty did too. The engine fired up and I saw Betty's lips moving. John Johnson gave me a big, wide grin and mouthed the words, "Good luck."

CHAPTER THIRTY-THREE

I stood outside on the porch staring at the cabin door. I heard Licker inside, scratching at the bathroom door.

My hand felt twitchy and I was acutely aware of the pain pulsing from the wounds in my leg and arm. My mind was actually calm, almost blank. It was not some Zen serenity or the peaceful acceptance one acquires when accepting certain death. It was not nearly that romantic. I realized I was, as John Johnson had put it, "fucking exhausted. Case closed."

Despite that exhaustion, my heart burned with a desire to finally have a resolution to this mess, to end the Lucastench, and to end it before John Johnson and Betty reached the City. Before my *friends* reached the City, I reminded myself. Standing on the porch of the cabin facing a massively more powerful, agile, and deadlier creature, I was reminded of something in the Bible that says, "No greater love than this. To lay down one's life for one's friends."

"Friends and love," I said aloud. In religious circles, love is viewed as the perfection of the human spirit. In psychological circles, love is viewed as both beautiful and dangerous. Too many psychologists have seen too much pain caused by love, for love, and because of love. When I was in graduate school and doing rotations at Norristown State Behavioral and Correctional Hospital, I heard love invoked for all things beautiful and sinister. *I only used the baseball bat because I loved my wife so much and I didn't want her to leave.* Or, *I loved him so much that I grabbed the razor and did this to myself.* Even, *I loved my children so much, I couldn't let them live in this sick world.* Etcetera and, sadly, etcetera.

Love is powerful, and as such, has the power to build and to destroy. As I pushed open the door to the cabin, I had love in my mind. "The power to build and destroy," I said aloud.

I know Licker's canine ears heard me enter, as her canine power of smell picked up the source of the Lucastench, and she stopped scratching, becoming focused, aware. I shut the door behind me and the room was perfectly quiet.

I spoke aloud, reciting 1 Corinthians 13, that one chapter-and-verse of the Bible I memorized after taking a Psychology of the Epostles class in graduate school. I suppose I was reciting it to Licker, but who really knows. Maybe I was speaking to Gwen. Maybe to my unborn child. Or Rick. Probably not Lydia. Maybe Officer McNally, whom I barely knew.

I spoke nonetheless. "Love is patient, love is kind," I said as I began to clear the center of the cabin, which looked like the battleground it had been and would be again in moments. Moving aside the clutter, I made a nice empty, vacant area for our combat. I threw aside all the clutter of thrown-about camping gear, pieces of sleeping bag, empty boxes, food supplies, and flashlight. With my shoe, I kicked aside broken glass from the windows.

I skipped ahead a bit in Corinthians. "Love never fails," I said very loudly. "Where there are prophecies, they will cease, where there are tongues, they will be stilled, where there is knowledge, it will pass away." I took off my jacket and my outer shirt, leaving me in just a white, bloodied tee-shirt.

I began aloud again, "For we know in part and we prophesy in part, but when completeness comes, what is in part disappears." I patted the large, Rambo-style hunting knife in my waistband and removed it from its sheath. It was as powerful and commanding as a tank. The sharp steel was reassuring. One edge of the razor was smooth, the other, jagged for gutting. *I'm God holding a lightning bolt,* I thought.

I continued Corinthians. "When I was a child, I talked like a child, I thought like a child, I reasoned like a child. When I became a man, I put the ways of childhood behind me." I took the .38 snub-nose from my waist band and smiled at it, thanking it for all the help it provided me. I then threw it out of one of the demolished windows.

I reached into my back pocket for my wallet. I flipped it open and took out the picture of Gwen. I tossed the wallet to the side of the room with the rest of the clutter. I stared at the picture of Gwen and kept my recital of Corinthians going. "For now we see only a reflection as in a mirror." I paused as I tucked the picture of Gwen into my pants pocket and reached for the handle of the bathroom door. Licker was silent. My hand fell to the door knob, and before opening it, I finished my litany. "Then we shall see face to face. Now I know in part, then I shall know fully, even as I am fully known."

I turned the door knob and the moment before I threw open the bathroom door, I screamed the last section: "Now these three remain, faith, hope, and love. But the greatest of these is love."

I swung the door open and I swear Licker was grinning before she lunged at me.

CHAPTER THIRTY-FOUR

I see John Johnson every few days. He stops by to see me. He often asks me about that final battle with Licker. He wants details of the combat. It isn't enough for John Johnson to know all of the wounds I sustained fighting Licker. He wants to know how I won, what exactly went down.

Since Gwen's death, I had few people left in my life. So I asked John Johnson to be my "Power Of Attorney" for healthcare decisions. It is a requirement to have a POA to live in the nursing facility that I am forced to call home. The ventilator breathes for me now and I am nourished through a tube that goes directly into my stomach. Licker had got me in the throat, destroying my windpipe beyond repair, along with the muscles that assist the esophagus in swallowing. So breathing and eating now require mechanical assistance.

I can talk in short sentences for short periods before I need to rest. So I spend my days in bed writing this story that you just read. The last time John Johnson visited me, I realized all I had left to write of this story was this final section. So, I felt it was time to tell John Johnson what I remember about fighting Licker.

It is really a montage of cluttered images.

Gwen. When I opened the door, I was thinking of Gwen. Licker lunged and I felt a sharp pain in my forearm. Felt thrashing and a warm cascade drip down my arm. I knew it was blood but I didn't look to see any. *Gwen was beautiful to look at when she smiled.*

I swung the knife in a sweeping motion as I thought of Rick

peeing in a long arch, practicing for his new eccentric life. The knife made contact and I felt it stutter as it slit through some flesh. Licker released my arm and let loose a whine.

We both backed up a step and I thought of Officer McNally. *How silly to get a graduate degree in ceramics and pottery. Rick would've loved the eccentricity of it.* Licker took a few stuttering steps toward me but retreated as I swung the knife before me in an arc.

I was thinking that I hope they have pottery wheels in heaven, when Licker made her move. She jumped, but jumped low, almost skidding across the floor, below the arc of my knife.

She caught not my ankle but the top of my foot in her massive jaws. The pain was unlike any I'd felt in my life. I thought again of Rick. *Don't land on your back, Rick. You won't survive if you land on your back.* Licker yanked her head with my ankle in her jaws, and I landed as I warned Rick not to land, flat on my back.

I used to imagine what Lydia would look like as I threw her flat on her back on a bed wearing only panties and a bra. I'd imagine climbing on top of her, a smile of delightful passion on her face. *You cannot think of another woman.*

Licker let go of my foot and sprang toward my chest and face. With my free hand I punched her square in the face. With my other hand, I swung the knife. An image of Betty popped into my mind, when she danced with the bloodhound, holding his paws, keeping her footing and keeping that damn dog at bay. I hoped she'd get her kids back.

Licker growled in frustration as my punches and swipes of the knife kept her mouth from my neck. *Don't aim for her face but the back of her skull*, Betty told me. *Punch through her face till you hit the back of her skull.* I felt a sudden surge of power and I clocked Licker so hard, square in the eye, that I'm certain I broke her eye socket.

I know I broke my hand. The pain radiated up my arm, across my shoulder and sent blinding shocks through my head.

Licker too seemed a bit disoriented and actually paused from her attack for a moment, looking blankly at the floor.

John Johnson flashed into my mind. Tough, confident, and fearless, John Johnson. That big-ass grin, those white teeth behind that dark skin.

Remembering John Johnson's grin I felt myself wanting to smile too. I took such comfort in John Johnson, his power and his kindness.

Licker had regained her composure. Her disorientation morphed into pure rage and standing nearly on top of me, she lunged, making a final push to triumph.

I guess you could argue that we both succeeded. Licker's teeth hit the flesh of my neck and secured a grip around my throat. My arm flew through the air and the knife plunged into Licker's neck.

One jaw, one knife, two necks.

I pulled the knife out and thrust it back in as Licker tightened her grip on my throat, her big incisors puncturing my windpipe, tearing the soft tissue needed for swallowing.

Stabbing furiously with the knife, I thought of my unborn child. *Was it a girl or boy?* I stabbed again. *Would he/she have been more like me or Gwen?* Again, I stabbed. *Would I have been a good father?* Stabbing. *Gwen would've glowed when holding our baby.*

That is the last memory I have of that event. I have a vague recollection of my arm moving wildly but relentlessly, plunging the knife in and out of Licker.

Poof, I woke up and Licker was lying on top of me. She died with her teeth still in my neck, which the doctors later told me was the only thing that kept me alive. Her teeth prevented the massive bleeding that normally would've occurred. The teeth kept the wound somewhat closed and though I passed out, the blood coagulated and I lived. If Licker had rolled off of me or released her grip on my throat, we would both have died. I assume Licker had the madness of the Lucastench till the very last flicker of her life. She wouldn't have let go for anything in the world.

I discovered later that when John Johnson reached the City and pulled into the Emergency Room parking lot with Betty, he saw a woman walking one of those pet-therapy dogs into the hospital. So he decided to perform a test. Telling Betty to stay in the car, he shouted to the woman with the therapy-dog—a Boston Terrier—before she could enter the hospital. The dog looked at John Johnson and then looked away. The dog was not enraged at the Lucastench. Wanting to make certain that the hex was over, John Johnson reached the woman and asked if he could pet the dog. She smiled and said that of course he could. Therapy dogs are made for petting and made to make people feel better. John Johnson squatted down and petted the dog and when the dog licked his face, he whispered to it, "Thank you."

Feeling confident that my battle with Licker was over, he placed a call to Bucks County 911 and told them why they needed to get to the cabin and where it was. Exactly twenty-three minutes later, cops and paramedics arrived at the cabin.

The doctors tell me my body is not tolerating the tube feedings anymore and I am losing weight. It confuses the doctors, since the inside of my intestines are fine. They should readily be processing the brown fluid that is fed into them for my sustenance. I just smile and nod and let them try different things to get my body to accept the feedings... but I know my body will never eat again. I am ready to go.

Love is patient, love is kind, Corinthians says. I agree and I have been patient long enough. I am ready to see Gwen and I have prayed for love to be kind and take me from this world.

Love is being kind.

There is one final memory right after my battle with Licker. I awoke for a brief moment, but couldn't move. Licker was dead and lying on top of me, her jaw locked around my throat. My eyes scanned the room. Carcasses of bloodhounds, Lydia's body under a shroud, pools of blood, chunks of flesh, and other remnants of a torn world.

Lying there, fading from that torn world, I surveyed the scene and wept at the gorgeous horror.

ABOUT THE AUTHOR

Christopher Grosso is the author of the novels *Godfat's Door,* *Mauled,* and *Mouth to God's Ear,* all published by Crossroad Press. His full-length play, *Odor of Sanctity,* is available through Monologue Bank. His poetry collection, Philadelphia Swank, won Thirty West Publishing House's 2017 Chapbook Competition. Having earned his MFA in Creative Writing from Brooklyn College and MA in Religious and Pastoral Studies from Cabrini University, Christopher Grosso now lives outside Philadelphia with his wife and stepdaughter.

Curious about other Crossroad Press books?
Stop by our site:
http://store.crossroadpress.com
We offer quality writing
in digital, audio, and print formats.

Enter the code FIRSTBOOK
to get 20% off your first order from our store!
Stop by today!